PRAISE FOR *the one that I want*

One of *Cosmopolitan* magazine's
Steamy Beach Tomes for the Summer

"[A] novel about the choices we welcome and the choices we resist."
—*Redbook*

"With a thriller of a conclusion . . . [*The One That I Want*] keeps readers in suspense until the final electrifying pages."
—*American Way*

"The real magic is Scotch's ability to create authentic moments between her characters that push this fast-paced story to the edge and joyfully brings us along with it."   —Examiner.com (Los Angeles)

"[One of] the summer's best beach books."   —*Star-Ledger* (Newark)

"Sweet, funny and thought-provoking—the perfect book for a long, relaxing afternoon by the pool."   —*Commercial Appeal* (Memphis)

"Don't you dare leave for the beach this summer with out it."
—WomansDay.com

"Well-told . . . a good choice for fans of women's fiction and book clubs. It's fast-paced and feels light yet still packs a satisfying emotional punch."   —*Library Journal*

"Scotch creates eminently relatable characters, with a particularly excellent understanding of the way sisters interact, and has the ability to craft scenes of real emotional weight."   —*Booklist*

"An aching, honest look into the death and rebirth of relationships . . . a wise, absorbing narrative."   —*Publishers Weekly*

Also by ALLISON WINN SCOTCH

The Department of Lost and Found

Time of My Life

the
one

ALLISON WINN SCOTCH

that I want

a novel

Broadway Paperbacks

NEW YORK

Copyright © 2010 by Allison Winn Scotch

All rights reserved.
Published in the United States by Broadway Paperbacks,
an imprint of the Crown Publishing Group,
a division of Random House, Inc., New York.
www.crownpublishing.com

Broadway Paperbacks and its logo, a letter B bisected on the diagonal,
are trademarks of Random House, Inc.

Originally published in hardcover in the United States by
Shaye Areheart Books, an imprint of the Crown Publishing Group,
a division of Random House, Inc., New York, in 2010.

Grateful acknowledgment is made to Hal Leonard Corporation for permission
to reprint an excerpt from "Human," words and music by The Killers,
copyright © 2008 by Universal Music Publishing Ltd.
All rights in the United States and Canada controlled and administered
by Universal-Polygram International Publishing, Inc.
All rights reserved. Reprinted by permission of Hal Leonard Corporation.

Library of Congress Cataloging-in-Publication Data
Scotch, Allison Winn.
The one that I want : a novel / Allison Winn Scotch.—1st ed.
p.   cm.
1. Married women—Fiction. 2. Life change events—Fiction.
3. Visions—Fiction. 4. Psychological fiction. I. Title.
PS3619.C64O54 2010
813'.6—dc22   2009039462

ISBN 978-0-307-46451-4
eISBN 978-0-307-46452-1

Printed in the United States of America

Book Design by Lynne Amft

2 4 6 8 10 9 7 5 3 1

First Paperback Edition

For my parents, who taught me everything
I needed to know and let me figure out the rest
all on my own.

Sometimes I get nervous,
When I see an open door.
Close your eyes, clear your heart,
Cut the cord.

—THE KILLERS, "HUMAN"

the one that I want

one

Imagine, if you can, that you are sixteen again. That first kisses are still a possibility, that the giddy anticipation of life's open roads is still fiery in your belly, that a perfect satin dress and a rose corsage can still make you feel more beautiful than you ever could have hoped for. Sit back and imagine all of these things: taste them, revel in them, and then understand that this—even at thirty-two, even happily married and desperate for a baby—this is why I love prom. I get why you might not, why you might think I'm some sort of stunted adolescent, why you might think that I'm one of those girls you'd have loved to hate in high school. But that's not it: I love prom for everything that it represents—hope, innocence, possibility. So before you judge me, before you hear my story, know that. Know that I get it, it's not as if I don't get it, don't get why I should have long since moved on from prom. But I can't help myself. I love the heady expectancy, the spiraling dance floor, the rush of adrenaline before the king and queen are crowned.

And now, once again, it's July, one school year behind us, another on the horizon, the wave pulling out the grads, the tide washing in new ones, and just as I have done for the past five years, I am planning prom. And yes, I freaking love it. I freaking own it. Welcome to my life.

Today, behind my desk in my office, I tap the eraser against my yellow notepad. *This one will be the best in memory!* I think. *City of Lights: Westlake Does Paris!* Last year we did Under the Sea, which felt a little tired, and the year prior, the prom committee nearly came unhinged when deciding between the Roaring Twenties and the Seventies, so before blood was drawn between the school president and the junior class social chair, they settled on the Fifties, which didn't work on any level. Half the kids ditched the theme entirely, while the other half showed up in poodle skirts and skinny suits that they borrowed from their parents and spent the duration of the evening looking decidedly uncomfortable, uncelebratory in every way.

But I'm giddy at the thought of erecting a faux Eiffel Tower in the gym, delighted at the proposed beret party favors. That none of us has been to Paris is beside the point. Or maybe that's the point entirely. I lean back in my chair, the wheels squeaking below me. Yes, come December, the City of Lights will be perfect. *Parfait!*

Westlake High School holds its annual prom in December, an aberration, but the tradition started nearly two decades ago when the teachers union was threatening to strike all spring, and the students rallied the principal to push the prom to the dead of winter, lest they were deprived of the culmination, the exclamation mark for the years they'd logged. The principal acquiesced and the students got their prom and no one bothered to change it back the next year. Or the years after that.

And though it is just July and though prom feels so very far away—with the heat wave that's pushed in from Montana that has us shedding all but the most necessary of clothes, and with the sun that doesn't sink below the skyline until nearly nine o'clock, and with at least a third of the student body begrudgingly enrolled in summer school—my to-do list for prom is long and getting longer. And yes, I have more pressing items on my desk—approving detention for Alex Wilkinson, who, on the third day of summer classes, has already been booted from algebra for trying to feel up Martha Connolly, and calling the parents of Randy Rodgers, whose GPA has torpedoed below the athletic requirement for the fall football season—but I'm brushing it all aside for prom.

I glance over my notes. *Crème puffs on trays? Baguette and cheese buffet!* Tyler, my husband, tells me to give it up, to stop pouring so much of myself into these kids, into this life inside the halls of Westlake High, and I suppose that he's partly right: maybe I'm a little too close, too tied up in my alma mater, but what the hell. If there's anything to get too tied up in at this place, it's prom. Because I've long thought that prom *matters*, has some sort of intangible, relevant effect on these students, their last gasp of childhood before we send them out into the adult world, where many of them, so, so many of them in Westlake—with unsteady jobs, with iffy paychecks, with perhaps shadowy prospects for the future—will be burdened with the complications that the post–high school world brings. So why not revel in it just a little bit? I'll say this to Ty when he mocks me. Why not make it as perfect as perfect can be? I'll answer to Susanna, my friend since forever who doesn't quite share my shiny optimism.

I scribble down, *"Check budget for cost of renting Arc de Triomphe,"* and spot a tiny spider wobbling along my keyboard. Lately, because the only thing hotter than the outside air is the air inside my office—with the school's faulty air conditioner—I've taken to leaving my windows open, and a family of spiders has taken up residence just below the sill. This one—no bigger than the tip of my pinkie finger—is slipping on the keys, flailing by the letter *Y*. I jimmy my to-do list under its weensy legs, and it panics, turning the opposite direction and attempting to flee right off the page. I rush to the window, just before he makes a suicide plunge off the paper, and drop him outside, back with his family, wherever they may be.

"Are we really doing this?" A voice calls out behind me, and I pull myself back inside. Susanna has thrown herself onto my lavender love seat, her cheeks too flushed, her skin a little too glistening, her tank top flat against her moist skin. "Jesus, is it nine thousand degrees in here, or what? I feel like my insides are boiling."

I reach for the Polaroid camera on my desk. "Say cheese!"

"God, not right now, Tilly!" she says, sweeping her brown hair into a bun off of her neck, trying to sound angry but mostly too hot to care.

But the camera has already whirred to life, spitting out a shiny white square that, in less than two minutes, will have captured the moment forever. It's a policy of mine, as guidance counselor: sit on my couch, risk getting snapped. On the wall behind Susanna, I've created a giant mural of all the faces who've sunk into my worn love seat, looking for answers.

"So really, are we honestly doing this?" she says again. "This musical? You're serious about it?"

Okay, another confession: I have a wee bit of difficulty saying no, refusing requests when I have reason, every right to refuse them in the first place. I am the person who other people know will invariably say yes, so I'm asked for a lot of things, which means that I also say yes to all of said things. So, two strikes against me, as Tyler would say, mostly because he likes to use baseball analogies whenever possible, but also because he's right, my will is not my greatest asset.

"Sue me," I say to him.

"Never," he answers. "It would be too easy."

So when Principal Anderson called me three nights ago at home, apoplectic that due to budget cuts, or as he put it in a tight voice that reminded me of someone who had pulled a groin muscle, *"If that stupid Department of Education actually cared about educating any of these children rather than their goddamned bottom line!"* he had to fire Jancee Cartwright, the music department head, and now he had no one to coordinate the fall musical, and did I know anyone who might be able to pitch in? *"Well, sure I do,"* I replied, and then promptly volunteered myself, as well as Susanna, who teaches ninth- and tenth-grade English.

"You starred in *Grease* our senior year, Susie," I say now, watching her cheeks turn from a shade vaguely resembling fuchsia to one nearly perfectly cherry red, a shift I decide to attribute to the heat. "You'll do great. It'll be super fun! Just like old times!"

"Old times were fifteen years ago, Tilly!"

"Thirteen," I say, correcting her. "And who cares?"

She sighs, her equivalent of a white flag.

"I'm just a girl who can't say no," I say, already giggling at my joke, ignoring the truthfulness of it, but she just looks at me blankly. I can see her eyelids sweating. "From *Oklahoma!* Get it?"

"Oh," she says, then closes her eyes. "I think I might have heatstroke."

"I know. Me too," I answer, reaching for the Polaroid, flapping the photo back and forth, back and forth, *flap, flap, flap,* the tiny, pitiful breeze from its makeshift fan offering no respite.

Susie's face is just starting to crystallize in the image when I feel something gush inside my underwear. *Crap.* I set the photo down on my desk, watching her features slowly come into focus, and mentally calculate how long it has been since I last ovulated.

There, her hair is pixelating. No, this shouldn't be my period, I think. *Not yet. And now I can see the slope of her shoulders, the way her collarbone has gotten too skinny with the stress from*

Austin. This was only our third try, but still, it's been hard to digest why I'm still not pregnant, because I want it so very, very badly. As if wanting something like this means that I can will it to fruition. *Here she is now, basically complete, with her clown-colored cheeks, her features annoyed and damp and weary.*

Tyler and I have waited eight years to start a family. While the rest of our friends in Westlake were breeding at the rate of one child every other year, we remained a duo—a happily intact duo, but a duo nevertheless. Tyler wanted to ensure that we could handle the financial burden, snip my father's purse strings, and because I understood his need, I waited too. Until finally, three months ago, he was promoted, and came home that very night and said, "Let's do it." Whether he meant that literally or in a more general sense, we did, we did it, and have done it many nights since, but still, there's been nothing to show for our efforts.

Something warm has definitely made its way into my underwear. *Crap, crap, crap, crap, crap, crap, crap.*

"Here." I toss the Polaroid toward Susie, flinging it like a Frisbee, and it lands on her stomach. "You're spared this time."

She holds it up, takes a quick glance, and mutters, "Good God," then dumps it into my purse on the floor by the couch.

"Meet me at the bathroom in five," I say, grabbing a pile of sheet music from the corner and dropping it on Susie's chest. "And take a look through these. Anderson narrowed our choices. *Oklahoma! Grease. The Music Man. The Sound of Music.* The rest is up to us." She grunts in reply as I swing my bag over my shoulder and head out the door, the eager faces of my students tacked up on the wall, watching me as I go.

The girls' bathroom smells like cheap tile cleaner and something slightly malodorous that infests all high school bathrooms. I drop a quarter into the tampon machine, but it's out of tampons, and I'm thus forced to settle for an industrial-sized maxi pad. The rusty hinge on the stall door creaks as I open it, and I tug down my skirt to reveal . . . nothing. No red splat to announce my period, no heavy spurt to tell me that I've arrived with the pad about fifteen minutes too late. Nothing. I fold myself over, peering closer, my pulse accelerating for the imminent arrival of bad news, certain that I felt *something*, but no, the lip of my underwear is unmarred, perfect. *Probably just a wayward giant ball of sweat.*

The door to the bathroom swings open, flip-flops flip-flopping their way into a nearby stall. The student quickly finishes her business, and the whoosh of the toilet is followed by her immediate exit. Teenagers have no time to wash their hands, no consideration of the germs that might plague them. They are invincible. Bright. Untarnishable. The world beckons. I hear it from them every day when they flop on my office love seat, their nonchalance practically oozing off them, their aspirations for the future simultaneously hopeful and ridiculous.

I press the pad into my undies, just to be sure, just in case I missed it, and shimmy my underwear back up my hips.

The bathroom door squeaks open again.

"Tilly? You ready?"

"Hang on, I'm coming." I flush the toilet for etiquette's sake.

"No period," I say, smiling at Susie in the mirror. "Cross your fingers."

"Are you late?"

"No, not yet, but you never know." I run my hands under the faucet, then my eyes, a momentary reprieve from the heat, and look at my reflection, wide-eyed and anticipating and ready in every way for what comes next. The prom. The musical. The baby that just might be brewing inside of me.

"Fingers are crossed, then," Susanna says, and I study her, noticing how faded she looks, how just a year ago, she, like the students here, was bright and shiny and not even close to used up, and now, how she's dulled, muted even. The gray circles, the pull of her jaw, her wrinkled skirt.

"Let's go," I say, grabbing my bag from the chipped Formica counter, its innards overflowing with contact names for follow-up calls for college applications and potential after-school job notices.

We stride down the empty hall of Westlake High School. Everyone, even the most delinquent kids, has been dismissed for the afternoon, for the long holiday weekend, full of barbecues and fireworks and cold beers with neighbors. Right now, though, mostly everyone is at the fair.

We walk by the athletic display, stuffed full of trophies from state championships past, and I catch a glimpse of the team photo from Tyler's senior year: he was the star shortstop and team captain and eventually MVP of the championship game. If you search the newspaper photo that's pasted up next to the trophy, you'll see seventeen-year-old me, my face distorted with sheer euphoria at Ty's victory, my body lithe and firm and supple underneath my cheerleading uniform. I rarely stop and gaze into the display these days, but still, just knowing it's there is enough to fill me with complete contentedness.

Susanna and I reach the exit, and I press open the heavy metal doors, which jangle behind us as we go. The outside air is suffocating, the sun relentless. I close my eyes and smile up at it, despite my open pores and my moist underarms and my best friend's cheeks, which are now red like army ants. I have the Arc de Triomphe, and I have the fall musical, and I have a husband who loves me, and my best friend beside me, and I might, oh, I just might, have a speck of a child growing inside of me.

I open my eyes and grin at Susanna. "Oh, what a beautiful morning."

"What are you talking about?" she says. "It's four o'clock already."

I start humming.

"Oh, I get it. *Oklahoma!*"

"It just wouldn't be the same if it were called, 'Oh, What a Beautiful Afternoon,' now, would it?" I say, waiting for her to unlock her minivan. "But it is." I smile wider. "A beautiful afternoon."

She rolls her eyes as the doors snap unlocked.

"Come on," I say. "This is going to be fun."

"More like trouble with a capital T," she answers, climbing into the driver's seat and igniting the engine.

"A *Music Man* reference! I didn't think you had it in you!"

We laugh together, an open, freeing joy that has glued our friendship together since kindergarten.

For a second, I consider asking about Austin, about whether or not Susanna has reconsidered taking him back, whether she thinks they can find a way to mend their marriage, stay true to their vows. But she is smiling now, enjoying the moment, and it feels so much easier not to ask. Later, I will. But no, not now. And besides, before I can even broach the subject, we have pulled out of the parking lot of WHS, our windows down, the air rushing through our hair, the radio already on, and for a moment, it's as if we are seventeen all over again.

Susanna makes a turn into the parking lot just after the home-made sign reading, JULY FOURTH EXPLOSION: WESTLAKE CARNIVAL.

By the time we hit the grounds, the fair is bustling. All of the local vendors hawk their eclectic wares from behind flashing booths, some playing country music, some blaring horns, some simply shouting for us to come over and have a gander. We stroll through the grounds, stopping to buy handheld battery-powered fans for two dollars each—a pittance against the heat—waving at an assortment of friends who have piled up over time. I've lived in Westlake since birth; we've all raised each other over the years.

The fairgrounds reek, as they always do, of an off-kilter combination of animal stink, fried dough, and human body odor, and the dust immediately layers our skin like spackle. As we walk by the petting farm, I pull my hair, the color of damp straw, into a tight ponytail.

"I'll meet you in a few," Susanna says. "Austin is here somewhere with the kids. We're doing a hand-off."

"Want me to come?"

She shakes her head. "It's fine. He actually came over for dinner last night." She shrugs.

"Things any better?"

"We'll see," she says, a little too grimly, a little more devoid of the forgiveness I wish she had for Tyler's best friend, who's not such a bad guy, but who may have made a marriage-ending mistake by fooling around with his office manager in her car after a very happy happy hour and having the poor sense to do so in his driveway when she dropped him off, just in time for Susie to catch a glimpse out their bedroom window. Not that I don't understand her bitterness; I do. But I don't want them to shatter, not the two of them. Not the four of us who have clung together, barnacles, since high school.

I watch her wander off and then scope around for Tyler, but the crowd is too packed to get a real sense of the landscape, so instead, I head for the ice-cream stand.

"Hey, Mrs. F."

I spin around to see one of my favorite students, Claudette

Johnson, behind me, in slightly too-short shorts and a slightly too-clingy T-shirt with a winking Mickey Mouse decal, which surely holds some sort of irony that's over my head. She is lean and tanned and well rested, and if you didn't know her, you'd never imagine that her prettiness has nothing to do with how she defines herself.

"Hey, CJ, how's your summer going?"

"Well enough. Last real summer before I'm out of here." She flashes me a genuine smile that illuminates her entire face, taking her from small-town beautiful to anywhere-in-the-world breathtaking. The same smile I see whenever she comes into my office to discuss launching her life on a bigger stage than Westlake can offer.

I wish she wouldn't be in such a rush. I always tell her that. *"I wish you wouldn't be in such a rush, CJ!"* That there are a lot of wonderful things about planting her roots here in town, near her father, who I know will despair at seeing his only child head out into the world that could swallow her whole; near the community who rallied around her and her dad when her mother skipped out seven years ago. But CJ never considers it, never considers a secondary option.

"And are you ready for prom planning? We're starting next week."

"I got your e-mail." She nods. "And I heard you might be doing the musical too." I notice several of the football players lingering behind her, taking in the view.

"Guilty as charged." I smile. "Don't worry; you'll be the first to hear about auditions."

The line inches us toward my awaiting Nutty Buddy.

"How's your break going?" CJ asks. "Do anything major?"

"Nothing much," I say, thinking of how Tyler has just expressed his regret that we once again didn't take advantage of my summer off, didn't take that virgin trip to Europe or at the very least, a drive down the coast to California.

"I wish we'd done it," he said a few nights ago, shortly after I hung up with Principal Anderson. "I've always wanted to surf in San Diego. We should have at least done San Diego."

I laughed as I stirred the tomato sauce for dinner. "I've never heard you mention *that* before."

He shrugged, flipping the channel from one baseball game to another. "I'm feeling old. Feeling like I'd like to try new things. Why not surfing?"

"Why not?" I agreed amicably, already relieved that he hadn't mentioned trying to squeeze it in during August, mulling over how difficult it would have been to find time for our baby-making sex, considering who would have watered the plants, who would have looked out for the house, how I would have organized prom and now the musical. *It's so much easier that we didn't go,* I thought. *Tyler can learn to surf another time.* But I swirled the sauce with my wooden spoon and said nothing. I almost blurted out that we'd see Paris at the prom, but I suspected he'd just turn up the volume on the TV. Not that Tyler doesn't enjoy prom; every year he dutifully holds my hand and slow-dances, but just last year, he mentioned that he was starting to feel a little too old for this stuff, a little more like a chaperone than an alumnus, and last week at dinner, when I announced the City of Lights theme with unhinged giddiness, I could detect the disinterest painted across his face. Though Susanna later said, "Who could blame him? He's thirty-two. Who still wants to go to prom?" I twitched and supposed she was right, all the while thinking, *Well, I do!*

I fork over three bucks for my ice cream and wave good-bye to CJ. The Nutty Buddy stands no hope against the swelter and starts melting down my hand as soon as I tug off the gold wrapping, so I swirl my tongue over the edges of the cone in a frantic race against the heat and suck in the flawless taste of vanilla ice cream, hardened chocolate sauce, and peanuts.

I roam toward the bumper cars, the squeals of toddlers growing louder over the bluegrass band that plays on the stage behind me. I spot Susanna with her six-year-old twins, negotiating a cotton candy purchase, Austin hovering near their huddle, but I let them be.

I'm wiping the sticky ice-cream residue off my hands when I notice a tent just behind the hot dog stand. It's a compelling, rich shade of purple with an elaborate fabric door dotted with gold stars that shimmer in the glare of the sun. I start toward it and feel the pad in my underwear shift. *Please don't be my period.* A silent prayer. *Please, please, please don't be my period.*

I pull back the velvet curtain and poke my head inside. The air is cool, so much cooler than the fairground, and for the first time in hours, my body calms itself, my pores shuttering, my pulse slowing in my neck. Incense burns in the corner, and a cloying scent of vanilla and clove overwhelms my nostrils.

"Hello?" I say, my vision taking a moment to adjust to the darkness.

"Just a moment." A voice calls out from beyond yet another swath of fabric hanging behind a wobbly folding table. "Yes, hello." A woman with a wrestler's body emerges, squat, compact, almost lithe but too bulky to be graceful. Her hair is so black, it's almost purple, and her skin, alabaster against it, is nearly translucent. She's about my age, though her overuse of eyeliner reminds me of some of the Westlake students who are still learning the art of makeup application. Suddenly, she is familiar.

"Oh my God, Ashley Simmons?" I say, squinting to make out the recognizable face.

She steps closer. "Silly Tilly Everett." Her lips purse together into a half smile. "I'm not surprised." *Silly Tilly*. My nickname from a lifetime ago.

"It's Tilly Farmer now," I say, then double back to her statement. "You're not surprised to see me here?"

"Not really." She shrugs. "You were always an easy read."

"I thought you moved away." I deflect, because I have no idea what the hell she's talking about. Ashley was the third part of my best-friend trio with Susanna up until the seventh grade. When puberty attacked, we—all hormones and budding breasts and *boys, boys, boys*—dismembered our triangle. Ashley gravitated toward the kids who lurked outside the middle school, cat-calling at the nerds, unmerciful in their teasing, and later graduating to the stoners and crew who smoked cigarettes in the parking lot, while Susie and I stuck to the jocks, the cheerleaders, the prom court. Last I'd heard, after two years at community college and then beautician school, she headed south to Idaho.

"I came back a few months ago," she says. "Quietly. Didn't make a big announcement." She pauses. "My mom got sick. Coronary heart disease."

"I'm so sorry to hear that," I say, because I am. "Please send her my hellos." Ashley's parents were always kind to me, even when she and I had long outgrown each other. In high school, when my family was fraying at all edges, they both showed up on our front porch, toting tuna casseroles and an offer for a home-cooked dinner at their place. I thanked them for their generosity but turned them down, saying we were coping and doing just fine. I'm not sure if I ever did return their Tupperware.

"What's up with the tent?" I say, glancing around.

"I do readings," she says, like this is supposed to make sense.

"Readings?"

"Yeah, you know, of people's destiny, of their future."

I feel my upper lip curl, my forehead wrinkling in bemusement, but then sift through my memory for a vague recollection of her saying much the same in high school—that she could read palms, predict when someone would die, eerie incantations that eventually branded her an outcast, even among the dweebs who were already outcasts enough. She'd brush by me in the hallway and whisper in my ear, "Tilly Everett, do I have something to tell you!" a hint of foreboding, a tickle of glee in her voice. I could never figure out if she was doing it because she resented me for becoming popular or if she still remembered our friendship and was only playing me, that tiny fragment of our childhood still a shared spark.

"Let me read you," she says. "You never let me in high school, and now's the time. I can feel it."

"Um, that's okay." I pause. "I have a pretty great life."

Her face morphs into a sneer. "You always thought that. You were always oblivious."

"I'm not oblivious!" I say, instantly defensive. "I love my life. I married Tyler, by the way. We're trying for kids."

"As if that's the answer to anything. As if Tyler and a baby are the answers to anything," she says, moving behind her makeshift table.

"Well, I think they are," I say. "Not that I'm looking for answers." I stop, annoyed at myself. "What's your point, Ashley?"

"My point, Silly Tilly, is that you need a little clarity, a little insight. And I'd like to help you get it." I wish she would stop calling me that, stop making me feel like I'm nine again.

"Sit," she commands, gesturing to a weather-beaten chair in front of her table. Inexplicably, I obey. She walks over with a glass bowl of water, two small candles, a vial of gray powder, and what appears to be some sort of vegetable root.

She drops in the chair opposite me, all of the lines on her face pointing downward, the sweat pooling above her lip into round, beady drops, and interlaces her fingers into mine, then closes her eyes. I wonder if I should follow her example, so I press my eyes shut, but then I open them again when she whisks her hands back from me, as if she received an electric jolt.

"Oh," she says with a firework of alarm. "Oh my." Then she smiles as if to mask her horror, reminding me exactly of the Cheshire cat. "I always knew there was something special about you, Tilly Everett." She reaches for a set of matches on the corner of the table and lights the tea candles.

Farmer, I want to correct her. *It's Tilly Farmer now. Tyler and I got married and we're having a baby, and that's all I need in the world to make me happy!*

"Tell me the most important thing about yourself, something that I wouldn't know, something that maybe no one knows," she says, her tone guttural, ghostly almost, a shell of what it was before.

"I don't have any secrets," I say without hesitation. "I said it before—I love my life. There's nothing to hide."

"Everyone has something to hide," she says, meeting my eyes roundly.

"Well, I don't. I'm happy. That's all that matters," I reply, half-wishing I'd never agreed to this in the first place. *Yes, why did you agree to this in the first place?*

She grunts in response, indicating absolutely nothing, and sprinkles the charcoal-like powder into my hands, tugging my arms closer, nearly pulling the elbows straight from the sockets and ignoring my protests of discomfort. She presses the vegetable root into my palms, inhaling and exhaling sharply. The scent of the incense mixes with her stale breath and the charred aroma from the powder, and I'm overcome with pulsing nausea, which winds its way up from the core of my stomach, and I swallow hard, certain I'm going to vomit. But then, just as I'm on the cusp of heaving, she pulls the root off my hands and dips the tips of my fingers in the bowl of cool water, and the sensation passes.

"Oh!" she says again, her voice a mix of alarm and euphoria, her eyes fiery as she stares, bearing down, boring into me.

"What? *Oh*, what?" I say, matching her panic because all at once, this seems a little too real, a little more creepy than I bargained for. I can feel the baby hairs on my arms prickling, at full attention. "Did you see my future?"

Don't be ridiculous, Tilly! I think. *No one can actually see the future.* Blood rushes to my cheeks, a visual confession of embarrassment at the stupidity of my question.

"It doesn't work like that, Tilly." She smiles, though it's all teeth, the affection gone.

"What do you mean? You said you could tell my fortune. So what is it?" *Leave! Just get up and leave. Ashley Simmons is a train wreck who can derail anyone who gets in her track.*

"Sometimes I can see something, other times, something else presents itself," she says, as if this is an answer to anything. "You might not understand."

"I don't," I say. "Honestly, Ashley, is this some sort of karmic payback because we weren't friends in high school or something?" I stand to leave.

"Sit down," she commands. "I'm not done. And not everything is about high school, Tilly."

Her bark surprises me, and my knees buckle into the seat.

"Close your eyes," she says. I hear her scurry behind me and then feel her rubbing that root of God-knows-what over my temples, then into the base of my neck, where my blood palpably beats. Her hands form a web over my scalp, and her fingers press, like staples, into tiny points along my forehead. I hear a vertebra pop in my spine, and my equilibrium is disrupted, and even behind the veil of darkness in my eyes, I feel myself spinning, being pulled down by gravity to the straw-covered makeshift floor.

But then she whips her hands off of me, and my vertigo is gone, whisked away, and when I open my eyes, the tent around me looks different, brighter, clearer in a way that I can't define at all.

"*Now*, we're done," she says through a heavy, broken breath. Sweat stains splatter across the collar of her shirt. "I won't charge you. Consider this a gift."

"A gift of what?" I ask. "You haven't told me anything."

"A gift of clarity, Tilly. It's what I always thought you needed."

"I don't get this at all," I say, rising to go, my legs unsteady below me.

"You will," she says. "You will get it, I'm sure." Then she moves to disappear behind her curtain without so much as a formal good-bye. "You'll understand soon enough, and then the next time you see me, you'll thank me for being so generous."

I start to reply, but she is gone. So I fling aside the fabric opening to the tent, squint my eyes to adjust to the sunlight, and head off in search of Tyler, already intent on shaking off Ashley Simmons, her ominous prophecies, the idea that she could somehow intuit the future, my future.

As if! I snort to myself. *Give me a break!* I think as I meander by the carousel, ignoring my shaking fingers, my anxiety flaring like a rocket grenade.

I scavenge around the grounds, putting it behind me.

Never once does it occur to me that Ashley Simmons might be on to something, might be the very thing that will unhinge me from the present and send me down a slippery slope of time.

two

Two hours later, just before the sun finally begins to tuck itself behind the horizon and grant us a small reprieve from the suffocation of steamy air, Ty and I have reunited near the Skee-Ball machines, and having gorged ourselves on turkey drumsticks and popcorn, we make our way back home.

As Ty drives, we wind our way through the town whose back roads, faded awnings, and seasonal crosswind scents are as familiar to me as a second skin. Past the elementary school where Susie and I spawned our sisterhood, past the Chevrolet dealership where my father bought me my first car, past the Italian restaurant that CJ's father has run since she was a baby, past the electronics store that my dad opened before I was born and nearly lost when he drank too much to know the difference between a washer and a dryer. Ty and I fall into a comfortable silence, the silence that is born from knowing each other for two decades, and I calculate how quickly we'll be home so I can check to see if the pad in my underwear is still spotless.

I know that I shouldn't be so obsessed. Ty tries to reassure me every time I really come undone over it, over another month of failed opportunity. He'll say, *"Everything happens for a reason, babe,*" which I know he means to be endearing, but it sort of irritates me all the same. *As if everything in my life has happened for a reason!* What an idiotic notion. As if I wouldn't rewind so much of it if I could. But I can't, and I know this, and I have lived my life knowing this, so whenever he espouses such things, I wrap my palm around the curve of his cheek and thank him. Because at the root of it, he's only doing his best.

Ty turns down our cul-de-sac, its elm trees bursting with flourishing leaves, sporadic wildflowers at their trunks, occasional tangled rosebushes nestled beside them, and as we coast into the driveway, I spot my youngest sister parked on our front steps, a bouquet of irises in her hand.

"Oh, damn it," I say, unsnapping my seat belt and opening the door in one fluid motion, the crest of air-conditioned comfort sucked dry immediately.

"What's she doing here?" Ty kills the engine.

"We forgot." I turn to look at him, but I can tell he has no recollection. "My mom's birthday. We totally forgot."

"Oh, shit," he says, though it's more of a sigh than an actual lament, and he readjusts his baseball hat, a microscopic delaying technique before we face the enemy. We both disembark from the giant steps of our Ford Explorer, bought used and at a discount, and drop onto the graveled ground.

"I've been waiting here for two goddamned hours," Darcy snaps as a greeting. "Do you know how long two goddamned hours can be when you're sitting by yourself with nothing to do?"

"Why didn't you call me?" I ask.

"Phone's dead." She shrugs. *Of course it is,* I think. Darcy never goes anywhere adequately prepared or equipped for the circumstances. "Besides," she continues, "I can't believe you forgot."

"I didn't forget," I lie. "I had a busy day. You know that the fair is the school's big fund-raising opportunity." *Not to mention the Arc de Triomphe. Why focus on her birthday when there is the Arc de Triomphe?* I think. "And I'm busy with the school musical," I add after a pause, like that might impress her, like I should even attempt to impress her.

"Whatever," she says, unimpressed. "It's not as if it's Mom's birthday every day or anything."

I flop my shoulders, unwilling to take Darcy's bait, as Tyler unlocks the front door and goes inside, abandoning me to mop up the mess. The screen bangs shut, and Darcy bites her cuticles while she waits for me to amend my wrongdoing. A pang of sympathy for my baby sister assaults me.

"Look, it's still light out. Let me run to the bathroom, and we'll go, okay?"

"Okay." She pouts, reminding me of how petulant she was as a child, how quickly her mood could turn from sunny to cloudy to completely tornadic with no warning at all.

"I'll be in your car." She rises, her dirty blond ponytail swaying back and forth, and I notice how skinny she's gotten while she's been in L.A. Her shorts drip off her hipbones; her breasts are no bigger than buds; her legs are gawky and slim, like a baby deer's.

The car door thumps shut behind her, Darcy symbolically shouting, *"Screw you!"* and I plod inside to the front hall bathroom and tug down my underpants to check the giant-sized maxi pad, which is still clear, unmarred.

I stand upright and glance in the mirror, and then look closer because something seems off. The pallor of my skin has a hint of gray underneath it, and the shadows under my eyes are an ominous shade of yellow. *Heatstroke*, I think, leaning over the sink to splash water on my peaked cheeks. I wipe off the lingering drops, dab my face with a towel, and when I gaze anew at my reflection, I see something even odder, something really out-of-body, freaking-me-the-hell-out strange: Ashley Simmons, with her coffee-colored eyes and layered black hair, staring back at me.

Jesus Christ! My heart nearly detonates inside my chest, and I squeal, jumping back, the hinges of my knees colliding with the toilet. I step toward the mirror once more, then double-bat my lashes, and, *poof,* with that blink, she's gone, just a figment of the memory of my afternoon. I stare again, just to be sure, but no, no, it's just me, grayish, sickly me, with a pissed-off sister in her SUV and her stomach churning at the thought of a failed conception. I shake it off with a quick flutter of my head. *Heatstroke hallucinations.* I remind myself to Google the symptoms later.

The car horn honks, snapping me to, and I picture Darcy sitting out there, impatient, her left leg bouncing, her irritation skyrocketing.

"Ty," I shout to his den. I know he's already absorbed in the Mariners game and won't notice my absence for at least an hour. We fall into this pattern every April and stretch it out until at least September, maybe October if the playoffs look like a possibility: Ty retreating to the TV to catch whatever game he can find, me enjoying the solitary bit of quiet time after a day of demands that are never once reciprocated, surfing over online picture galleries, pretending like I might actually pick up a camera again, my photography career derailed much like Ty's baseball aspirations, though for very different reasons.

"We're leaving!" I shout even louder, hoping to make it above the fray of the Mariners crowd. But I hear nothing, so I grab the car keys from the entryway table, close the front door firmly behind me, and join Darcy in the car. We are off to visit our mother.

• • •

Westlake, population 81,000, has forever been a town on the cusp, a town whose sparkly name always belied its more dilapidated reality. Ask most residents, and they'll tell you that our city is only one lucky break away from prosperity. One great apple-harvesting season or one new factory opening, and the gods would rain down on us. It's been this way for as long as I can remember. Most of us never made our way out of here, content with our lot in life, maybe not the best lot, but still, we're grateful for what we've got. The sign at our city limit that greets travelers, most of whom scamper through without a glance back on their way west to Seattle or east to Boise, implores, WELCOME TO WESTLAKE! STOP AND STAY FOR A WHILE. But none of them do. None of them do stay. It's the rest of us who stick.

Darcy was an exception in many ways. For one, she actually left. I begged her not to go, and I watched my father's face wash with a mix of admiration and heartbreak when she packed up her Toyota and drove off, literally, into the sunset, but there was never any rationalizing with Darcy. So we let her go and hoped that she would find what she was looking for. Or at the very least (and maybe we hoped this more than anything), that she would come back to us.

For two, Darcy and I, along with our middle sister, Luanne, were fortunate, if you could take the sum of our collective history and actually see it positively, which I choose to do. My father's store was never impacted by a winter that froze too many crops or a Boeing plant layoff that landed some of our neighbors on the unemployment line. People always craved a new TV, their biweekly paycheck be damned, always needed a new refrigerator when theirs sputtered to an out-of-nowhere death in the middle of August. For many years, early on and then again later, when he recovered from his self-destruction, my father has been a man about town. A member of the Elks Club, a sponsor of a Little League team, a beloved, gregarious bear with a riotous laugh and a moderately supple bank account that afforded Darcy that Toyota and Tyler and me our two-bedroom-plus-den colonial, which my dad bestowed on us as our wedding gift.

Tonight, Darcy and I weave past the faded homes, which grow increasingly bleak the farther we trail from my own neighborhood—their front porches dotted with American flags and drying laundry—and I try to forge a bridge with my sister.

"How long are you here for?" I ask, hoping she'll say forever, hoping that she'll finally abandon this incessant need for freedom, for something *"bigger than here!"* (Her words, not mine.)

"Just another week," she says, her eyes like lasers out the window.

"You're at Dante's?" I ask.

"Uh-huh," she says. "He has a great piano. I can play all night." Dante Smiley, born Daniel Smiley, changed his name during a passing Goth phase in ninth grade, and the moniker stuck, though he's now a staid paralegal at the attorney's office in the strip mall next to Target, and occasionally moonlights as a drummer in Murphy's Law, a not-even-good-enough-to-be-deemed-garage band that manages monthly-or-so gigs at bars around town. Darcy gutted him the summer of their senior year when she announced she was leaving for Berklee College in Boston in September and had no intention of staying faithful to their two-year romance. And now, whenever she's back, he flings open his door with a salty mix of hope, redemption, and second chances. The guidance counselor in me thinks he's perilously naïve, while the sunshiny optimist in me admires his romanticism.

"How's it going in L.A., then?" I ask.

"Fine," she answers.

"Any closer to a record deal?" I say gently, as this is usually the point in our conversation when Darcy's temper sparks like a blowtorch.

She sighs and glances over at me. "Please, Till, I'm tired. Can we not do this now? I'd like to just respect the moment."

I nod and smile at my sister, so heartbreakingly young at twenty-three, with so much to unearth. She smiles back, though her eyes are lush with sadness, and it's all I can do not to release the steering wheel and smother her with every ounce of myself.

"Did you call Lulu to meet us?" I flick on the blinker to signal a right turn down the long lane leading us to our mom. The sun lets off a sudden, last-gasp flare for the evening, and both of us reach to lower the windshield shade, moving together like synchronized swimmers.

"She went by earlier," Darcy says without rancor. "She was working tonight."

"And did you touch base with Dad?" I hold my breath.

"He doesn't know I'm back."

I pull into the parking lot and kill the engine.

"Darcy." I meet her gray eyes and affect a tone I hope she doesn't find patronizing. "You should've called him."

"Would've, should've, could've," she says, opening the passenger door and grabbing the almost-wilting irises. "Welcome to life. Now let's get on with it."

Darcy leads the way through the maze of headstones. Dusk has settled into darkness, and the caretaker, lurking but never seen, has thought to flip on the slightly too-bright lights, which give the cemetery a shiny sense of false daylight, and the overhead beams bounce off the headstones and the sad reminders of the tragedies that inevitably await all of us. We tread through the winding path in silence, an old habit from Darcy's childhood when she still believed in ghosts and always shushed Luanne and me if we chattered, the better to keep the spirits away. Sometimes the air wafts with the scent of cut grass or heavy rain, but today it smells of mulch, of dirt, the sign that someone else's family recently laid a loved one to rest.

As I approach her headstone, with a solitary bouquet of roses resting at its foot, I unconsciously slow down with a complicated mix of dread, respect, and the sense that even after so many years, I never quite get used to the words MARGARET EVERETT, BELOVED MOTHER, WIFE, AND TEACHER, carved into the granite, staring out at me, unable to respond to all of the things I've told them in the fifteen years since she's been gone.

"Oh, Mom." Darcy plunks cross-legged, swooping down into herself like a comma, while I stand behind her and give them their moment. From my view, she reminds me so much of the child she used to be, sitting out here for hours, just eight years old, imploring our mother to come back, eyes full of tears I didn't even know she still had.

"Happy birthday," Darcy whispers, her head bowed to her chest, and I step back even farther, too embarrassed to intrude on whatever secrets Darcy will pass on to the only person who could ever seem to tame her.

When she finishes, I move forward to have a quiet moment with my thoughts and my mother, whose departure left its scars on me as well. When she first died, I visited all the time. I asked her how to cope with my father, who had begun to drink himself into a blind stupor, left with a household full of too much estrogen—and communication skills that were stunted as best—and I'd share how I was doing all that I could to shield Darcy from the agony of what had now become our life. When Ty and I started dating, just a month after she passed, I sat for hours, pulling grass up with my fingers and casting it about, pouring out all the details of heady, teenage love.

But eventually, time found a way to move on. I headed to college in the next town over and spent my weekends visiting Ty, who'd been handed a baseball scholarship to the University of Washington. As the years went by, I still visited my mother, but life also got in the way, which is what I always thought she'd want for me anyway. Weekly visits turned into monthly, and soon monthly turned into special holidays, and sure, I missed her so terribly at times that it felt like my heart had been exorcised, but I also found a way to move beyond it. Burrowed safe in the enclave of Westlake, where life repeated itself like Groundhog Day—no rapid movements, no figurative earthquakes that sent damaging fault lines through our world—I found a way to mostly feel complete.

Darcy, though, never forgot. Never let time get the better of her. She marked my mom's milestones and dates like they were her own, boomeranging back to Westlake seemingly at random, though it was never actually at random, because it was always for an anniversary of Mom's death or her diagnosis or her wedding date or, like today, her birthday, and then fleeing as soon as the town started to infest her psyche, as it inevitably would.

The crickets, who must not mind the heat, have taken up residence on the lawn, playing their night music that serves as our only background noise. The cemetery is deserted: everyone is still at the carnival or at the minor league game at the stadium in Tarryville or settling in for a night of *Deal or No Deal.* I wish my mother the happiest of birthdays and run my hand lovingly over the smooth stone of her resting place, and wish, as I always do when I actually take the time to visit, that somehow things had been different, that someone had told us way back when that her intestinal cramps and her bloating and her general malaise hadn't merely been what she figured as simply a weak stomach. That someone had had the foresight, a map of the future, to intuit that no, it wasn't a genetically lousy digestive tract. That, in fact, it was ovarian cancer, and that by the time she was diagnosed, there was really no time left at all. Four months, two of which were spent mostly sleeping, borderline unconscious. *Why didn't someone have that map?* I think. *Why couldn't someone have seen it coming?*

I consider it briefly, as my fingers run themselves over the etchings of her headstone, MARGARET EVERETT, in and out of the *M*, and then the *A*, and then the *R*, how different all of our lives might have been if someone had known better, if someone could have seen the future.

But then I come back into myself and remember how much I love my life, how much I love my husband, how elated I am at my own shot to be a mother, and how grateful I am that we all, mostly, came through it as well as could be hoped. My father is sober. Luanne has coasted as if it never happened. Darcy, well, maybe not Darcy.

"Dad obviously didn't come today," Darcy says as we head toward the parking lot. "The only flowers were Lulu's."

"He's in Mexico," I answer, before realizing my mistake.

"He went to Mexico during Mom's birthday? God, he's an asshole."

"Darce, to be fair, it was a long time ago." *Shit, shut up, Tilly!*

She stops abruptly, just before the parking lot, and turns toward me, that look—*Ugh, do not give me that look, baby sister*—of righteous indignation, of over-the-top roiled anger that explodes from her like a speeding tornado.

"You *do not* get to imply that this shouldn't be important!" She wiggles a finger toward me, her words echoing in the emptied lot. "This is *Mom*! This is her *birthday*, for God's sake! Dad should be here. We should *all* fucking be here. Together. As a family. Not in Mexico lounging on the beach like an eff-ing whale!"

"Darcy, I was only trying to say that Dad's moved on. It doesn't mean that he doesn't love her or remember her! It just means that we all have our lives to live."

"Mom doesn't!" she cries, a needling way to shame me into conceding to her.

"Oh, come on," I say, instantly angry. "Like I don't know that! Like I really don't know that she's gone! For God's sake, Darcy, if anyone knows that, it's me!"

"Oh, here we go," she says, disdain dripping from her edges. "Oh, I forgot. You won the prize on martyrdom."

She brushes past me across the lot, flipping her cell to her ear, then remembers it's dead. But because she is Darcy, because she will not relinquish even a moment of weakness, she just shoves the phone in her pocket and keeps walking, without even a glance behind.

"Darcy, come on," I shout to her fading figure. "You're not going to walk back to Dante's! It's at least three miles!"

She doesn't answer, just turns the corner onto the main road, leaving me to scamper into the Explorer and chase after her. I pull up next to her, rolling down the window, trying to appease her.

"Darcy, get in. I didn't mean it like you think I did."

"Yes, you did," she answers. "You think we should just all move on and get over it, and I'm sorry, but I think you suck." Her voice is weighted dead.

"Darce, *please.* Let's not do this today."

"Too late," she says, stubborn to the end. "Honestly, get out of my face. You ruined this for me."

"I *ruined* this for you? God, could you be any more melodramatic?" The car is rolling slowly along now, and I check the rearview mirror to be sure that no one is nosing up behind me.

"Grow up, Darcy. Just freaking *grow up*. We all have lives to live, futures to look forward to. That takes nothing away from Mom!"

"Yeah, well, good luck to you then." She spins on her heels and darts into the parking lot of the Exxon station by the side of the road. I call after her—"Darcy, get back here! We are not finished!"—but she tucks herself into a phone booth, fishes a quarter from her pocket, and punches a number into the phone.

"Darcy!" I try one last time, but my voice just reverberates in the car. And even if she could hear me, she wouldn't listen anyway. So I shake my head, gun the gas, and fly down the road. Darcy will find her way back home with or without me. She always does.

three

Tyler is deep into slumber when I crack open the den door. He's fallen asleep with the game still on—he's been doing this nearly every night these days: collapsing here on the couch, too lazy to haul himself upstairs.

"Ty." I try to shake him awake. "Ty, get up for a sec."

He grunts and his eyelashes flutter, but he is too far gone to rouse now. So I unfold a blanket from the hall closet and carry it over to him, wrapping him like a newborn. I flick off the TV and then the light, but the room doesn't quite fall black. Tyler's breath is patterned, measured now, and I stare at my husband, the one boy whom I've loved for just about forever, and I marvel at how he is mine. His brown-black hair still thick on his head; his tanned cheeks that never fade, even in the coldest of months; his broad, defined torso still as agile as it was when he was the star shortstop. He will make such a capable father, this I know; his bear-paw hands will swallow up his child with his love. I want to wake him to bitch about my irritation with Darcy—how she always makes it about herself, how she refuses to cut any of us any slack—and also to beckon him to come even out the weight on our mattress, tether me like a buoy.

I move to kiss him good night, that last flicker of a moment of our evening together, when I'm seized with a cramp in my foot. It shoots through me like a lit wick, before I can even think to grab on to something steady, exploding through my temples, and then, *blam*, it's gone. Stars splay themselves on the back of my eyelids, and my gag reflex kicks in as I choke back suffocating air.

"You okay?"

I look down to see Tyler peering up at me, his eyes half-open from the disturbance.

I exhale through my mouth. "I'm fine. Just upset over a fight with Darcy."

"What happened?" He sighs, his words slow with sleep.

I start to reply, but the open window has shut: he's already gone, slipping back in his dream world, slipping out of consciousness entirely.

I pop three Aleve, yank my dress over my head, and fall into bed. The air conditioner whirls and hums as I try to temper my anger with Darcy and her ever-present immaturity. This begrudging, this I'm-so-stinking-pissed feeling is foreign, unfamiliar, and I want to let it go, but it's stuck there, taffy in my bloodstream, emotional static cling. I consider calling Susie but know she has her own burdens to bear, and Luanne is working the night shift. *Just get over it, Tilly. You know she was just upset because it's Mom's birthday.* I run through a list of my prior grievances with her: how many times have I let her off the hook for bad behavior? I didn't even realize I kept a list, but now, with my annoyance primed and ripe, the list, I conclude, is long.

My leg twitches restlessly, and I throw a pillow over my head, but shut-eye eludes me. I mull my prom to-dos and mentally flip through my list of baby names, but still, sleep won't come. That goddamn list of Ways Darcy Pisses Me Off is caught on replay, so I right myself, slide my worn plaid slippers over my feet, and pad to my bureau, crouching by the bottom drawer. It creaks when I wrestle it open. Over the years, the stacks of photos have toppled over into each other, so while they were once aligned precisely — delineated by high school, by pre–Mom's death, by our wedding— now, they're one amalgamation, the proof of the life I have lived.

I have taken the bulk of these pictures. Not all, but most. I discovered photography at twelve, at sleepaway camp, when we were mandated to attend all of the afternoon activities whether they interested us or not. And photography was certainly a *not* for me—not for *Silly Tilly*, that girl I haven't thought of in years, who was better primed to flirt with boys in the dining hall or cannonball into the pool on the days when the temperature nearly melted us from the inside out.

Our bunk trudged to the photo hut and the counselor gave each of us our own camera and told us to explore the grounds, snapping at whatever grabbed our attention. We wandered into the woods, and I just snapped and snapped because I was really thinking about kissing Andy Mosely later after canteen and how to avoid the horror stories I'd heard about locking our braces. But then the instructor asked us to unspool our film, and in the near blackness of the camp's darkroom, he demonstrated how we were able to turn those passing glimmers of moments into something concrete, something that would mark that second in time forever. And I was captivated—Andy Mosely and his braces flew right out of my brain. And soon, while my friends were working on their canoeing skills or lanyarding bracelets for the bunk, I could be found in that semidarkness, turning a blank paper into a piece of history.

Tonight, I scour the mess of photos, running my fingers over the chronology of my life, until I find the one I'm after.

It's a black-and-white shot. I'd set the timer on the tripod and rushed back to our front porch, throwing myself next to Luanne and plastering a panicked smile across my face just before the click of the camera sounded. My father's arm is casually thrown across my mother's shoulders, and we, the trio of sisters, are sitting on the steps at their feet, though my body is somewhat disjointed from my rush to make it in time. The paint is slightly cracked on the frame of the porch, and an American flag falls limp in the background, waiting for a breeze to blow it to attention. But our cheeks are all flushed, and our eyes are all glowing, and together, the five of us, we are a family.

I feel the pinch of tears, and slowly one, then two, then three roll down my cheeks, where they nosedive onto the carpet. It was the last summer before my mother was diagnosed, before everything changed, before I started hoping that someone could freeze time and point us in a different direction. Before Darcy hardened herself, before we talked around each other, before I ever even thought to make a list of the times that I'd had to save her.

I rise gingerly to go back to bed, still clutching the photo and running my fingers over my father's face, marveling at how much he's aged, how poorly he's withstood the damage that time can bring. And then I feel it again—there's no mistaking it now, a cramp in my toe, then my leg, then upward as it whooshes through my heart and then my head, and I can't free my mind from Ashley Simmons' face and her knowing smirk and the sensation of her fingers interlocked with mine. And then, I am falling, falling, falling, unable to fight against the paralyzing pull of gravity. I hear a disconcerting crash, and then, it all goes black.

My dad has sidled up to the bar at Mickey Mantle's, the sports bar off of Route 17, nestled in a strip mall between Applebee's and a nail salon. I watch him from a corner, the air bursting with wafts of smoke from the patrons, who suck in their cigarettes, their lips pursed in concise cylinders. Rick Springfield's "Jessie's Girl" plays on the jukebox from the game room, and if I listen closely, I can hear the smack of two pool balls colliding.

The black-leather-topped stools on either side of my father are empty, though a huddle of men are perched at the end of the countertop, their eyes glazed over as they nurse their longneck beers and stare at the extra-innings Angels-Cubs game that's coming in via satellite from L.A.

No one notices me, even though I'm the only woman in the vicinity barring Cindy Heller, who was three years ahead of me in high school and looks about two decades older. She got pregnant straight out of her senior year and now has three kids with two different dads, neither of whom have stuck around long enough for her to pin them down for child support. Her frown lines twitch as she makes her rounds with overflowing drinks, the occasional order of nachos.

My dad raises his hand to signal for the bartender, and I see two shot glasses delivered in front of him. I scream for him when he reaches for one glass, then the other, and pours them down his throat as if they were water, as if they were air, as if he hasn't been sober for nearly a decade, and as if the very poison he just knocked back hasn't nearly killed him many times over. I scream again, but no one turns to look at me, no one even seems to hear. I try to move toward him, to rip those shot glasses straight from his hands, toss them on the floor where they'll shatter into tiny, penetrating shards, and haul him the hell out of here. But as I implore my brain to lift my legs, to thrust forward, I discover that I'm weighted down, paralyzed, and I can scream and scream and scream, and try to run and run and run, but I am both silent and frozen, invisible and helpless all at once.

My father throws one final shot down his throat and then stands, grabbing hold of the mahogany bar to steady himself, and as the crowd in the corner salutes a run scored, my dad bobs and weaves himself to the exit. Before he wanders out into the warm starry night, he plunges his hand into his side pocket and pulls out his keys, triumphant, like a fisherman with his catch. I try to shout above the din, above the ruckus, For the love of God, stop, Dad, stop, *but still, I am voiceless, so all I can do is watch my father stumble out of the bar and into the parking lot, where for a sliver of time until the door slams shut, I hope that he'll be alright, even though I know, as well as I've ever known anything in my life, that nothing will be alright about this at all.*

four

"Till, Tilly, are you okay?" Someone is gently slapping my cheek, and I squint my eyes open to find Tyler hovering above. "Till, Jesus, are you okay?"

"Urf," I say. My body aches, muscles sore and bent in ways they didn't ask to be, and I slowly cast about for my bearings. I'm on the floor by the bureau, a lamp broken to my left. I run my fingers over my face and feel the pockmarks from a night spent pressed into the carpet.

Tyler slides his hands under my armpits and lifts me, effortlessly, to the bed. I want to stay like this forever, but he releases me against the pillows.

"Jesus, what happened? I just came in with your coffee." He pauses and hands me a mug by the nightstand. "And found you like this."

"I . . . I don't know," I say. "I had the weirdest dream. About my dad."

"Lie down." He cuts me off. "I'll call Luanne."

"Lulu's a delivery nurse. She's not exactly the cavalry," I say, sucking down a long, necessary sip of caffeine. "Besides, I feel fine.

I don't know. Maybe I just fell asleep there." We both look at each other, wondering if either of us believes me.

"From the look of it, you fainted."

"No. It wasn't that." I try not to think of my dream, with my father having tumbled down the black hole of his alcoholism, of his near-suicide spiral ten years back that could have come at a much higher price. No, my dad is in Puerto Vallarta with his girl-friend, a trip they've made the past three summers, drinking virgin margaritas, wearing ridiculous touristy sombreros and fanny packs.

"Are you sure you're okay?" he says.

"I am." I nod. A memory of Ashley Simmons bolts through me. *"I'm giving you clarity."* I shake my head again and toss the image free.

"You still want to do this barbecue? Because it would be totally fine if you canceled. We should probably cancel."

"What? Yes, of course!" I tilt my head toward the window to check the weather, and a joint in my back—still angry from my night on the floor—pops loudly. I notice the sweat ring around his T-shirt, the pit stains under his arms. Tyler's already been out for a run while I lay here splattered on the floor.

He turns toward the mirror, tugging his damp shirt over his hair in one smooth motion and sighing the tiniest of sighs that only his wife of a decade can detect. I know he'd rather not go. I know that he's weary from making small talk with the same people he sees day in, day out. That he'll perk up when the conversation turns to baseball, and that everyone will thump him on the back at the memory of his championship ring, but still, he'll suck down his beer and wish that he were someplace where he didn't have to justify himself to himself, because—as I have told him too many times of late—he's the only one who feels let down with who he's become. Everyone else thinks he is king of the world.

I linger in bed, watching him strip his sweaty clothes, tying a towel around his waist, when the phone rings—too early, too loud, and we both jump. The coffee spills on the white duvet, spreading like a pool of blood at a crime scene. Ty recovers before I do and takes one lone, giant stride toward the nightstand, and flips the receiver onto his naked shoulder.

Darcy, I think, remembering our fight, how we left things. *Maybe she's calling to apologize.* Until I realize the absurdity of that idea, because Darcy would never call to apologize. My anger breeds itself all over again. *How many times have I apologized to HER ass? Not this time! No, for once, not this time.*

"Hey, Timmy," Tyler says, mouthing "Timmy Hernandez" to me, his brow furrowing.

"What?" I whisper, but he raises his index finger, telling me to hold on, my thoughts of my delinquent, stubborn sister evaporating.

"No, no, I understand," he says to the phone. "Sure, yes, she's right here. Hang on." He passes the phone to me, covering the receiver with his palm. "It's your father. They arrested him this morning when he plowed his car into a tree off Harbor Road."

"What?" I say shrilly, my dream needling its way back into my consciousness, right alongside a dark swath of fear that I conjure up so quickly, too quickly, a mirror of my past. "He's supposed to be in Mexico!"

"He was drunk, Till," Tyler says softly, but I barely hear him. My stomach rises up and my tongue convulses, and I dry-heave over my coffee-spattered comforter. Then I move the phone to my ear to listen to Timmy Hernandez, the town sherriff, tell me everything I already somehow seem to know.

Three hours later, my father is snoring in our guest bedroom, as he has been since I brought him home from the station. His right eye is the color of grape jelly, but otherwise, he looks mostly okay, though, of course, I know that he is anything but.

I've instructed Tyler to run to the grocery store and pick up all the pound cake and premade cupcakes he can find. We're still due at Luanne's this afternoon, and it's too late to cancel. She and Darcy would know something is wrong, and then they'd press me, and then I'd have to either lie or tell them the truth, and neither of those options seems palatable. I would tell Luanne, but not today, not during her annual can't-miss Fourth of July blowout. And Darcy—we aren't speaking anyway, and this news would be like the match to her TNT: combustible. The last thing I need. My head hurts enough as it is. My father, well, I can manage him for a few more hours, probably a few more days, until I figure out a plan to tidy this up.

"This is what I do," I said to Tyler earlier, while he listened to me skeptically. "I *take care* of things for people. I'll handle this, just please, go to the store because I can't be two places at once." He popped his eyes at my chiding, at my bite, which was unfamiliar to both of us, but it had stuck with me through the night—this edge, this razor blade cutting through my psyche. *Jesus Christ, Tyler! Just go to the goddamn store and pick me up some freaking pound cake! How hard is that? Get your ass up from the couch and turn off ESPN while I manage the nitty-gritty. Is that too much to ask?* I handed him the keys, and he left without another word.

Now, I'm tucked on the velour armchair in the corner of the guest room, keeping my father company, my feet curled under me, a blanket draped over my legs. The open window blows in pleasant, soothing air, a balm after yesterday's torrid onslaught.

While I wait for my dad to come to, to offer some sort of rational explanation, I try to focus on work. I reach for CJ's grade report—she's amping up to apply to Wesleyan this fall; she'll mail the application off to the university so far from here and send every last hope for her future along with it. As I tug out the file, the Polaroid of Susanna from the day before slips out of my purse. *Just yesterday?* I think. It feels like forever ago. Before my ungraceful run-in with Ashley Simmons. Before the explosion at the cemetery with Darcy. Before my father got up and drunk and became one with a tree. Before I intuited that he would do so in the first place. That last one, that's the stickler.

I drop the photo back into the bag, abandoning hope of distraction while waiting for my dad to awaken. My dream from last night keeps pressing into the corners of my brain: how it seemed so tangibly real, how I blacked out without warning. My father gasps a deep inhale, and I glance up at him, waiting to hear his excuses, waiting for something more than Timmy Hernandez could offer under the fluorescent lights at the sleepy police station that never sees much more action than the occasional DUI or domestic violence call.

Timmy was generous enough not to press charges.

"Tyler and I go a long way back," he said to me, touching my elbow and leaning in close enough that I could smell the stale coffee on his breath. If I didn't know better, I'd swear he was trying to get a peek at my boobs. "You know, the team and all that. So this is a personal favor to him." Peering at him now, you'd never recognize the once ace pitcher for the '95 Wizards. Timmy's paunch flopped over his fading leather belt and his hairline was beginning to resemble the Great Lakes, looping widely above his forehead.

"I appreciate that very, very much," I said, searching over his doughy shoulder for my dad.

"The thing is, Tilly—" Timmy paused and rubbed the crux of

his neck. "From what I understand, this isn't the first time it's happened."

"No, no, you're right." I waved my hand, pressing my fingers to the bridge of my nose. "After my mother died . . ." I trailed off.

"No, what I mean"—Timmy lowered his voice—"is that this isn't the first time it's happened *of late*. We spoke with Cindy Heller over at Mickey Mantle's, and evidently, he's been in nearly every night the past few weeks."

At the mention of Cindy Heller, I felt the blood drain from my face, as if someone had stuck a vacuum up my nostrils and flipped it on high. A wave of my dream ran through me, an exorcism.

Now, the front door slams shut, and my father bristles in his sleep. Tyler peeks his head inside the door frame, holding up two grocery bags as evidence. I glide from the chair and go into the kitchen.

"We shouldn't leave him," he says, dropping the bags on the dining table. "What happens if he wakes up?"

"I threw out all of the alcohol in the house," I say, like that's the only thing I need to worry about if my off-the-wagon father wakes up in our guest bedroom while I'm at my sister's Fourth of July party, sucking on ribs and flicking buttered corn on the cob out of my teeth. Ty glares at me, fleetingly, then it is gone, the idea of his beloved beer going down the drain. *Oh, grow up!* I think, then shake it off. *What is wrong with me?* I exhale, purging my negativity, attempting to inhale a fresh outlook.

"I'll stay here with him," he offers, like this is in any way a selfless act.

"I don't want to go without you!" I crack open the plastic cupcake bins, and Ty hands me a serving plate.

"I think you should," he says as we unload each cupcake

onto the plate in tandem. "To be honest, I'm beat from the fair. Talked out. And I think someone should be here when he wakes up."

Yeah, I *should*, I think, annoyed at his cop-out, abandoning my attempt at positivity.

"Fine," I say with a sigh, because I don't want to argue with him, because we stopped arguing years ago, each of us recognizing that it's just easier to let the other one be. And besides, I don't trust myself right now, this unfamiliar anger nipping my tongue, begging to be unleashed. "Luanne and Ben will be disappointed. And Charlie, he'll ask for you."

"I know," he says, kissing my cheek and sliding toward the guest room to check in on my dad, and then he'll likely go on into the den, where he'll slip once again into the clatter of the baseball game, the background noise of his life. "Tell them I'm sorry. Tell them I wasn't feeling well."

I reach for the tinfoil to cover the plate, wrapping it securely, glancing down for a moment, catching a glimpse of my reflection, tangled and angled and mashed up like a fun-house mirror, looking back at myself, resembling nothing like the me I've come to know.

Later that night, after the barbecue, I unlatch the door and shuffle into the dark foyer, the kitchen lights bouncing off the umbrella rack, the shadows heavy. My flip-flops drag under my sullen weight. I'm still not feeling right. Whether it was the burden of forcing a frozen smile while chitchatting with Luanne or avoiding Darcy, who refused to make eye contact, stuck on her side of the great divide of our fight, or the gravity of watching little Charlie and his toddler friends chase each other, whirling like spinning tops through the front yard sprinkler, or the loneliness I felt without my husband beside me, I'm bone-weary, tired to the core, fatigued in that way that you feel in every one of your cells.

"Tilly." My father's voice is a croak. He is waiting for me in the kitchen.

"Jesus!" I shriek, not expecting him, not expecting anyone. "You're up! I almost had a heart attack."

"I'm sorry," he says, his face haunted, then adds, "For scaring you." Because we both realize that the breadth of his apology could extend for miles, for years.

"What happened?" I say, regretting it instantly because I just want to tumble under my covers and close my eyes for three days straight. A muscle twitches in my eyelid, a spontaneous, uncontrollable cry for rest.

"I hate to ask, but do you have anything to eat?" my dad says, like he isn't perfectly capable of moving to the pantry and finding out himself. I open the refrigerator and prep a plate of meatloaf I made two nights ago.

I set the food in front of him and pull out a chair, hoping he'll make this easy for both of us, though, if I were to really think about it, my father's strong suit was never making it easy for anyone. He forks at the meatloaf, pushing it around the edges of his plate, occasionally spooning it in for a morose, thoughtful bite, his jaw working and working and working, as if he could chew forever because then, surely, we wouldn't have to talk.

Finally, too exhausted to wait much longer, I say simply, "Dad, please, tell me what happened. You've been sober for so long."

He runs a few fingers through his tufted graying hair and shoots out his breath. He's hesitating, wondering if he can spin this into some tale in which he is the victim, in which the bartender held him down and poured those shots down the back of his throat, while he thrashed around and tried to refuse. Metaphorically at least. My dad, though a former football captain and two-time Westlake businessman of the year, is a portrait of contradictions, the epitome of the adage *Don't believe what you see*, because what you see of him is often a bluff, a flimsy excuse for what is really happening at his core. Tonight, though, he surprises me.

"Adrianna left me," he says, eyes casting down at the oak table.

"Timmy Hernandez told me that you told him she was in Mexico. Not that she left you," I say, confused, disbelieving.

"She is. Now. But she left me three weeks ago. She went down there without me." He sighs. "We already had the tickets and pre-paid for the condo." He looks so very, very old as he says this, like his joy for living has been vaporized, like he's ready to call it a day. The creases sink lower around his mouth the circles around his eyes are black holes. I think of the picture from the bottom drawer in my bureau, the one in which our family seemed unbreakable, and even though I'm armed with the map of how he got here, it's difficult to reconcile the snapshot of that man with the one sitting here now. My father listlessly nudges a chunk of meatloaf, and I rise to get him a glass of water.

"What happened?" I ask, holding the cup under the faucet for too long, distracted by my thoughts. The cold water spills onto my wrist, and I splash it off me, a damp dog after the rain.

He shakes his head. "She was diagnosed with melanoma."

"What?" I say. "Why didn't you tell us?"

"No, no, it's not as bad as it sounds. Stage one. Very early. They caught it, she'll be fine." Even as he says this, his face turns ashen, his mind casting about for a drink. I wipe the butt of the glass with a paper towel and set it down in front of him. He sips long and deeply, like he's arid ground grateful for a storm.

"So if she's going to be fine, what's the problem?"

"I just . . ." He stumbles, looking for any sort of reasonable way to explain how far he's fallen. His eyes burn red, his lashes batting furiously. "I just couldn't accept it. That it was fixable. With your mother . . . it happened so quickly with her, and when Adie told me this . . . I couldn't accept that she'd be okay."

"Why didn't you call me?"

"I thought I could handle it. And Adie just wanted to deal with it and be done with it, move on like it wasn't a big deal." He waves his fork in the air, as if informing me that his girlfriend has cancer would have been a nuisance. "Anyway . . . I picked up a beer one night to relax, thinking it would be just one. And then it was more than one, and then it was the next night . . ." He drops his head. "And so on."

"And Adie?"

"You know she has a zero-tolerance policy," he says, his voice weighted in guilt. Adie's first husband was a nasty drunk, and much as she loved my father—and she did, she did love my father—she'd told him from the start that she'd spent too long rebuilding her life to see another man tear it down all over again. I can't blame her for jetting it to Puerto Vallarta. If I were a different person, I would too.

"So now what?" I ask, reaching over to clasp his free hand, because I'm not that different person, even if for a glimmer of a moment, I wish I were.

"Now I stop," he says.

"Come on, Dad, it's not that easy."

"You'll help me," he says, locking our fingers together.

"Dad . . ."

"Please, Tilly, please. You always help me." His voice cracks. "You're the one who helps me the best."

I start to protest, because I've done this with my father before, because the guidance counselor in me knows better, knows that a one-person army in the face of this particular enemy isn't enough. But he looks at me with his runny eyes and his worn skin and yes, I see it there, his shame, and my heart cracks open for my father, the victim, whether or not he shares some, if not the bulk, of the blame for his burdens.

Of course I'll help him. This is what I do best.

five

My father, Ty, and I work out a plan. Or, at least, I work one out and explain it over coffee on Sunday morning, before Tyler leaves for his annual fishing trip with his old crew from the UW. Because Sheriff Hernandez has revoked his license for a month and because I don't trust my father enough to leave him unwatched, on his own, until he's proven to me that he's capable of going straight, my dad will remain in our guest room until his thirty days of probation are up. From there, we will reevaluate, examine his sobriety, explore what we all feel up to tackling next. I mention a treatment center, tentatively, with gentle feelers, but my dad balks, his ears red with angry contrition.

"I'm not going back to that place," he snaps, referring to the rehab facility that I finally shipped him off to the summer between my freshman and sophomore years in college. When everything came to a head and it became too obvious to ignore; when Darcy called me in a terrified, whispering frenzy, locked in her closet as the house was pillaged by a meth head in search of something worth selling, and my father was dead drunk on the downstairs couch, dead to the world around him, oblivious to his daughter, cowering and alone.

It is not the sturdiest of plans, I realize on Monday night, as I navigate the SUV to Susanna's to retrieve her and the twins for the Fourth of July fireworks show, but it is the compromise we can all live with for now. I still haven't spoken to Darcy. Even though I know that she won't wave her white flag and that eventually I'll need to wave mine, I still can't stomach it. *I'll call her tomorrow*, I think, just like I told myself yesterday. *I'll call her and pretend that this didn't happen, and we'll all move on, and eventually, I'll find a way to tell her about Dad.* This is how it's always worked, yet I'm annoyed at myself for the concession. Or maybe just at the concession itself. Who knows?

I beep the horn and the twins jet from the house. Susie lumbers after them, like she might rather be in bed, though I'm happy to see that her hair is washed, brushed shiny, a dollop of lipstick and blush spread across her face.

"We have to make a decision, you know," I say to her, once the kids are safely buckled in and we're speeding down Route 72 toward the lake.

"Shhh," she says, casting a quick glance behind her. "I don't want to talk about Austin in front of them."

"No, not a decision about *him*, a decision about the musical. Which one. Anderson needs to know by Friday."

"Oh," she answers, like she's contemplating a million reasons why she should back out. "Well, I don't really care." She pauses. "Whatever you think will be the most fun."

I glance over at her before flicking my eyes back toward the road. My best friend. No, she hasn't had a little fun with much in a while. The boys are yammering to each other behind us, and Susie just sighs, stares out the window, looking like she'd like to sink into the seat and *whoosh*, be invisible.

When she first discovered Austin's indiscretion, I had to talk her down from maiming him. Now, as the reality has seeped in, as she's discovered that she might not be made of enough grace to forgive him, and, with this discovery, realized this thing might shatter every last vision of her future, she's shifted from angry to broken. Not vengeful, not grief-stricken. Just broken.

"Then I vote for *Grease*," I say, hoping I can bolster her. "Remember how much fun it was senior year?"

She shrugs.

"Come on," I say. "It's time to anoint a new Sandra Dee. You can pass over the crown." I pull off the highway, turning down the bumpy dirt road toward the lake. The same road I drove down a million times back in high school, our summers spent working the day shift at the grocery store, at the diner, at a local construction job, the nights spent building bonfires and sipping wine coolers and listening to Pearl Jam on the dock.

"I think I'd be passing over the spandex pants, actually," she says, smiling. "Like I could ever fit into those again. God, yeah, okay, that *was* fun." She pauses, awash in the memory of *Grease* and of everything that has come after, as we turn into the clearing that opens to the lake. "Okay, why not. I could use a distraction."

"There are worse things you could do." I grin, giddy, shutting down the engine.

"Enough," she says at my *Grease* reference, tugging the twins from their car seats and stepping out into the night, though she laughs in spite of herself.

Though there are easily several hundred people gathered, I spot Luanne flagging us down almost immediately. Her hand flap-flap-flaps, her skinny arm waving us over. Charlie, her three-year-old, sits on her foot, munching on a cheese sandwich, and Ben, her husband, stands to kiss us hello.

"Hey," she says breathlessly as Susie goes about spreading a

blanket and unpacking a picnic dinner of peanut butter sandwiches and Oreos for the kids. "Come here." She tugs my wrist,
dragging me away from the fray.

Luanne and I look almost exactly the same. Smoky blue eyes
that are set about two millimeters too far apart, small rounded
noses that we inherited from my mother, milky skin that burns on
the spot without sunscreen but, as I learned in high school, can be
nurtured into just the right type of tan. Yet, despite our resem-
blance, she is subtly prettier than I am. Her features fold into each
other more smoothly; the lines around her eyes have yet to seep in.
Though the lines around my eyes have been earned over the years.
She never had to do the heavy lifting.

"First of all, how's Dad?" she says.

I'd called Luanne after the barbecue and broken the news, but
only after she swore not to tell Darcy, not to honor the sister code
of always sharing secrets. As the middle one, Luanne had a buffer
on either end of her when Mom died and Dad spiraled into an alcoholic haze. She kept going to soccer practice or taking her extra
biology lab because I was busy writing checks for the bills that my
father would forget to pay or dashing to the store when we ran out
of toilet paper or reading *Nancy Drew* with Darcy come bedtime,
when my dad was "still at work," though presumably, in retro-
spect, he was at a bar instead.

Luanne, as expected, absorbed the latest news with the even-
keeledness of a middle child. *"Let me know what I can do to help,"*
she said, as if he'd come down with a bad spell of allergies. *"Maybe
I can come over and talk with him,"* she said, her professional
nursing tone on full display. I could hear Charlie clamoring for
her in the background and Ben shushing him until Mommy was
off the phone, and I was certain that as soon as we hung up,
Luanne would be just fine. Yet another disaster that she'd review

from the outside in, while her older sister stuck herself smack in the middle of the chaos and buffed it clean.

"Sober," I say with a shrug. Which he is. Home and sober and taking up residence on the den couch, watching the Mariners game, plopping right into the dent that Tyler left this morning. "We'll see."

I've already written off my dream, my *freaky premonition-like* dream, as nothing more than coincidence. I've heard about this before: that if you really home in on someone, on their energy, their body language, their patterns, you might somehow develop a sixth sense, intuit the future or what they might say next or what they're thinking. Which is, I supposed when I thought about it last night while trying to fall asleep, *exactly what must have happened with my father.* And as far as this seed of anger? This breeding irritation with the world? *Well, I mean, come on, who wouldn't be a little put out,* I think, *a little damn pissed off at things, even if it's entirely against her nature to be so?*

"Okay, good," Luanne says, an afterthought, like the bow has already been tied around my father's recovery. An electric pulse of annoyance surges through me. "So listen, I have news. I'm pregnant."

"Oh, Lulu, that is so, so *wonderful*!" I pull her toward me, clutching her tight, then pushing her back to take a look. "You're not showing yet."

"I'm only five weeks," she says, her voice a whisper, right as the announcer, Steven Sommerfield, who runs the local radio station, steps up to the mike and declares the festivities nearly ready to begin, and I have to lean in closer to hear her. "So don't say anything just yet. I just got the blood work back today."

"Five weeks! Oh my gosh," I say, louder now, above the din. "I might be pregnant too, actually!" Casually, though, like I haven't been running to the bathroom and checking my under-

wear every other hour in the past two days. My period is due
any day.

"Wait, *what?*" She squeals. "You're pregnant too?!"

"No, no. I mean, I guess I could be."

"That would be *amazing,*" she says, kissing my cheek,
squeezing my hand. "Wouldn't Mom just love that?"

I smile openly at her, because that is my middle sister—so
seemingly simple and then out-of-nowhere deep. Before I can answer, a thundering *boom* explodes above our heads, crystal lights
forming a layered flower soaring in the sky, then twinkling down,
fading, fading, fading into nothing.

Darcy is planted on my front steps when I pull into my driveway
after dropping Susanna and the twins back at home.

"What?" I bark, still angry, that bass note of disharmony
beating in me, alive, present. I reach in the backseat to lug a grocery bag I'd earlier forgotten. "Is this your peace offering or something?"

"Fine," she says flatly, standing and holding up her open
palms. "Yes, I'm sorry. Get over it." She hesitates. "Also, I have to
crash here."

"Of course," I say. "Always with the catch." I trudge up the
porch, the bag full of canned beans and peas and corn, cramping
my left bicep.

"Look, *I'm sorry,*" she says. "Jesus." We both know it's not
like me to hold the grudge, to make her work hard for her contrition. But the sticky anger isn't letting go. I push past her. "Come
on, please? I had to pack up from Dante's, so I just need to stay
here a few days before I head back to L.A. My ticket isn't for another week, or trust me, I'd be out of here."

"Oh, Jesus Christ, Darcy! Pull it together!" I drop the

bag—too hard—by my feet, and the cans clang together, a cymbal punctuating my thoughts. "I mean, look at you! What are you doing with your life?"

Her eyes flare and she steps backward, as if the force from my unexpected ire has literally propelled her away, and *bam!* She trips over the suitcase that I'm just now noticing and is on her ass in a second.

"Shit!" Darcy yells.

I chew the inside of my lip, willing my pulse—a metronome in my neck—to slow. *What is wrong with you, Tilly Farmer?* I think, at the exact moment that Darcy shoots me a *What bug crawled up your ass?* look. Finally, when I'm certain that I won't resort to physical harm, I exhale and sit down next to her.

"What happened?" I sigh.

She wipes her dirtied palms on her shorts. "Eh, I slept with him last night." She looks up at me, all wide-eyed and innocent, like she didn't know that Dante has been pining for this since she bolted to Berklee. "Turns out, I probably shouldn't have. He told me he still loved me." She shrugs.

"Oh, *Darcy*," I say, exasperated, too tired for a you-should-have-known-better lecture, my rage finally poofing out of me. "Fine. Come on."

It's only then that I remember my father. *Oh crap.*

Darcy has never quite meshed with our dad, or maybe it was vice versa, but more likely not. But my mother, either consciously or unconsciously recognizing this, quickly made Darcy her favorite, a fact we all just tacitly accepted. She was the one who was blessed with my mom's gift for music, and they'd spend hours pressed against each other on the piano bench, playing in harmony, playing solo, or just giggling with their shared love of melody. And when she died, well, surely, any child would be scarred at the loss of her mother at such a young age, but for Darcy, it was a pox that has never been erased. That my father compounded her alienation with his drinking was, in her mind, unforgivable.

The screen door bangs against the frame, and we shuffle inside, the wheels of Darcy's suitcase squeaking along the hallway. Before I can even think of what I'm going to say, how I'm going to explain this to her, and what could possibly temper her anger at my father, he walks out to greet us. He is wearing Tyler's faded hunter-green robe and carrying a glass of what I know is water but also suspect might be vodka, just because, well, it's the sort of thing you worry about when your off-the-wagon father moves back in with you.

"Darcy!" His arms open into a wide embrace as he pulls her in closely. "I wasn't expecting you. Did you just get into town?" He says this with the nonchalance of a man who has mastered the art of overlooking the obvious: that he is standing in my foyer in my husband's robe, with his hair askew, his undershirt dank, a purple welt under his eye, hoping against all rational hope that people around him won't point out the myriad of problems with this picture.

"You need a shower," she says, wiggling her way out of his hug like a worm down the sidewalk. She steps back and stares at him. "What are you doing here?"

"What are you doing here?" he asks back, and winks at her. Actually winks at her.

"Darcy," I say quickly. "Dad is staying with us for a while. Tyler's on his fishing trip, so I wanted the company. Why don't you go put your stuff in the den?"

She squints at our dad, then looks from him, to me, to him again.

"Why does he look messed up?" she asks me, with her eyes still pinned on him.

"Messed up how?" I say, fervently wishing that my father had taken my suggestion to shower this morning, when it appears that he actually slept the whole day through.

"Puffy eyes, gross skin," she says, her words like steel. "Like he's recovering from a bender." She isn't dumb, this sister of mine. We long ago learned to recognize the signs.

"Darcy." My dad starts to speak, then, surprisingly, chokes on his words. His hands flop listlessly at his sides, reminding me of dying, gasping fish.

"Oh, fuck me," she says as the transparency of the situation clicks into place. "I cannot believe you!"

"Darce." I touch her elbow gently. "Take your suitcase to the spare bedroom."

She hesitates, eyeballing my father with vitriol, fury that I haven't witnessed since she left for Berklee, intent on never casting a second glance back. I see Darcy consider her options—return to Dante's, camp out at the airport, buy a new ticket that she can't afford—before she realizes the certainty of her situation: she's stuck. She grabs for the handle of her suitcase, and then, *squeak, squeak, squeak,* I hear her carelessly dragging it, the contents of her life, down the hall.

She's stuck, I say to myself.

And then surprisingly, despite the fireworks, despite the possibility of hope in my womb, despite everything, an alien, tiny germ of a voice, that same one that's been tailing my psyche since I blacked out on my bedroom floor, echoes back, *Aren't we all?*

 My father's house is musty—a mildewed cloud hovers over the living room—like someone hasn't slept here in weeks, or, at the very least, someone hasn't cared enough to tend to the housekeeping details that comprise the basics of domestic hygiene. A tower of unread newspapers has fallen like playing cards in the foyer. A mountain of letters—shoved into the mail slot and ignored—has amassed on the floor; an overflowing pile of garbage tumbles from the kitchen trash can. Mostly, though, the house looks dead, un-lived in. *Why didn't Adie call me? At the very least she could have called me.*

My irritation rises up, a tiny pebble rubbing against my sole, uncomfortable, present, impossible to ignore. I'm starting to feel like the Incredible Hulk: one minute entirely normal, the next minute turning green with anger, ripping off my shirt, and storm-ing down the streets in search of a brawl. Or Dr. Jekyll and Mr. Hyde. Maybe one of them.

I nab several wayward socks that are squashed next to the baseboard, trying to remember who is who—which one goes crazy? Jekyll? Hyde? I can't decide. I throw the socks against the couch, where they land with a pitiful thwop.

Dad still lives in our childhood home. It's too big a house for him now, with its five bedrooms and its pool out back that mostly stays covered the year through. Adrianna wanted to sell it; she tried to convince him to buy one of the condos in the new complex that had been built a few years back near the mall with the Penneys in it. New construction wasn't too common for Westlake, and mostly, those condos sat empty. My dad kept telling Adie that he was waiting for the price to drop, but Luanne and I always knew that she'd never get him to move, even if he won one of the damn things for free.

I run my fingers over the wallpaper in the kitchen. My mother applied it herself, just before she got sick. We all piled into the car and went to the décor store, and oh, did it take hours upon hours for us to agree. Finally, Darcy flipped the page to a creamy paper with tiny green and pink flowers that swirled in such a way that they almost looked as if they were dancing. We huddled around our baby sister to get a view of it and then fell into a bubble of silence. "This is it!" Darcy shouted, and we murmured our approval. And then, soon after, the diagnosis came, and even though our kitchen looked much the same as it had before the gutting news, nothing, of course, was ever the same. Even those tiny pirouetting flowers seemed to lose their bounce.

I tuck the strewn garbage back into the can and then flip the lights off and tread down to the basement for a suitcase to stow enough of my father's clothes to last the month. The too-steep steps creak as I gingerly make my way down, my hand grasping the cool cement wall. The main lighting long ago burned out, so I tug the rusty brass chain that swings near the bottom of the stairs and click on the solitary lightbulb for illumination. My eyes take a moment to adjust to the dimness.

The dank underbelly of the house is a compilation of my father's life. Despite the passing years, he hasn't had the stomach to part with many of my mother's belongings; instead, on the one year anniversary of her death, Luanne and I finally picked up the actual pieces, stowing the bulk of her closet in cardboard boxes that we then dutifully hauled down here. Darcy was out cruising the neighborhood on her bike, and my dad was mourning at Shecky's, a bar within walking distance of our home that has long since closed.

I haven't ventured down to the basement in years, and now the boxes are all stacked just as they were from ages before, my teenage handwriting scrawled on the sides: *"Sweaters," "Coats," "Shoes."*

In the half light, I navigate through the archives. *"Shirts." "Jeans." "Pants."* All tucked away in a time capsule, like if he never gave it away, she might still somehow make it back to claim it. I spot another box behind one that says *"Misc."* and recognize not my own handwriting, but that of my mother.

"Tilly's photo stuff." A rush of heat rises in my cheeks, the memory of her frail, beaten shell of a self, insistent on taking me shopping for a new camera, and then that same afternoon, when we plopped on the floor in my room, loading the old gear and some old pictures into this very box, the idea to organize my photos and equipment, not to part with it forever. But later, only weeks later, she passed, and with so many other more pressing matters to deal with, I slipped down to the basement and slid the box to the very back corner, where it sat hidden, untouched until now. That second camera, the one she bought for me on a summer morning before she died, smashed one day when it tumbled out of my car, a crack like a storybook lightning bolt right through the lens, and I never worked up the nerve to ask my dad for a new one. A new camera seemed infantile when the very skeleton of my world was shattering.

A fat film of grime has spread itself across the top of the box.

My nose sucks in the dust and just as I'm repressing a sneeze, my cell vibrates in my pocket.

Tyler. Finally. I haven't heard from him since he dropped off the radar and into Nolan Green's parents' lake cabin two days ago.

"Hey, what's up?" I say, unsnapping my phone and tucking it under my shoulder as I separate the musty cardboard flaps of the box and look inside. Urine-colored newspaper, balled up and decaying, peers back at me.

"Sorry I haven't called," he says. "Reception up here is spotty. And we've been on the lake most of the time anyway. You should have *seen* what I hauled in yesterday. It's on ice. I'll bring it back for the weekend."

I plunge my hands under the newspaper and feel something smooth.

"How's your dad?" Ty continues.

"So-so." I pause, only half-focused on the conversation, because, truth told, I never enjoy the newly gutted fish that Tyler totes home with him, with their glassy eyeballs and their tiny bones that inevitably poke into my gums when least expected.

What is this? My fingers shimmy beneath the surface and tug out a stack of black and white eight-by-tens.

"How are you?" Ty asks.

"Fine," I say. "A little tired, but fine." I start to tell him about Luanne, but the line crackles, and I hear his voice lob in and out, *"Hel—lo, hel—lo, Til, hel—lo?"*

"I'm here!" I say loudly, my voice reverberating off the damp walls.

"I can hear you," he says, clearly now. "So, yeah, anyway, I caught this incredible bass, and oh my God, you won't believe the stories Nolan has about the team now." Nolan, because he was never quite good enough to play for the minors, just barely qualified for the bench of the UW team in college and now works in the back office, recruiting new prospects, new hopes, new blood to invigorate them.

Distractedly, because there were few things I cared less about than Nolan Green—who once got so totally wasted in college that he passed out naked next to me while I was already asleep in Tyler's bed and didn't have the decency to apologize the next morning when I rolled over and snuggled with him for a good five minutes until I realized the difference—I flip through the eight-by-tens to a shot of my high school crew that I took down by the lake. It must have been July, maybe early August: Susanna and Austin and Elizabeth Childs, whom I now run into at the post office, and Darren Lewis, who enlisted in the army and came home from Iraq a hollowed-out shell of a man, and of course, Tyler, in board shorts, with his arms flung open in a victory stance. In the background, the lake is a metal gray, with streaks of summer sun bouncing off the ripples. I stare at the sixteen-year-old Tyler and remember the pangs of longing that I had for him that summer. How our friendship evolved into something more for me, and how we'd all convene at the dock after our shifts ended at our summer jobs, and how I'd watch him, as surreptitiously as possible, hoping that one afternoon he'd discover the same pangs inside of him.

"But it's pretty awesome here," he says. "Pretty amazing. Just mostly solitude. Good time to be alone with my thoughts."

"I'm sure." I roll my eyes. As if Nolan Green ever found the solitude in anything.

And then, out of nowhere, I feel it: the cramp building from my little toe. *Oh, shit,* I think, as the pain snakes its way through my limbs—worming up from my calf to my thigh to my bowels and clamping around my heart until it shoots into my brain, and I feel like my head might implode into a hundred thousand little pieces.

"Ty!" I say, though it is nothing more than a whoosh of a

whisper, and I pray that he can hear me, pray that somehow, he can snap me out of this, snap me back to the present, eradicate the temple-splitting pain. But then it feels like water is filling my ears and the dim basement walls are asphyxiating the air in my lungs, and then I feel the cool concrete floor against my cheek, and I close my eyes and block out the hurt, and then, I feel nothing at all.

The rain is pit-pat, pit-pattering off of the roof of the SUV, which is parked in the driveway, adjacent to a U-Haul, whose back door is flung open and is half-stuffed with mismatched cardboard boxes and one gray, fraying duffel bag that I recognize as Tyler's from college. To be honest, I didn't even realize that he still owned it. He must have dumped it in the back of the hall closet when we moved in, and I must have overlooked it through the years.

I am on our sidewalk, staring at the house, the driveway from the outside in. I run my hand through my hair and notice, startlingly, that though the air is pregnant with moisture, I'm dry, bone-dry, an apparition in this reality.

Our front door swings ajar and Austin emerges, carrying yet another box. He waddles to the U-Haul, drops it with a grunt, then leans against the vehicle to catch his breath. Tyler comes out a second later, his hands empty, and surveys the truck.

"Alright," he says to Austin, then zips up his puffy down coat, one that I bought for him last winter. "We're done. Thanks, man."

They slap each other high fives and then readjust their baseball caps in unison. It's then that I notice that Austin's ring finger is stripped of his wedding band, a tiny and yet enormous naked symbol of where I am, of when I am, and what's transpired, and suddenly, I'm acutely aware that I've once again been thrust into the future, into a time warp that hasn't yet unfolded.

Moving? *I think.* God damn it, we're moving! How on earth are we moving and where on earth are we moving to? *I tangibly feel my blood race, and I wonder how Tyler got me to agree, what promises he must have made for me to cave, to make such an enormous concession.* Maybe it's because I am pregnant, *I consider.* Maybe I got pregnant, and we need a bigger house. *I peer down to my stomach, to see if it has pillowed, but no, I am still the me from the past, not the me from the future, so there are no clues to be found. And besides, I remember almost as quickly, this house is perfectly adequate for a family of three, and even if it weren't, it's not like we could afford something bigger anyway.*

I stare at the front door and hope that I will soon see myself waddle down the steps, toting a cup of hot tea, maybe chocolate chip cookies for their hard labor, signs that I am happy to leave this place—this house? this town—that I won't resent Tyler for the disruption to my perfectly planned life. But there is no movement at the entryway, nothing but torpedoing water spilling from the gutters onto the porch.

Tyler and Austin ease themselves on the edge of the U-Haul, despite the rain, and both emit long, exhausted sighs. Tyler is just a few feet away from me, and I so want to call out to him, ask him for some answers. What the hell, *I think, and give it a go.* "Ty-ler!" *But when I do, when I do call for him, of course, he doesn't turn toward me, can't hear me, can't see me. I shout his name three times and then quit, defeated. And then I try one last time, screaming,* "Tyler," *throwing the weight of my body behind it, and he flinches, yes, I see him flinch, and I wonder if I'm on to something.*

But then they stand and head inside, and I am once again left alone with only this open truck bed and the rain, pit-patting its way around my bubble.

Suddenly, the door flies open, and Darcy races out. She is wearing old leggings and flip-flops that must leave her toes instantly frigid, and though she needs a jacket in this dreary, freezing rain, she's wearing only a sweatshirt. She flips her hoodie over her now dark purple hair and wipes her smeared mascara, making more of a mess down her cheeks than before. There is a stain down the front of her, wet and blotted, and it reminds me of a Rorschach test. She rushes past me, so close that she nearly brushes right against me, and I smell the unmistakable scent of vodka. I try to reach out to her, to grab her forearm and cling tight, but of course, I am helpless, and soon, she has fled down the driveway, down the road, gone.

I turn back and stare at the contents of the truck, of my life, so tidy, so easily mobile, and as the drops accelerate from a passing steel cloud, thundering down in sheets upon sheets, I wonder if it is possible that I might actually drown.

seven

"Jesus, Tilly, wake up!" Someone is rubbing pepper beneath my nose, and a burning sensation sparks up through my nostrils.

"Ow! Stop, stop!" I wave my hands in front of my face and push myself into a sitting position. The back of my head is pulsing, and I run my hands over my scalp; a monstrous welt is growing like an infected zit. My eyes are paperweights, but I force them open to find Susanna and Darcy crouched beside me.

"What are you doing here?" I say; my voice is sandpaper.

"We have to get you to the hospital," Susie says.

My eyes scurry around me. *What is going on? What the hell is happening?* Slowly, my memory clicks on, *Why is Tyler packing up our house?* I swallow hard, my lunch, a drive-through hamburger, reappearing in my throat. *Oh, no. This can't be good.* The memory of the first time this happened crests through me: my visions of my father and how I somehow saw the future that hadn't yet unspooled itself. *No, no, this is probably nothing. Yes, no, it's nothing. Maybe it's a coincidence. Two blackouts, two visions.* I fight back my gag reflex for the second time.

Darcy rubs the nape of my neck, a feeble attempt to soothe me.

Then I consider something more alarming: the vision itself.

Tyler. The boxes. Why would I dream that we're moving? *We're moving? We can't be moving! No, no, NO. This must be a fluke, must be some weird sort of hormonal reaction perhaps related to being pregnant. Yes! Yes, that's it! I am pregnant, and as a result, my brain is spinning off the deep end.*

"I think I might be pregnant," I say. "I'm thinking that my hormones have gone haywire, and I bet it's just that I'm pregnant! It's happened before." *Yes, it must be because I am pregnant, because what else could it be? That I can somehow intuit the future?* Suddenly, I remember Ashley and her stupid, insipid, self-righteous prophecies. *Shit.* I exhale. *No, no, I am pregnant. That is it! That. Is. It.*

"Ty mentioned that, that it's happened before," Darcy says, her voice cracking at the idea of some sort of medical catastrophe. She's already been through that once, once being one time too many. Plump tears bobble on her lower eyelids. "But you think you just might be pregnant? You think that could be it?" She tries to force a smile out from the weight of her concern, and she looks so heartbreakingly much like she did as a toddler. Wide blue-gray eyes, even bigger than mine or Luanne's, a quivering lip, bursting with the emotion that she was never capable of masking.

"Ty told you?" I ask. I feel like I'm drowning, slipping around in time, slipping around in the gravity of my fears.

"He called me when you stopped talking to him on the phone and he heard a crash," I hear Darcy saying, as she and Susie each clasp an elbow and pull me upward. My brain is zipping, speeding, trying to keep up, and I have to forcibly home in on her lips to understand the words coming out. I feel like I'm existing inside some warped science-fiction novel with two dueling existences: one in which I am completely losing my mind, in which the world has spun off its axis, and another in which Susie and Darcy speak to me in slow, garbled words, as if life is operating in slow motion, as if life is simply moving on. "You had the car, so I called Susie. We got here as fast as we could."

"I'm fine," I say again, though my face feels bloodless and drawn. "I'm sorry you guys had to come get me. Suse, when you got pregnant, did you have . . . weird dreams?"

"Yep." She nods. "Oh my God, did I. The weirdest, all about Donnie Parker, who, remember him, I dated before Austin? All the time. Like, every night, I dreamed about the past."

I swallow, because the one thing I'm not dreaming about is my past.

"But that aside, you're not fine," Susie says, reading me clearly. "I can see it. You're not fine."

"I am," I exclaim, shrilly, sharply, a little too defiantly for anyone to believe. I lumber down onto the lowest step and fold my body over my knees. "Please. Can't we just go home? I'm exhausted. I'll take a pregnancy test tomorrow. That's all this is. I'm sure."

I bristle at the thought of home, of Tyler packing up all of our belongings and whisking us away. Tears announce themselves behind my eyes, then tumble down my pale cheeks, an admission of my despair at the thought of leaving, even though, yes, *it was just a dream, a figment of an idea that must have planted itself inside of me, right along with that fetus, a reverse-nesting sort of thing that splays out my fears of being uprooted now that I have to, critically, actually root myself.* I wipe my face and tuck my head beneath my legs and hope that the world rights itself when I pick it back up.

"Okay, well, maybe this is good news," Susie says. "Maybe you really are pregnant! People do faint when they're pregnant!"

"Yes," I say, "that's probably it." I see Ashley Simmons in my mind, mocking me, telling me that of course I'm not pregnant, that babies and husbands aren't the answer to everything! I pull my head out from its cocoon and fold my hands over my face, and a crest of nausea sparks in my bowels. "Can we just go home? It smells like mold down here, and I'd like to get some sleep. I'm sorry for this."

"Don't apologize again, for God's sake." Susie's hand moves in concentric circles over the spot between my shoulder blades. "I bet it's that you're pregnant!"

Slowly, I unfold myself and grab the banister to stand. My legs feel anchored, as if someone has tied concrete slabs to my ankles and then said, "So what, walk anyway."

Susie takes my hand and says, "Let's get going," and I wearily force my legs to comply with my brain and head back toward the bright lights up above.

Darcy brings me a cup of peppermint tea when we get home.

"I checked in on Dad, and I called Tyler to tell him you're okay," she says as she passes me the steaming mug. I raise it to my mouth, but the lip is still too hot to sip. She nuked the mug in the microwave, even though I asked her to use the teapot.

"Thank you. I'll call him tomorrow," I say. "How's Dad?"

"Asleep." She shrugs. "I guess that's how he stays sober. It's tough to drink when you're asleep."

"Cut him some slack, Darcy." I blow my breath over the tea. "He's trying his best. And he's here so that I can help him."

"Don't you ever get tired of that?" she asks, plopping on the bed, bouncing the mattress.

"It's been a long time," I answer. "And besides, we all do what we have to." I brace myself for another rehash of the same old fight. "Please. Just don't start. I don't have the energy for a fight."

She inhales, and I know she wants to say something more, but in an unusual second of self-awareness, she dials herself back.

"So what's really going on with you?" she says finally. "Are you really pregnant? Am I actually going to be an aunt?"

"You're an aunt already," I point out.

"That's true, but I meant for you," she says.

"I don't know—maybe," I answer. "I'll pick up a test in the morning." I squeeze her hand, and we grin loopy grins at the thought of that tiny seed sprouting inside of me. Any of the rancor from the past few days is whisked away; we are sisters, after all, and have spent a lifetime breaking—and then forgiving—each other.

"You'll make a great mom," Darcy says, touching my knee. "Really, you will."

I stare at her for a beat, grateful for her momentary kindness, with so much unspoken between the two of us, and then I watch her beautiful porcelain face, making a mental map, a frozen image like a photograph I would have taken so many years ago. Now, maybe a Polaroid that I'd paste up on my office wall, a remarkable face in a sea of some less-than-remarkable ones. *When did she become such a grown-up?* I think. Behind her blackened eyeliner and her ever-present pout, she's evolved into an honest-to-God adult. I never noticed it until now. I look at her, with her face half-illuminated by my nightstand lamp, and her still blond hair falling every which way below her shoulders, and I snap a picture in my mind, an image that I hope will linger for as long as I can remember. She holds my glance more firmly than I realized she was capable of, and I can feel her bolstering me, offering me her back on which to lean.

A knock on the door surprises us both, and Darcy squeaks. Dad edges the door open.

"What?" she says to him.

"Anyone want to join me for a late movie on the tube?" he says, the loneliness and desperation in his voice too obvious to ignore.

"I'll pass," Darcy says, rising to leave. "Tilly, we're testing tomorrow." She leans down and kisses my forehead. "Good things are coming, for sure." I nod, a rush of thankfulness for her loyalty passing through me.

She brushes by my father, each of them tilting their bodies ever so slightly so they don't physically collide, and then he looks at me and offers a little shrug. *You know, just one of those things,* he shrugs, that his youngest daughter will likely never forgive him for the sins of his past. I shrug back at him, my own admission that for now, in an unusual turn of events, I don't have the answers we're all looking for.

He scoots out of the room, his slippers shuffling against the wood floor, and then I hear him thwop-thwop-thwop down the hall to the den, where he will fall asleep on the couch, the noise of the TV lulling him into slumber, just like Tyler, for whom sleep seems to come so easily, so unencumbered. But me? No, I won't sleep. Not tonight. Not now that I fear that my dreams might be haunted, not now, when I no longer trust myself to dream at all.

eight

The next morning, Darcy tails me like a delinquent puppy dog through the hushed hallways of Westlake High. She hasn't returned since the very day she graduated, and now, I can't tell if she's nervous or repulsed to be back here.

"It still smells the same," she says, while I tell her to hurry up, and we scuttle over the linoleum floor. "Ugh, I might barf. It's like half-cooked cheeseburger or something."

"Shhhh! Summer classes are in session," I say. "I told you this was part of the deal. And please, I'll remind you again, make yourself as inconspicuous as possible."

"Don't be mad at me for wanting to support you!" she says, buoyed with indignation.

"I'm not; I'm sorry," I reply. "We're just late. And you know I hate being late."

Darcy was up this morning at an hour I'd never actually seen her awake, insisting that she join me today.

"I always thought you might actually be a vampire," I said to her over morning coffee.

"Tyler is away, and I want to share this with you, since he can't," she said back, her words remarkably prescient for someone whom I mostly view as a stunted adolescent. I informed her that she'd subsequently be held hostage with me for the duration of the day because I wouldn't have time to drop her back at the house before my meeting with CJ and then with Anderson to finalize the details of the musical. Darcy just stuck her tongue out and said, "Fine," as good an example as any of our newly forged peace.

On the way to school, we swung by CVS to buy a pregnancy test, where Louis Lewison (yes, really, his parents named him that) worked behind the register and took forever, *forever!* on a price check for the Ensure that the elderly couple in front of me was buying in bulk. And now, we are late.

CJ is waiting for me when we rush into my office. Her softball-toned legs are too long for the purple love seat, so her knees angle awkwardly upward, reminding me of a parent sitting in a pre-schooler's chair.

"Sorry, I'm late, CJ. It was my fault." I thud my bag onto the floor and rifle through the contents for her folder, ignoring the pink First Response test that I tucked into the inside pocket and the visceral beat of my heart when I consider what that tiny plus sign might bring. I need to be pregnant; I need to cling to the idea that Tyler and I could be, are, in fact, becoming a family, not just two people who met more than a decade ago and somehow now belong to each other. Because last night, when my body implored me to sleep, my mind refused, and all I could do was replay that bleak, waterlogged scene over and over again—the U-Haul, the boxes—like a movie reel caught on a skip.

"No big deal," CJ says, then looks at Darcy. "Hey, you're Darcy Everett, right? I remember you."

"I am," Darcy says, making a little curtsy, a symbol of her delight at getting recognized, as if CJ were a member of her fan club.

"I was in seventh grade when you were a senior," CJ says. "I heard you're out in L.A. now, landing a record deal or something. Cool."

"Pretty much," Darcy says, ignoring the minute detail of the factual inaccuracy of the rumor.

"That is so, *so* awesome. Like, seriously, you're like my hero. Getting out of Westlake and becoming famous."

"Oh, well, yeah," Darcy says, suddenly interested in invisible lint on her T-shirt. "It's nothing. I mean, it's pretty great, but it's not that big of a deal."

"Do you think I could call you sometime? Get your number from Mrs. F? I'd love to hear how you did it."

"Sure, definitely." Darcy smiles, her composure regained.

"Are you helping out with the musical?" CJ says. "Auditions are next week, right?"

I nod and Darcy gives a noncommittal shrug. "Maybe," she says. "I'm not sure how long I'm staying."

I shoot her a glance—another one of Darcy's flaky nonanswers, when we both know that she'll be long gone to Los Angeles by the time CJ and the cast line up outside the music room and warble for a shot at the lead.

"And with that, Darcy, please excuse us." I sigh, plopping into my chair. "CJ and I have a few things to go over."

She scoots out the door, with a "call me" motion to her ear for CJ's benefit, and I move my college application folder to my lap.

"Okay, so, I reviewed everything this past weekend, and I think we're almost there." I flip through the pages. "The only area you might be lacking is some sort of community service. Wesleyan is big on that." I look up to see her defeated, punctured, on the sofa. Her face sags like a basset hound's.

"It's not such a big deal, CJ," I say. "We're way ahead of the game. It's only July; that's why we're doing this so early. There are loads of places to volunteer, and if you start ASAP, you can include it on your app."

"I barely have time to squeeze in my shift at the restaurant. How the hell am I going to manage this?" She shakes her head. "It's like everyone is conspiring against me to keep me here."

And what's so wrong with here? I want to shout. *Why does everyone seem so intent on going anywhere but here? Darcy! CJ! My own freaking husband!*

"We'll make it work," I say, a false confidence in my voice. "I'll make some calls, you make some calls. This is doable."

She pauses. "Johnny dumped me." Her throat catches.

"I'm sorry, CJ." I reach over and pat her knee. To the best of my recollection, she's been dating the basketball forward since late last spring.

"It doesn't matter." She shrugs, belying her crumpled cheeks, her scrunched nose, staving off her breakdown. "Ms. F, you have to get me out of here. I can't be stuck. I can't be stuck here with Johnny Hutchinson and his stupid friends, and this life in this stupid town."

We're all stuck, I think again.

"You won't get stuck," I say reassuringly, as much for her sake as for mine. "You'll get into college, CJ, even if for some reason it's not Wesleyan."

"I can't be," she whispers. "I can't be stuck." Then she looks at me with alarm and says, "No offense, Ms. F. I think you're awesome."

"None taken," I say, perplexed a moment, until I realize that, in fact, I symbolize the very thing she's fleeing.

"Anyway"—she sighs—"I'll see you next week for auditions

and for prom-committee meeting right after." She smacks a plastic, empty smile on her face. "Which dessert to order, which punch to make. Good times."

"It *is* good times. Did you see the e-mail I sent around about the Arc de Triomphe?" I grin—genuinely this time—drunk on the memory of my own prom, me in a powder blue dress, Ty in his dad's tuxedo, slow-dancing to "I Will Always Love You," with the lights in the gym spinning, a wine cooler warming my senses.

"I did," she says, pushing up her own smile that never quite meets the rims of her eyes. "You're right; it'll be amazing."

After CJ turns out the door, I try to refocus on other work, on busywork, but I keep replaying her pitying, despairing gaze. "I'm not stuck. I'm *not* stuck." I say it over and over again, a leftover habit from childhood when I thought that if you repeated something enough times, you could somehow make it true.

I stare out my side window onto the playing field, which will sit empty, quiet, and untouched until the softball team tramples it this afternoon. I run my hand down to my belly. A sign, an inkling, a hope. A chance for Tyler and me to become invincible. Because, despite what I've been telling myself—yes, maybe, if I really dig into it—I can acknowledge the fissures. His discontent. But Tyler and I were already supposed to be invincible. From the very first time that he kissed me—we'd all had a few beers and had broken into the football field to blow off some steam on a crisp September night—I knew that we were invincible. I'd been pining for him all summer, the well of emotion catching me off guard.

We'd been friends since elementary school. My mother was barely hanging on. He'd just broken up with Claire Addleman, who was a co-cheerleader and to whom I thus owed friendship fidelity. And yet, we'd kick our feet off the dock of the lake or we'd huddle together at a bonfire in the late hours of the evening, and none of that mattered, especially not my mom. In the little bubble that I inflated around us, Tyler shielded me from all of the anguish that crashed down upon me as soon as I ventured outside of his protection. So when we lay down on the football field, staring at the clear night and its crystalline sky, and he pressed closer to me, and then rolled his head sideways and then took his hand to move my chin toward his, and then molded his mouth over mine, I knew that it was forever. That bubble, rising around us, washing everything else away.

I knew that we were lucky to meet so young, to avoid the mistakes that some of our friends made: pregnant in high school; divorced at twenty-six; miserable—like Austin—until you make that cataclysmic mistake that shows you that you don't really know what misery is until your wife emotionally castrates you and kicks your ass out. It wasn't that it was easy for Tyler and me—the weekends in college driving back and forth, the drunken frat party temptations, the fact that we had to grow up together rather than meeting when maybe each of us already knew who we were separately. But we did it, we endured, in spite of it all.

The bell clangs, tugging me out of the memory.

We're all stuck, I think again, picking up the phone to check in with Ty, hoping to reach him and say, *I might be pregnant, and please, I wish you were here and not up at Nolan Green's parents' lake house, and didn't feel so far away.* But I'm sent to voice mail, an empty greeting that offers little reassurance that he is out there, missing me too.

A spider suddenly winds its way up the leg of my desk and onto my prom files. I fleetingly consider granting it reprieve, returning it to its wayward family outside, but instead, I reach down, remove my sandal, and *smack*, gone, it is gone.

• • •

Darcy, always easily distracted, has nearly forgotten her well-intentioned, sisterly determination as we amble down the hallway during lunch period toward the girls' locker room, the pregnancy test concealed in my hand.

"God, it's scary how little it's changed," she says, eyeing the placards above the gym upon which various team captains' names are carved. She bites into the peanut butter sandwich I packed her this morning and swirls her tongue over her teeth when the bread lodges itself in her molars.

"You only graduated five years ago. How much did you expect things to change in five years?" I say, my mind on a million other things.

"Don't kid yourself. This place is, like, frozen in a time warp," she answers, one finger mining for stuck bread.

I hold open the door to the locker room, and she saunters in, head bobbing every which way, absorbing all the tiny memories that she thought she left behind.

"Jesus." She inhales. "Do you know I nearly lost my virginity in here?"

"No," I say. "And that's probably something you can keep to yourself." I walk by the first stall, clogged with toilet paper, and into the next, then latch it behind me. My fingers tremble as I peel back the box flap, then unwrap the stick that could deliver the news of all that I've ever hoped for. My perfect baby. My perfect husband. My perfect life.

I read the instructions twice, and both times, they assure me that even though I'm barely late, if late at all, this perfect combination of science and technology can determine if I'm pregnant *even before I know it myself*! And then, with Darcy still muttering under her breath in the background, I squat, aim, and fire.

"You okay in there?" she says, shifting gears like a trucker, one moment consumed with her personal angst, then next, nothing but open concern for her older sister.

"Fine," I answer, staring down at the plastic fortune-teller, watching the water line to see if, by maybe a little touch of magic, it ebbs from a clear demarcation to something sort of pink, something sort of life-changing. "Just waiting."

Her footsteps tap over to me, so I can see the nose of her dilapidated black sneakers poke under the door. She slaps her hand up on the outside of the stall.

"Whatever happens, Til, it's not the end of the world," she says. My sister, ever the pessimistic pragmatist.

"Of course it's not," I mutter, focused on that damn pink line. "Watch the clock out there, tell me when three minutes have passed."

"Will do," she answers, and then we both fall silent, the seconds moving forward, though I feel like I might be frozen in time. Finally, Darcy exhales and says, gently, kindly, "Time's up," and though my eyes haven't strayed from the pregnancy test, I still force myself to look again, as if I might have missed something while I fixated on it for the last 180 seconds.

But no. It's empty. The same as it was in the box on the shelf at CVS. No perfect baby inside of me, no perfect husband to call and share in the joyous news. I'm surprised at the depth of my disappointment, at the gutting pang that echoes all the way into my bowels. I hold my hand gently on the door, mirroring Darcy, intuiting her resolve, thankful for her company, until finally, my mind grants my body reprieve, and I find the will to step forward, to step all the way the hell out of there.

* * *

"Come on," Darcy says, grabbing my elbow four minutes later, her solemn mood replaced by a forcefully sunny one. "It's not the end of everything. Let's go cheer up."

She hangs a left down the hall and steers toward the music lab, the place she ensconced herself through much of her high school years. Sometimes, she'd lose track of the hours, and before she had her driver's license, I'd be dispatched to pick her up. I'd head toward the room and hear her playing long before I saw her, the melody weaving and whispering, booming and beckoning, her angst, of which she had so much, dissolving under the ivory keys. My mother always said she had a gift, but none of us really gave it much merit. We indulged Darcy's endless hours of playing because to see her there, on the bench huddled over the lip of the piano, she morphed into someone so different: someone who hadn't been scarred by all that she'd been scarred by. She was rounder, softer, rapt, and innocent all at once. But a gift? It was only when she was offered a full scholarship to Berklee that we understood just how precious her talent was. The letter arrived in the mail, and she held it up and said, "I told you so." And then she walked out the front door, most likely to Dante's, and it occurred to me just then that what should have been a triumphant moment in Darcy's life was instead yet another hollow one. Even now, five years later, I remember so clearly wishing in that broken minute that I had known, that I had paid more attention to her talent, nurtured it rather than overlooking it, embraced it rather than assuming it was simply one more complicated yet maybe not quite remarkable attribute of Darcy.

"So you're really gonna do *Grease*?" She strides into the dilapidated music room.

"Yeah, I think so. It'll be fun. Like when Susie and I were seniors."

"Not exactly groundbreaking," she says.

"Why does it have to be groundbreaking?" I retort. "It's just a musical. It's just supposed to be fun."

She shrugs. "It's just boring. That's all. Typical Westlake."

"Hey." I bite. "I love it here."

"Of course you do," she says, pulling out a piano bench and plunking down. "Of course you do."

"Meaning what?"

"Meaning nothing ever changes," she says, and then her fingers curve over the keys and her shoulders melt into her upper back and her entire body shifts, almost imperceptibly, into an alter ego of sorts.

I want to dig back at her, but I clamp down because I know she can't help herself, that she's simply wired to rebel against the straight and narrow, against the choices I've built my life upon. And anyway, she is lost in her music.

It's a tune I don't recognize, likely one of her own. She hums under her breath, and I lean into the wall and watch her, this contradiction in the flesh. Her music weaves its way into me, too, transports me to a time when Tyler and I had just married, heady with lust and assuredness and hope for everything that had yet to unfold. Our bubble still intact. On weeknights, we'd sometimes convene at my dad's house. Luanne would rush back from nursing school, and Tyler would pick up a six-pack after his shift at the store. After my dad grilled T-bones out in the yard, the scent of broiled, barbecued meat loitering through the back windows, Darcy would polish off a bowl of ice cream and play for us. Sometimes it was jazz, sometimes it was Mozart, sometimes it was improv—the melodies taking shape per her mood, offering us insight into whatever was going on inside of that tangled mind of hers—and we'd all recline in my dad's living room, sink into the cushiness of the couch, and listen. In those cloudless moments, it was easy to think that life could be sunny forever. Or could be sunny again. Maybe that's what it was: that if you pieced everything back closely enough, you wouldn't actually notice the seams that exposed themselves when it all had ripped apart.

I watch her now, folded over the piano keys, and want to shake her from her trance. I want to pull her up and scream, "Don't you understand that if nothing changes, nothing will ever go astray!" But then she starts in on some bass notes, like a harbinger of my frustration, and I realize that of course it's too late; everything has already twisted loose, even if I can't pinpoint where or why or how it even began.

The door beside me jiggers open, and a lanky man sporting faded cords that fall low on his hips moseys in. He doesn't see me, just Darcy, who takes no notice of him, so he rechecks a paper he holds in his hand and shuffles around in a semicircle, like a broken compass, lost.

"Can I help you?" I whisper.

He pushes his tortoiseshell glasses up the bridge of his nose and flits his free hand through his cropped, burnished blond hair.

"I'm sorry," he says in a muted tone echoing mine, and then he smiles, a white, wide, beckoning beam. "I'm looking for the art room. Kelsey in the front office drew me a little map." He holds up his crumpled piece of paper. "But I think I've missed it."

"Oh, I can show you," I say. "Follow me." I slip out the door and click it closed behind us. The door has been soundproofed, so, just like that, *poof*, Darcy and her music evaporate.

"She's amazing," he says, gesturing behind us.

"She is," I say with a grin that I then let slide, that solitary pink line and the hopes I'd placed on its invisible twin pressing into my mind. "Um, if you don't mind my asking, who are you?" I start toward the direction of the arts room.

"Oh, apologies." He extends his right hand. "I'm Eli Matthews. Taking over for Mr. Ransom for the summer and into the fall."

"Oh, I forgot!" I say, reciprocating his shake. Mr. Ransom, the arts teacher at Westlake for over thirty-five years, has taken leave to tend to his wife, who was recently diagnosed with Alzheimer's. "Well, welcome to Westlake High. I'm Tilly. The guidance counselor."

"Ah, the guidance counselor. You always know what's up with everyone. You're the one I have to get an in with." He smiles again, and I'm immediately at ease, leaving my shadowing gloom behind me.

We turn a corner to the farthest room in the right wing of the school. The bell bleats above us, and doors down the hall all spring open, teenagers swarming like bees from the hive.

"Well, this is it," I say. I jimmy the knob, but it sticks. I bend down to eyeball the tiny widget next to the knob that used to automatically unlock the door from the outside. "Give me a second. When I went here, I figured out how to break in." I rotate my neck to crane up at him. "I spent a lot of time back here until my senior year."

"Art nerd?" he says jokingly.

"Closet art nerd, I guess. Recovering art nerd, maybe. More like a cheerleader," I say. The lock won't give.

"Keys," he says, tapping my back and tugging them from his pants pocket. He wiggles his eyebrows as if he has just the cure for what ails me. Oh, Jesus, like he might have anything *close* to the cure for what ails me.

The bell rings again, indicating five minutes until next period, and I remember Darcy, lost in her haze of melodies in the music lab.

"I better go," I say. "Glad you found it."

"Glad you helped," he says as the bolt unclicks itself.

"Anytime," I answer, doing my best to reciprocate his cheer, and then head on my way. *Of course I helped*, I think. *That's what I do.*

nine

Tyler calls and wakes me the next morning. I am dreaming that I'm pregnant, that my belly is round as a watermelon, my breasts like swollen gourds, my cheeks rose-petal pink, and that Tyler and I are still perfect. My cell vibrates on my abdomen. I fell asleep waiting for him to call, with my hands cupping my stomach, my phone tucked inside my palms.

"Hey," I croak.

"It's nine thirty. I woke you?"

I swivel to face the nightstand and my alarm clock. "I haven't been feeling well. I guess I slept in. Didn't have to work today."

"Sorry," he says. "Everything okay?"

I think of the failed pregnancy test. *No.*

"Yes," I say. "Everything's fine. How's fishing?"

"Good, great, so good we thought we'd stay through Sunday if you don't mind. I don't have to be back at the store until next week."

"Oh, I thought we could spend the weekend together." I close my eyes because they seem better suited to being shut right now.

"I know . . ." He pauses, waiting for me to make it easier on him. "It's just, you know, prime trout season. They're practically jumping out of the lake for us."

"Okay." I sigh. "Sure, it's just a few days." I throw my free hand over my face, wishing I could block out the light entirely.

"Awesome. I love you." He hesitates, his voice catching. "Um, listen, there's also something else." He coughs twice, which doesn't sound like a real cough, more like he's biding his time. "So, yeah, um, Jamie Rosato called."

I sit up quickly, too quickly, and my bedroom spins at the back of my eyes. *Jamie Rosato!* He and Tyler played together at the UW, back before Tyler blew out his left ACL and never fully recovered, watching his sure-thing prospect for the majors, or at the very least the minors, dissipate in one agonizing slide to home gone wrong.

"He called, you know, like he does every year, and wanted me to come out and take a look. Their assistant fielding coach just quit to go to Oregon State." He wavers, waiting for my response, of which I have none because I am too busy trying to process this, trying to figure out why the hell this feels a little too close to déjà vu when I know, *I know,* that, other than discussing Jamie Rosato's annual phone call in which he tries to get Tyler to move to Seattle and coach at the UW, we have never had *this—this exact—* conversation before.

"So, um, the thing is," Tyler continues, "I think this year, I might consider it. Consider going. You know, maybe take a trip to Seattle and see what they say."

"We can't move to Seattle!" I squeak, finally having found my voice.

"I never said anything about moving to Seattle," he says, a little too composed, like he envisioned this conversation and already has his answers, his bullets, wedged inside his armor. "I just, you know, want to go see what they're offering."

My mouth is dry, too dry, my rotten morning breath sticky on my tongue, and I can't answer, can't speak.

"Till? Tilly? Are you there?"

"I'm here," I say, feeling like I might be sick, feeling like I might just puke all over this perfect crisp white comforter in my perfect bedroom in my perfect house, minus my perfect freaking stupid husband. I start to launch into him, my newfound temper anxious to be test-driven, but he's already beaten me to the punch, cut me off before I can steer us down that road.

"It's not a big deal. Not like I've committed to anything," he repeats. "But listen, we're driving into town for some tackle. The line gets shitty here. We'll talk about this on Sunday, I promise." His voice cuts in and out on those last few words, *I promise*, more like, *I p—om—is*, but I know what he's saying, even though I don't believe him, don't believe one single word out of his stinking mouth.

The line goes dead, and I hurl the phone to the other side of the bed, where it lands on his pillow, then somersaults off to the floor.

Slowly, then very very quickly, the events, the visions, this sickness that is eating away at me, these germs of anger and of honesty that are flaring inside of me, crystallize in my mind. *No, no, no, of course I'm not pregnant! That would have been way too easy. How could I have been so stupid? How could I have kept telling myself these stupid, stupid fucking lies, deluding myself like being pregnant was the answer to anything!*

I replay my dream about my father and how I somehow intuited the events that had yet to happen, and then I consider Tyler and that U-Haul and the boxes toting the anthology of our lives, and it is all too clear what has happened. Ashley Simmons—her insidious, duplicitous, wan, sweaty face—flashes in my mind, and I am sure, *I am as certain as I have been about anything*: she changed something inside of me, virtually *promised*, with that smug tone of voice and omniscient mumbo-jumbo, that she was going to alter me, alter my destiny! *Is this what she did? Yes, yes, yes, yes, yes, yes, yes!* I want to vomit, I want to punch something, I want to fly up and roar and rip someone's face off. Instead, I grab a pillow and slam it down, which makes a pathetic thud on the bed, nothing at all representative of my fear, of my bafflement, of my anger at what she has done. *It was Ashley Simmons and her idiotic judgments of my life! With that subtle smile of condescension! "I'm giving you clarity," she said! Shit, shit, shit, shit, shit!*

This isn't clarity, I think. *This is a curse.*

It's only later, much later, long after I've thrown a mishmash of clothes over my jittery limbs, long after I've hurled the SUV down the driveway and am on my way, long after I've replayed Tyler's words and my vision and then his words again, that I stop to wonder what the most cursed part of this is: that I have started to see the future, or the future that I have started to see.

Thwack. Thwack. Thwack.

My knuckles have gone white from the force with which I am pounding on Ashley Simmons' front door. The best part of living in a town like Westlake is that even at 9:30 A.M., you are always able to track someone down via the local gossip grapevine. One call to Susanna, who made one call to Eleanor Franklin, who then made one call to Alyson Martin, and by the time I was done with my coffee, Ashley's address—a run-down apartment complex three blocks from the high school—was mine. She lives on the second floor, the guardrail rusty and rain-faded, with a view of the Dumpster in the parking lot. The air just outside her door smells like pot, a tiny cartoonlike mushroom cloud of marijuana fumes.

Thwack. Thwack. Thwack.

I hear a rustling from inside and someone distantly muttering, "Hang on, Jesus Christ," and then two locks unlatch, and the door swings open.

"What the hell time is it?" she says, her hair matted into a giant knotty ponytail smack on top of her head, like Pebbles from the Flintstones, her face smeared with yesterday's makeup. When she glances up to see me, though, her expression evolves from chagrined to delighted, as if there is no one she'd rather greet on this early summer morning than me. "Silly Tilly Everett! I was almost expecting you!"

From two feet away, I can smell her breath, like meat left out two days too long.

"*A)* Stop calling me that. And *B)* whatever you did to me, undo it," I seethe. *There it is, that seed of vitriol that is spreading inside of me, that venomous bug that she unleashed when she cast her spell. Stupid, stinking Ashley Simmons!*

"Impressive," she says, as if transcribing my thoughts. "I didn't know you had this in you. Sweet Tilly Everett. I've never even heard of you losing your temper." She smiles, cunningly, knowingly. "Never once during cheerleading practice, never once during student council, never once . . . ever!" She giggles, accelerating my discontent to a perilous, dangerous threshold.

"I'm serious, Ashley! You're messing with my brain, with my *life,* and you need to fix it!" The urge to throttle her nearly overcomes me.

"I didn't *do* anything, Tilly." She pouts. "I just opened up some things for you. Whatever's happening, it's all because of you." She pauses and lowers her voice. "So, what exactly is happening?"

"I'm seeing the future! I'm seeing into the goddamn future!"

Sweat has started to pool in my armpits; I can feel my T-shirt, ten years old, from a sorority party, cling to the sides of my body.

"And what do you see?" she asks calmly, the mirror opposite of my unraveling. "What is it that has so unnerved you that you insisted on coming over here so pissed off and waking me at this ungodly hour?"

"Okay, first of all, it's ten o'clock in the morning," I hiss, and three pieces of spittle erupt from my mouth. "And second of all, I am seeing . . . things . . . not good things . . . things that *I don't want to goddamn see!*"

"Well, how is that my fault?" She shrugs, and I want to belt her, take my fist and shove it right down her throat.

"I want to take my fist and shove it right down your throat," I say, to which she cackles. "What's so goddamn funny?" I scream. "Because this isn't funny at all to me!"

At the ruckus, her neighbor's two locks unlatch, and a heavy-set man in a greasy white tank top pokes his head out his door. The light bounces off his shiny bald head, and I squint my eyes.

"You okay?" he says to Ashley. She nods, and he nods in return, and then *slam, latch, latch,* two locks are secured right back up, insulating him from the world, from his psychotic next-door neighbor or maybe just her psychotic visitor.

"I just—" she says, her laughter now aborted, though it still mocks me in the cusps of her smile, "I honestly didn't know that you could be this angry with *anyone.* Did you?"

I actually stop to consider it. *No, no, I'm not this angry. I am not the person who shoves her fists down people's throats. Those are the kids who end up on my couch, those are the kids whom I fix, who look to me as an example, for God's sake!*

"So help me, Ashley, if you screw things up for me, I will track you down and make you regret it," I say, tugging at the hem of my shirt, now pocked with abdomen sweat. The humidity is clinging to my temples, my hairline, my belly button, my wrists.

She laughs again, a high-pitched, hysterical yelp, as if anything about this is remotely amusing. "Tilly, you realize that you're only seeing what's going to come. This has nothing to do with me or what I've done. Come on, lighten up. I didn't change anything. I didn't *alter* a single damn thing. It was just clarity, that's all." She smiles, pulling her gums back to reveal perfectly aligned, crisply white teeth, a sign betraying her middle-class childhood, complete with orthodontia and parents who cared enough to correct her overbite in the first place.

"We're not done with this," I say, turning to head down the stairs.

"I'll see you around." She waves, flashing her purple-painted nails, lingering in her doorway, watching me go. "And why not enjoy it? Why not use this, you know, to give you some insights, instead of getting so fucking, you know, in my face about it?"

I haul myself into the driver's seat, slamming my door as a response, then cast my gaze back at her one last time. She's still there, that clownish smile plastered on her face, a harbinger—a noose around my neck—that follows me long after I've sped out of the parking lot and gone on my way.

ten

Later that afternoon, Susanna and I are on our way to finalize the *Grease* decision with Principal Anderson; he bounced us yesterday due to a last-minute budget meeting with the district superintendent, and maybe twenty-four hours ago, I would have cared a bit more about getting this shindig off the ground, about *greased lightning!*, but now, today, with my life literally flashing in front of me, this is just about the last thing on my to-do list. But I already lectured Susanna on the phone last weekend: *"I cannot stand to watch you sit around for one more second feeling sorry for yourself,"* which is exactly how and why I showered off the invisible cloak of juju stink from Ashley's and have landed in my car, headed toward Westlake High to discuss a silly revival of a musical that I really didn't give two shits about in the first place. Well, actually, in the first place, I did. But now, in the second place—in this newly carved, less idealized afterplace—no, I really don't.

Darcy, because she has nothing better to do now that she is home and pissed off at everyone or has pissed everyone off, hops in the backseat and joins us.

"So Tyler called," I say to Susie, who is staring but not really looking out the window. "He said that Jamie Rosato called. Wants him to come out for a recruiting trip."

"Ugh, sweetie, I forgot. I heard." She reaches over to touch my shoulder. "You okay?"

"You heard? How'd you hear?" I stare at her for a beat too long, then turn back to the road, swerving to stay in my lane.

"I, um." She nibbles her index-finger cuticle. "Austin told me?" She phrases it more like a question than the statement of fact that it is.

"Austin told you that Jamie Rosato called Tyler? When? When did he tell you?"

"Um, yesterday? I think." She pauses. "I'm sorry, I should have called. I've been so flaky these days. I know."

"Wait, he told you yesterday? Tyler just called me this morning!" I snap off the radio to be sure that I'm translating this correctly. "How did Austin know before I did?"

"Uh-oh," Darcy says from the backseat, suddenly interested.

Susie gnashes into her cuticle even further, her giveaway for her little white lies, ever since she was six.

"Susanna Nichols, I am your best friend," I say, flipping on my blinker, trying to focus on the road, changing lanes without careening right into poor Jessica Hughes, whose dented maroon Honda Civic just pulled up next to mine, likely on her way to her pharmacist shift at the drugstore. "And you better tell me right this very minute what the hell is going on."

"She means it." Darcy pipes in from the peanut gallery. "Do you hear her? She practically pummeled me the other day on the front porch. She's like Rambo these days."

"Well, I do mean it!" I huff. "I'm pretty goddamn pissed off right now."

Susanna does a double-take at me, and Darcy offers a puzzled glance that I catch in the rearview mirror. "What?" I continue. "I don't have the right to be a little fucking pissed?"

"You do," Susie says. "We're just not used to hearing it, that's all." She sighs, a purging, what-the-hell sort of sigh. "Okay, well, Austin swore that I wasn't allowed to tell you, but I guess Ty's been feeling a little antsy here in Westlake, and I guess that's why he called Jamie a few days ago to ask about a job."

"Jamie called him," I say, correcting her.

"Um." She hesitates. "Okay."

My stomach plunges like an unhinged elevator and something intangible clicks into place. *"I guess that's why he called Jamie a few days ago to ask about a job."* He called Jamie about the job. The words replay around my brain, circling and circling, trying to make sense of themselves, but they cannot. *He called Jamie about the job.*

"Why would he do that? Why would he possibly do that and lie to me?" I turn off Route 43 toward the school, like a plane on autopilot, driving without even realizing where I'm going, driving without stopping to even think, because if I were to stop and think, I'd pull the hell out of there, pull far the hell away from here, where the truth is suddenly revealing itself to be nothing like what I thought it was, and flee. "Why didn't he tell me? Why am I hearing this third-hand from Austin?"

"I don't know. . . ." I feel her eyeing me from the passenger seat. "He mentioned it to me casually, then said to keep it to myself. I didn't really think to ask more. I'm sorry. I should have. I've just been preoccupied."

"He's an asshole," Darcy chimes in.

"Shut it, Darcy," I say, and her eyes flare, but she does.

"So you and Austin are talking now," I say to Susie, exhaling, trying—desperately—to pick this news up and set it aside, distract myself from the gravity of the moment, because the weight of it is simply too much. "That's a good thing, Suse," I add, because I can't help myself.

"Sort of, I guess." Susanna shrugs, her seat belt shifting on her shoulder. "I made the mistake of pouring him a glass of wine last night when he dropped the kids off, and he took it as some sort of invitation. He tried to make out with me." She erupts into staccato, vibrant laughter, as if there were anything funny about the idea of her estranged husband, the one man she'd devoted herself to since high school graduation, making a pass at her in their old kitchen. But because I am so desperate to taste a morsel of distorted joy, I join her, my eyes focused on the road, the rest of my face cramping with pained, unrelenting, sick, ironic glee. She doubles over, tears running from her eyes, at the inanity of the situation, and I picture Austin, with his brash swagger and his mauling hands, trying to paw Susanna over a glass of Chardonnay, falsely convincing himself that he ever stood a chance. Even Darcy joins in, because while there is nothing truly funny about any of this, our laughter is infectious, like a plague.

"Man, remember a time when the only thing in the world we wanted was to make out with those guys?" I inhale at the memory of driving down to the lake with Ty and pressing myself up against him in his truck, or of lingering on my porch, eking out one last minute before my curfew, tasting his salty mouth in mine, and suddenly, here in my old SUV with my broken best friend and my lost, wounded sister, nothing is funny at all. We all clip our laughter, as if a suction cup inhaled the levity right out of us. "But anyway, try to remember that time, Susie. Maybe you can forgive him." *Because if they can be okay, maybe we can also, all of us, the four of us, be okay,* I think, until I hear Ashley Simmons, a tick in my ear. *"Silly Tilly Everett! Like husbands and babies are the answers to anything!"*

"Hey, listen, *you* guys will figure this out. Us? I don't know," Susie says, flipping the radio back on, just as I pull up to school. "Seattle isn't so far. You can do weekends, and then he can be here for the off-season."

I don't answer, because while I don't know much about what is unraveling, I do know that I'm not interested in sharing a life with my husband solely in the off-season. The question, I mull to myself as we step toward Principal Anderson's office and Darcy takes a left down the east hall toward the music room, is why my husband doesn't know this, and if he does—and I'm certain he does—why he's moving forward anyway.

When Darcy and I arrive home, after Anderson agrees on *Grease*, rolling his eyes and seeming like he'd rather be anywhere than bartering his options for a high school musical, my father is planted on my front porch swing. *Ironic*, I think. It was, after all, this very swing on which I first discovered the depths of his drinking when I was seventeen and he was numb to the world around him, a beached whale listing ever so slightly back and forth, while I ushered my eight-year-old sister—home from school early with a raging stomach flu—past him and upstairs, where she'd be none the wiser.

When Dad bought this house for Tyler and me, he also bequeathed us the swing from my childhood home, a memento of his lingering love for my mother, of the memories they built nurturing their marriage during quiet twilights over their many years together. Of course, it's a memento of a hell of a lot more—at least to me—but I've found a way to bury those memories, and yet today, they pop out, uninvited, a champagne cork in a silent room. He waves to us, and Darcy, still strapped in her seat belt, grunts in reply.

"What are you going to do about him?" she asks.

"Keep him here for now. Until Ty gets back and we can form a plan," I answer, quieting the engine, enjoying a gasp of silence. "He seems a little better, though," I add.

"It's been, like, half a week," she says, scorn drenching her words.

"And he hasn't touched a drink. That's something."

"So this is the plan? Count the days that he hasn't been drinking and hope that it keeps up?" She hurls open the passenger-side door but makes no move to get out, so eventually the alarm starts dinging, a sharp, constant beat that worms its way into my temples. I think of Tyler with each beep—*Beep-Tyler! Beep-Tyler! Beep-Tyler!*—and try to consider how I can talk him out of this ridiculousness, how I can change the future, turn the clock back, only not turning the clock back, turning it ahead or sideways or *something*! What can I do to shift everything so that what I saw won't be what I'm forced to see *when it actually happens*?

"Shall we?" I say to Darcy when the beeping gets to be too much, and then together we purge ourselves with expansive, cleansing breaths, each for our own reasons, unsnap our seat belts in unison, and slog inside. Darcy shuffles down the walk ahead of me, her feet sliding over the crimson bricks, in no hurry to greet our father, when the front door opens and Dante emerges from behind it.

"Shit," I hear her whisper, loudly enough that he likely hears it too.

"Hey," he says, offering her a weary, half-cocked grin. "Your dad told me you'd be here soon, so I waited it out."

"How'd you know where I was?" Darcy stops abruptly at the bottom step, and I nearly collide with her.

"Pretty obvious." He shrugs, then stares at his beaten navy

Converse. Darcy offers nothing, no reciprocating words to ease his discomfort.

"Hey, Dante," I say finally from over Darcy's shoulder, then brush past her to kiss his pallid cheek. "It's been a while. Nice to see you. Want to stay for dinner?" I can almost sense Darcy impaling me from behind at the suggestion.

"Oh, no thanks, Tilly. But thank you. I actually have rehearsal tonight." He scuffs his toes against the porch railing; his eyes wander up to meet mine, then dart away.

"How's the band going?" my father chimes in. I'd forgotten he was there, and given the way that Darcy shivers when he speaks, so too had she.

"Good, good, thank you, Mr. Everett. That's actually why I'm here." He focuses on Darcy, and I notice how easily he's able to match her gaze, as if she's the tonic that soothes him. "I left you four messages," he says.

"Battery's dead." She shrugs, and now she's the one who's discombobulated, whose hands duck into her pockets because she doesn't know where else to put them, whose nervous tick of chewing her bottom lip reveals itself.

"Well, whatever. We have a gig next Wednesday night."

"I can't make it," she says too quickly.

"Yeah, I figured as much. That wasn't what I was saying. I thought you might want to *play* it," he says, exasperated. "It's a good gig—Oliver's—and you could fill the place. We'd split the money." He pauses. "Which I know you could use."

She turns her right foot inward and considers it.

"You should do it, Darce. I'll round up my Elks buddies and we'll make a night of it," my dad says.

"You're not stepping foot in a bar!" she snaps, a little too virulently, a little too exposed.

"She's right, Dad," I say as he excuses himself inside.

"Look, Darcy, I know why you didn't call me back," Dante says.

Rather than respond, she offers him a hard stare and then thumps up the wooden plank steps and glides past both of us.

"This isn't about you and me," he says, sighing. "We need to fill the house if we want them to ask us back. And besides, you never met an audience you didn't like."

"Fine," she says, turning back toward him. "I'll do it. Just don't think I'm sleeping with you again afterward." The metal slams against the door frame, and Dante turns a deep shade of crimson.

"Don't worry," I say. "I hear much worse in my office at school."

He sighs. "This wasn't about her and me," he says, as if the more times he repeats it, the likelier it is I'll believe it. Or he will. I know that trick, *oh yeah*, do I know that trick. As if he couldn't have passed up a gig or found someone else to play with. As if I haven't watched him painfully pine for her, excusing her various misdeeds, her stormy behavior, her dismissive attention, for the better part of their adult, or nearly adult, lives. We're not too different, Dante and I, I realize.

"I'm sorry," I say, rubbing his shoulder before heading up the stairs myself.

"Not your fault." He shakes his head and offers a pathetic sliver of a smile. *That's true, it's not.* I consider. *And yet here I am, like always, apologizing.*

"I'll see you Wednesday," I say from the door. "We won't miss it."

"Tyler will make it?" he says, without a sniff of a motive, without any complicated meaning behind it. "I heard he's being recruited at the UW."

"You heard?" I ask, my surprise betraying me. *I didn't even realize I used "we." "I." "I" is what I meant, of course. I won't miss it. Though Tyler won't miss it either. We. I. Us. Two. One. Does it really matter?*

"Everyone knows." Dante shrugs. "Pretty awesome. Coaching for UW."

"Word travels fast," I say, my vision reverberating: the U-Haul, the packing, the boxes, the damp, depressing beat of the steady rain. *What can I do to rewind that? What can I do to make that record skip, throw it off course?*

"You know this town." He shrugs. I nod because I do. There are no secrets here. "Anyway, still pretty awesome. And I don't even care about stuff like that. I hope it works out for you guys." He strides toward the street. "Anyway, thanks. See you Wednesday."

His skinny frame lopes down the block, fading smaller, then smaller still, until I see his doll-sized figure exit on a side street. Though of course, I remind myself, it's not an exit at all. Not out of here, anyway. *We're all stuck.* For once, maybe Darcy is right.

eleven

On Saturday, I wake up to my underwear sagging—clinging and uncomfortable—and as I mope to the bathroom, I know this can mean only one thing. I tug down my underwear and yes, there it is, a quarter-sized stain, ruby red and nearly a perfect circle, reminding me, irrationally, of cranberry sauce. Because, I suppose, as I splash cool water over my cheeks and stare at myself for a beat too long in the mirror—my puffy, exhausted eyes, my sallow cheeks—a Thanksgiving side dish is much easier to stomach, figuratively, of course.

The house is muted, though I can hear a faint echo of a newscast humming from the guest room. My father has taken to waking early, and on the days when he's not needed at the store, he more or less parks in the den with CNN as his only company. I know he's attempted to woo Adrianna back—I overheard him pleading his case two nights ago when I shuffled into the kitchen on a quest for a one A.M. Nutter Butter pig-out—and I also know that she has rebuffed him, so mostly, he sits there, quiet, not asking for too much, minding his sobriety like it is something that requires constant vigilance—a science project, a soufflé.

It is already about a million degrees outside, though barely past 7:30 A.M., and the leather on the seat of the SUV sets my shoulder blades on fire. I crouch over, leaning on the steering wheel as I drive, the town mostly still asleep, or if not asleep, mostly still stirring behind closed blinds, deserted front yards littered with baseballs, drooping petunias, the occasional smashed shards of an old beer bottle.

My dad's house is much like I left it a few days back. The mildewy stink is now so offensive, it's nearly visible, the humidity intensifying it like gasoline to fire. I inhale, hold my breath, and scamper through. I'd meant to come over and clean, of course, but in light of everything, it doesn't seem to matter. In light of the fact that I might suddenly be able to see the future and not at all relish what it is that I am seeing, well, his mounds of dank socks and his molding pizzas in the fridge can wait.

The basement, though, offers reprieve. No smell, other than that pungent, stale, basement-y smell. No heat—it's been trapped outside the cellar door. I'm not quite sure why I'm back here, what I'm looking for, only that when I woke up this morning, with the cranberry sauce in my underwear and the dread *(dread!)* of my husband returning home later this evening, I jiggered my brain into thinking that maybe I could find an answer here, start to un- cover what it is that Ashley Simmons has done to me and how, maybe, I can change it back. Or how—and this may be what I want even more—how I can change what it is that I'm seeing.

The box, that old one my mother had packed up before either of us knew that she'd be gone so quickly, is right where I left it, just before I blacked out. The Tyler picture, of all of us down at the lake during that last gasp of summer, has fluttered to the floor, landing perfectly upright against a jug of old paint.

I grab it and yank it toward me, peering closer for clues. But it looks exactly as it did before: a portrait of ruby-cheeked teenagers, inhaling the sunshine of that unmarred summer day, no consideration for the future that had yet to unfold. I toss the yellowed newspaper out of the box, digging in deeper, looking for answers. I unearth my old camera, my old 35 mm, manipulating it, examining it, an archaeologist filtering through the past to reason with the future.

I mull over my premonition of my father, of the night before he drove into that tree, before Timmy Hernandez called with the news. *Where was I?* In bed. No, no. At my bureau. Looking at old pictures. *Looking at old pictures!* I throw my hands inside the box, faster now, furiously, searching for another one, another photo that can confirm whatever just clicked inside of me. Frantically, my fingers latch onto something, and I pull out an old black-and-white shot of Luanne. The image is too close on her face, mostly nostrils and eyelashes, so she's virtually unrecognizable. But I remember it, I remember that shot, remember handing the camera to Darcy on an early June afternoon, when the three of us were entertaining each other in the backyard, bored, making our own fun. Back before everything, back when I was still Silly Tilly. A lifetime ago. Luanne had splayed herself on a towel and fallen asleep sunbathing, and Darcy flitted over, pressing—*click*—right up into her face, just before I ran over and showered her with frigid hose water. We laughed and laughed, and Luanne pretended to be mad, but she never had it in her to stay mad for long, so pretty soon she joined us, and then we went inside for Cokes.

I stare at the picture, willing something to take me over, something other than this memory of an easier, freer life, but nothing comes. *Darcy took this one*, I think. *Darcy took this shot. Not me.*

And then I remember the Polaroid, the one of Susanna that's at the bottom of my purse. I spin toward the stairs, taking them double, checking my watch. I have exactly eighty-seven minutes before I have to meet Luanne for breakfast. She called last night looking for a solid, sound, hopeful voice, and I knew she didn't trust her body to maintain this pregnancy, not when she'd miscarried three months ago, so we agreed to meet for pancakes once Charlie went down for his nap. *As if pancakes—and babies—are the answer to everything.*

Eighty-seven minutes. I have no idea how long I was out the other two times, but maybe not that long. Or maybe longer. But I have to test it, I have to see. I find my bag nudged under the leg of the front hall console table and snap it open, fishing my fingers to the bottom, where I pull out the Polaroid in triumph.

I dash to the couch and sit and stare at the image of my best friend, depleted that day on my purple love seat, depleted, really, over the course of so many days. I stare and I sit and I stare, and I wait for it to come. I feel it then. The cramp. The pain. The jolt of the fever spreading through me, through my limbs, through my guts, through my core. And then, I lay back, and I let it happen, hoping desperately that what I see won't ruin me; hoping desperately that I haven't gotten myself in too deep.

～

The auditorium is dark, whispers smattering across the crowd, programs rumpling, younger siblings stirring in their seats. Darcy (Darcy!) glances toward the stage and, with a quick nod, begins the intro to Grease; I'd know the melody anywhere. The dilapidated garnet curtain pulls back, then gets stuck halfway, and then gets tugged all the way back, to reveal the motley Westlake cast. Wally Lambert, the senior class theater nerd, is sporting a cheap-looking leather jacket that the costume department has had on hand for decades, too-tight jeans rolled at the hem that do his hourglass figure no favors, slicked-back hair that's been infused

with way too much hairspray, and blindingly white Nikes,
which, I suppose from my perch just offstage, his mother
bought for the new school year and he's wearing now be-
cause costuming forgot to budget for his shoes. CJ is behind
him, center stage, in a waist-hugging poodle skirt and pink
cardigan, tapping her feet from side to side, making faux-
googly eyes at him—her Sandy to his Danny.

Backstage, Susanna is next to me, and because I do not
yet understand what I am capable of and equally as impor-
tant, what I am not capable of in these time warps, I reach
out to touch her shoulder. I tap her, and then I pat her, and
then I nearly shove her, but she doesn't respond. It's as if I'm
not even here, I think. Yes, I realize, I am mashed in an in-
comprehensible space between mind and matter, memory
and perception, now and then.

Wally is snapping his fingers and grooving his body—the
best that he can, because while he was born with a killer
tenor, his sense of rhythm is always slightly off—and then he
jumps into a stance, pointing his finger and furiously whirling
himself into the big moment. "Go greased lightning, you're
burning up the quarter mile!" *CJ and the rest of the Pink*
Ladies pop up: "Greased lightning, go greased lightning!"
The crowd starts clapping along, and Wally, with his zest for
the overdramatic, runs with it, his finger flaring out now,
taking on a life of its own, the Pink Ladies, most of whom are
just trying to keep a straight face, cooing behind him.

The audience is getting into it, and I hear Wally's mom let
out a "Whoop!" so I peek out just beyond the curtain toward
them. Darcy is furiously pounding out the chords, as if her
mettle as an artist is actually being measured in any way by
this production, while three band members, freshmen whom
I vaguely recognize but can't yet name, struggle to keep up,

struggle to stay in tune. The saxophonist hits a particularly rancid note in that final Greased lightning! *chorus, but Wally is singing so loudly that I might be the only one—well, and Darcy, yes, her with her perfect pitch—who notices.*

I scan the crowd before the lights dim for the next scene and spot my father toward the back, looking slimmer, less drawn, content. I see Eli Matthews crouching near the middle aisle, snapping a camera up toward the stage. I search for Tyler, but either he is not there or he simply can't be seen from my angle. Then I find Luanne, looking plump, not too uncomfortable, just a tiny burst of a stomach giving the first public hint of her pregnancy. And I feel myself relax, knowing her fears are unfounded, that the tiny embryo that has latched on inside of her won't give way.

I am slipping back; I can sense that I am running out of time and falling backward into reality, when I turn again toward Susanna, though it takes a moment to find her in the darkness. There she is, back near the scrim, the light from the stage bouncing off her flushed skin, her flourishing cheekbones. Her hands are knotted around a man's waist; his back is to me, but already, because I have known him for so many years, I know that this isn't Austin. This man is more wiry, his posture more upright, thicker, wilder tufts of hair on his head.

I want to yell out to her, to say, What the hell are you doing? *but it's too late for that, and I'm in tune enough by now to know that there's no point anyway. The sands in the hourglass have whittled down to nothing, and as the last grains fall through this void of time, they take me with them, and just like that, I am gone.*

I insist that Luanne get her pancakes to go. She is less than pleased, disgruntled even, but because I'm so adamant, jiggling my knee at the checkout, barking at old Marian Heckly, who has punched the cash register here since we were teenagers and whose hair has gone from brunette to faded brunette to midnight blue to steel-wool blue, to hurry the heck up with our change, Luanne acquiesces.

"You're going to be fine," I say to her as the car overruns the curb outside Susanna's house. "Trust me, you're going to be fine."

She chases me down the walkway, my spare keys to Susie's poking out like a joist from my fingers.

"How can you be so sure?" she says—with good reason, I suppose, though it annoys me all the same. Because since when does Luanne start questioning me, and since when is she the one to worry about anything?

"Because I saw you," I snap without thinking.

"Because you what?" She tails behind me.

"What?" I realize my mistake immediately. "No, what? Of course I didn't *see* you! I mean that I *see* you now, and you're fine! Ha! Yes, I mean, look at you, you're great!" I stutter over that last part, and she cocks an eyebrow, but then I plow open Susie's front door, nearly tripping over Kyle, who is nude but for a Superman cape. Christopher flings open the closet door, in nothing but tighty-whities. He wields a light saber and screams, "Back, you enemies, back or you're dead meat!"

Luanne and I both shriek out of true surprise, which brings Susanna running into the entryway, her hands matted with flour, her apron covered with what appears to be raw cupcake batter, and Luanne, I think—or hope—forgets about my near giveaway.

"What are you doing here?" she says, then says to the boys, "Take this outside."

"They're naked," I say.

"Have you felt how hot it is?" she answers. "Besides, less laundry."

Luanne nods like she understands, so I nod too, as if sending naked boys into the backyard to play is a reasonable accommodation for another sweltering day, but given that I have neither a child nor any real clue as to when childhood nudity becomes pervy, I follow Susie into the kitchen and say nothing.

"What's up?" she says, her back toward us as Luanne pulls out a kitchen chair, its legs scraping on the tile floor, and pours an ungodly amount of syrup into the Styrofoam container with her lukewarm pancakes.

I toss it out, an angry almost-whisper, before I can stop myself. "Are you having an affair?"

"What? What are you talking about?" She spins around, a scraper in her hand, sending tiny smatterings of batter across her cabinets. I see Luanne watching us, her chewing at a standstill.

"I need to know . . . are you having an affair?"

"Are you *f-u-c-k-i-n-g* crazy?" she says, spelling out the word like moms of young kids do, turning back toward her mixer. "Do I look like someone who has either the time or the energy to have an affair?"

I cast a glance over to Luanne, who raises her forehead as if to say, *Good point,* and then shoves another forkful in her mouth, muttering, "Sorry, starving. The hormones."

I retrace the vision, retrace what I saw and what I'm certain is true—or is going to be true in October. Something sticks.

"So, what is it?" I ask quietly. "Are you leaving Austin?"

She stops stirring the batter, her shoulders sagging, her breath expanding outside of her.

"I am," she says, setting down the scraper and shuffling to the table, where she drops next to Luanne, clouds of flour billowing around her lap.

"You can't leave Austin!" I say.

"Of course I can leave Austin," she answers. "And besides, how much of a choice did he give me?"

"People get beyond this stuff all the time!" I cry, as if this is my marriage, though part of me feels like it might be.

"Tilly, look, I don't want to. I don't want to be in that marriage where I've gotten beyond stuff like this. He cheated. I can't get beyond that."

I flop next to Luanne at the table. "No, I know. You're right." I sigh. "You should have said something, though."

"I only just decided. This morning." She shoots me a puzzled look. "How did you know?"

"I'm your best friend," I hiccup, careful now after Luanne. "I guess I can just sense these things."

"You're weird." She shrugs.

"I know." I nod, wishing that I could confess more, everything. But I can't. Not until I've figured out what this all adds up to, what the future has planned for me, and most important, how on earth I can possibly slam on the brakes to stop it.

twelve

Nolan Green's truck has barely deposited Tyler back at the house when I find him ensconced in the upstairs closet. Darcy is off rehearsing with Dante for their big debut—an e-mail went out, got forwarded, then reforwarded, and now, it feels like at least half the town will be in attendance next Wednesday—and my dad has actually left the house with Abe Collins, his assistant manager, who swung by to take him out for fifteen-dollar-steak night at Genuine Steaks.

"Just leave your laundry in the bathroom," I say to Ty, his sinewy arms outstretched for the top shelf. "I'll do it tomorrow." I try not to think of my vision of the U-Haul and its implications, but it's there, stubborn, mocking me. *Screw you, you stupid U-Haul! I am not going down without a friggin' fight!*

He tugs down his duffel bag. "I already threw it in. Thanks, though." He squeezes by me, tossing the empty bag on our bed, moving to the bureau to take out whatever clean undershirts remain.

"What are you doing?" I stand in the door frame.

"Packing," he says without glancing toward me. "I told you. Jamie called. Recruiting, they're flying me in tomorrow."

"But you just got back!" I exclaim, my pulse throbbing a little too wildly at the idea of *packing*, of all that it conjures up. Even though I have confirmed with Susanna that what I saw, what I am *seeing*, is as real as anything, still, what if I can stop it, what if I can undo what has yet to be written? And besides, I think, *He did not call you! You called him, you little liar! You called him!*

He looks at me now and shrugs. "It's when they needed me. I guess they have a star freshman shortstop who needs some coaching. You know how it goes. I'll only be gone a week."

"You know damn well that you'll be gone longer than a week!" I shout, him surprised at my decibel level, me surprised that I haven't ripped his face off at his lies.

He sighs and plunks on the bed, reminding me of a flaccid noodle.

"I just . . . I just want to test it out, see what kind of offer they can make me. That's all."

"That's all? That's not all. That's a lot!" I hear myself and wish I didn't sound so hysterical. The pre–Ashley Simmons Tilly would never have gotten this hysterical! But that fury is inside of me—*Out, damned spot, out*—and it isn't coming undone. "That's a huge frigging lot. And we're not moving, for God's sake! We had an agreement! We had a pact!"

"Well, I mean, can't things change?" he says simply, as though asking his wife to abandon the only place she's ever called home is like swapping in a new pair of snow boots. "I mean, I know that we agreed . . ."

"I know that you know that we agreed!"

"Can you stop? Please?" he says, tired, worn out, fractured. "I know that this isn't something we talked about, but he called, and it seemed opportune."

He didn't call, you little weasel. My fingertips shake. My jaw clenches to a lock. I stare at him, and yet he refuses to engage, refuses to spill the truth. Refuses, most important, to acknowledge that he is breaking our agreement to build this life together here, in Westlake, because this is the life that I need. This is the life that soothed me. That *soothes* me still. Why can't he see that? Why can't he understand what he is taking from me? I clench my palms into furious balls.

"What is so opportune about making me move to Seattle?" I think of Austin and those boxes in the rain, and yes, I am sure of it, I am going to stop him from going if it kills me, if I have to fall on my knees and draw blood. His blood, my blood, who the hell knows. Someone's blood. "Because our life is here! Everything we love is here! We are starting a family, for God's sake!" I still haven't told him that I'm not pregnant again this month.

"Your life is here," he says quietly.

"My life *is* your life," I cry. But he pales when I say this, the color sliding from his cheeks, his chest visibly tight. He sighs and rubs his hands over his face, then slinks toward the bathroom, the door closing firmly behind him, the lock latch spinning, clicking into place.

Tyler and I never fight anymore. We used to, sure, in our early days, but now it's so much easier not to. Tyler's fighting technique back then was the silent treatment, while mine was to glide by our hiccup without even so much as an acknowledgment—*If I pretend not to see it, maybe it won't exist in the first place.* Or something like that. I thought it added up to something sort of like that. But suddenly, now, it feels like I shifted the rules of our agreement, of our détente, and I stand alone in our room, unsure of what to do now, now that I no longer have that ability to strap on the blinders that ironically helped us navigate our way.

Finally, the door unlatches. Ty emerges, walks silently toward me, and pulls me next to him on the bed.

"Till, here's the thing," he says, looking straight into my eyes, resolved. "I'm thirty-two."

"I know," I say. "Like I don't know that you're thirty-two."

"I'm thirty-two and I've been here nearly all my life . . . and I cannot wake up another morning and know that this is all there is for me."

"What are you talking about? We're trying to have a baby! That's what there is for you." My rage is abating like a punctured balloon.

"That's not it. Listen to me." He shakes his head. "I was supposed to be something great. I was supposed to set the world on fire. And . . . and . . . and now, I sell mountain bikes to people who can't afford them and who will never use them anyway. That is what I do: sell bathing suits to mothers for their aqua-aerobics. Do you think this is how I wanted things to go? Can't you see that this isn't how I wanted things to go? Can't you give me that?"

"But we have a great life," I say, pleading now. "I love our life."

"I know." He nods. "I know you do."

"Isn't that enough?" Nothing is making sense; his words are annihilating everything. *How is that not enough? It is more than enough for me! Why can't I stop things?* Anger has ceded ground to panic, and the room feels too close, claustrophobic, the air around me shoving its way down my throat.

"The thing is, Till—" He inhales sharply. "The thing is, is that I don't know who I am without you. Without this town."

So what? I think, but instead I say, "Don't be ridiculous! You're the same guy I fell in love with at sixteen. The same guy *everyone* here loves."

"But that's just it," he answers, and two real tears roll down from each eye. "I don't want to be that same guy." He pauses. "Don't you ever feel this way? Don't you ever feel the tiniest bit confined?"

I stare at him. *Who are you?*

"No," I say firmly. "I don't. What is there to feel confined about? Why would I need to know who I am without you? I know who I am *with* you, and that's what matters."

"I think other things matter too. I think it *matters* that we're able to define ourselves outside of our marriage." He shrugs. "I . . . I just can't do it anymore."

"Do what? Our marriage?" The anxiety is spinning freely, cascading, a crescendo. *What is happening here? Just what in the hell is going on? I wake up one morning and my father is a drunk and my husband wants us to move and my best friend is making out with a man she's not married to, and I can suddenly see this without actually seeing it!* Ashley Simmons' voice replays itself, an echo in my inner ear. *"A gift of clarity, Tilly. It's what I always thought you needed." Screw you, Ashley Simmons, screw you and your ridiculous prophecies!*

"No, no, *no*," he says. His eyes rise to mine, then drop all over again. "Well, I don't know. It's this, just this. All of this!" He flaps his arms in a wild circle. "This life, this town, this same old shit, different day. We've *done* this before, been through all of this before. Your dad turning up drunk, your sister crashing on our couch." He stops to pull together the thread of his thought. "I need some air, you know." He looks at me now, fully. "It's only a week. It's just a scouting trip. We'll figure something else out. Something where we're both happy. Where we both feel satisfied."

I want to respond. I want to say, *How the hell did I not know you weren't satisfied? Where is this coming from? What the fuck is wrong with you?* But I find that my words are tucked somewhere inside, frozen in the back of my throat, unable to free themselves to ask what needs to be asked. Back to the old Tilly, who thought if she never confronted anything, maybe she'd never have to fight it in the first place.

We sit in the unnerving silence, and I hear the tick-tick-tick of the hall grandfather clock, until finally Tyler says, "Tilly, I love you. But do you ever stop to think about whether you're happy? Not just on the surface, but deep down, are you really, *really* happy? Whether this is really the life that you want?"

"Yes," I answer quickly, rising to leave before he can see me shatter. "Of course this is the life that I want!"

I rush into the hallway bathroom and plop on the toilet, coiling into myself like a fetus. Because his question stings me in a way I didn't even realize I was capable of being stung. Because happiness isn't a goal, isn't something I strive for. It simply is. My life is happiness; I choose for my life to be happiness, whatever that means, however that is defined. If someone were to ask me if I were happy, I would answer without hesitation, *yes*. That flicker of a moment of consideration is one flicker too many, a frozen beat that doesn't need to be mulled: why bother? *This is my life. This is happiness.* The two are one and the same. This, since I was sixteen and my mother died, is what I did, how I functioned, how I constructed everything around me; as sure as I breathed, I was happy. This is the life that I want, the one that I want. How is it that my husband doesn't know that?

I tread water through the auditions on Wednesday. *Yes,* I nod at Susanna, *Wally Lambert was excellent if a little bitchy about Darcy's piano playing, which he deemed too "three-quarter time, which threw me off the second chorus,"* and *Yes, it goes without saying that CJ will play Sandra Dee.* But Susie seems to be enjoying herself well enough, and for this, I'm glad. I ask her again to reconsider forgiving Austin, but she shakes her head no and yells, *"Next!"* which I know she means for the next auditioner but also uses it as a capper on her life. *Okay,* I nod, *point taken.* I'm too broken to argue.

Outside, the clouds are closing in, pregnant, full, poised to explode with torrential rains that our neighboring crops so desperately thirst for, that our pores, so exhausted from the unrelenting heat, will be thankful for.

After Susanna and I have agreed on the casting, I send her home, toting Darcy along with her.

"Thank God," Darcy says with an extra-zealous roll of her eyes. "Finally, release me already! I have a real show to get ready for."

I wave them off and then sink into my office chair, the shadow from the impending storm so low it hovers outside my window, a mirror of my mood.

Tyler and I have barely spoken since I dropped him at the airport. I've tried to call him, but he's always on the field or with their ace freshman shortstop or being taken out for beer and wings with the staff. (*"I can barely hear you,"* he shouted last night. *"Did you say you got some cereal?"* when, in fact, I had finally announced that I got my period.) And when he did find some quiet time, it was always after I'd fitfully forced myself into sleep, too haunted by the gravity of everything—my father, my visions, my marriage—to really slumber soundly, but annoyed all the same when he called and shook me from my half-dreaming state.

But he's coming back on Saturday, and I've resolved that I will figure out a way to make him stay, find an answer for his feelings of stagnation and a compelling reason for him not to uproot us to Seattle.

The box from my father's basement is nestled under my desk. I packed it into the SUV after my vision of Susanna, lugging its dusty contents up the stairs, tucking it beneath the back-row passenger seat. Now that I have a vague idea of how this whole thing works, I need more answers, need to dig deeper into the how, the what, the why. For someone who has spent a lifetime answering other people's questions instead of asking my own, this newfound curiosity feels insatiable, powerful almost, a germ in my stomach that's spreading inside of me, hungry and alive.

I wrestle the box to the sofa, and it lands with a soft thump, stirring up a light puff of pollutants and dust that unkempt teenagers have left in their wake. Tiny fragments of crumbs tumble to the floor, and I kick them underneath the couch for the janitors to deal with later.

A cracking clap of thunder explodes outside, and out of nowhere pellets of rain begin to pound the window, flying droplets eking their way inside the open frame and dripping down the back wall toward the radiator. I drop the stack of photos on a pillow— the ones from that summer, the one with Tyler in his board shorts and his arms held aloft, triumphant—and gingerly unwrap each element of the camera, placing them ever so carefully back on my desk. Here is one lens. And here is another. And here is the flash that I'd sometimes use in the day, just to overexpose the shot and give everything an awesome burst of light, such that it looked angelic, heavenly almost. I turn the lenses over in my hands, shifting the focus wheels—*click, click, click*—accelerating them until the sounds become meditative, transcendent, and I remember the calm that this ritual used to provide.

Click-click-click. Then faster. *Click-click-click-click-click.*

I spin the wheels over and over, replaying how easily irritated I was with Tyler when I reached him last night at the bar, with Quiet Riot playing in the background and half-drunk men hooting at some stupid baseball game on the bar TV. I'd mentioned my period but hadn't even told him about the depressing, demoralizing failed pregnancy test and how he was so far checked out of our life—*listening to Quiet Riot over pitchers of beer!*—that I had to sit on the toilet in the girls' locker room, with my baby sister hovering outside the door, and embrace her generosity because my husband, the man who should have been beside me, wasn't there.

Click-click-click. The camera lens spins easily in my hands. How is it possible that I've spent half my life with a man who now seems to be veering so far off course from what I—*we*—had planned? *Click-click-click.* I can see into the future now, but how could I not have seen this coming a long time ago? *Click-click-click.*

Someone clears his throat behind me.

"Sorry, bad time?"

I snap my head up and find Eli Matthews hovering in the door frame, his hands shoved in his pockets, his shoulders curved downward, shaving two inches off of his six-foot frame.

"W-what? Oh, no, hey," I stutter. "Sorry, just thinking about something."

"Everything okay?" he asks, stepping inside just a nudge. His brow furrows in concern, and I press back a tornado of tears at the way he has read me so quickly, so effortlessly. *No, nothing is okay! Nothing at all!*

"Fine," I say, setting the focus lens down on my desk, batting my left hand. "Just . . . lost in a thought."

"Wow, old-school camera!" he says. "I haven't seen one of these in quite a while."

"You shoot?" I ask, then remember my premonition of the musical. Right, of course he shoots.

"Went to grad school for it, actually," he replies, moving closer to finger the lens. "Now, I teach in between paying gigs, whenever I can get them."

"So that's how you ended up here? We don't get a lot of new blood in Westlake."

"Yeah." He smiles. "So I've gathered. When I said I'd take

the job—I was down in Portland shooting a few things for their paper when the agency called—I could tell they were a little surprised." He shrugs. "But I kind of like it here. People are friendly."

"We are," I say in agreement, wondering how one even begins to find a paying photography job, much less make a life of it. Not that it sounded like much of a life for me. It sounded like the life of a nomad.

"But this camera . . . no one uses this anymore. It's all digital. I used to love the darkroom, but gone are those days."

"We don't have a darkroom anymore?"

"Not that I've been told," he says. "Just a few computers now. Sad, isn't it?"

"I guess it's time for a new model," I answer, moving back behind my desk.

"I have a digital one I'm happy to lend you," he says. "Give it a test drive before you spring for the real deal."

"I'd love it," I say politely, though the thought of relearning what was once so inherent feels burdensome, and I already know that I likely won't follow through.

"I'll bring it in tomorrow," he says. He smiles that open, freeing smile, and something opens in me too.

"Why don't you bring it tonight?" I hear myself saying unexpectedly. "My sister is playing at Oliver's. The bar off of Downing Alley? Why don't you join us?"

He shrugs a happy shrug. "I've got no plans. I'll be there."

"Sounds good." I feel my cheeks flush pink.

"Oh, I forgot," he says after turning to leave, then turning back again. "The entire reason I stopped by in the first place." He fishes in his pocket and hands me a solitary key. "I had a copy made to the art room. So you're never locked out again."

He rests it on the edge of my desk and with a flick of his hand, waves good-bye. After he goes, I clasp it in my palm, wrapping my fingers around so tightly I can feel the honed brass edges embed themselves into my flesh. Finally, I uncurl my hand and look downward. There, right inside my lifelines, are tiny pockmarks, nipping little indents, that alter the look of my palm entirely, shifting the smooth surface to something rougher, something a little more daring, something that might be in need of repair but might be worth exploring anyway.

The skies are cloudless by later evening, the flooding on the streets the only sign of the day's unrest. A respite from the storms, which, the forecaster warned on the six o'clock news, are going to trail us all week, just before another slamming heat wave spills our way from back east.

By the time Susanna, Luanne, and I arrive at Oliver's, the bar is a virtual replica of Darcy's high school yearbook. Nearly every booth is taken, so we ensconce ourselves at a table to the left of the stage with a shoddy view and an oversized speaker sure to muddy our inner ears. Smoke puffs like cirrus clouds; the nubile among us suck on cigarettes that they are too young to yet give up. The creaky wood floor is sticky, beer soaked, a distant reminder of the basement of Ty's fraternity, the stench of spilled alcohol wafting upward.

I think of Ty and his return home Saturday. How I will wait for him with his favorite meal, spaghetti carbonara, and pretend that I don't know that he's going to rescind on his promise, that it won't be *just a week*, that he will ask me to abandon Westlake, move to Seattle, because our marriage should trump everything. *Maybe it should,* I think. *But maybe, also, it shouldn't,* an unexpected consideration echoes just as loudly. I will try to pretend that I don't still remember how Tyler had promised me that we could stay in Westlake forever, how after I nursed Darcy's fragile psyche back to as close as it could ever get to normal, when she finally started sleeping through the nights again, keeping her nightmares at bay, Tyler swore to me that we'd never have to leave my family, never let them go unguarded on my watch. Because I was out with Tyler that night, the night that Darcy, just ten years old, tucked herself into her blackened closet and held her breath as the meth head sifted through her room, through her life, in search of something he could pawn off as valuable, and she was hoping, furiously, that he wouldn't find her, hear her whimper, and do something much worse.

I should have been there. Of course I should have been there, but I was instead steaming the windows of Tyler's truck, screwing his brains out for those few summer months when we were at last together again in between our college semesters, and so, when Darcy finally reached me on the phone at Tyler's—after failing to rouse dad from his stupor on the couch—so hysterical I could barely understand her, and when I finally collected her at home, both of us shaking, her more fragile than I realized was still possible, I made Tyler promise. And he, rattled and pale, promised himself equally. Promised that we'd be in Westlake forever. That I'd be here to watch over them, over *everyone*, so no one, my little sister most of all, would ever feel so violated, so utterly neglected again. That Darcy eventually left didn't change anything, at least not to me. Tyler *knows* that Westlake is my balm, is the glue that keeps me whole. And yet he wants to leave anyway.

Tina Sacrow, who was three years behind me at State, strides over to take our order, breaking me free from the memory.

"Congrats," she says, after scribbling down my Coors Light and Susanna's margarita, straight up.

"I'm pretty proud of her," I answer. "She's never actually played a gig in Westlake before."

"Oh, I meant on Tyler and the new job," she answers over her shoulder, already on her way to make the rounds.

I stare at the peanut bowl on the table and feel my temples twitch.

"Just wait to talk to him when he gets back," Lulu says, intuiting my thoughts, though she's already told me that if given the chance, she'd move to Seattle in the flash of a second. *Which of course she would say*, I thought yesterday when I told her how sick this whole thing made me, how I wanted to puke my guts out, but by then she'd switched to discussing her morning sickness, her tender breasts, her already too-tight pants. Which only reminded me of how we stood on the opposite sides of the chasm, how my insides were seeping out onto a full tampon while she was busy gestating. *You're not me. You're not the one who made the promise to take care of everything!* I thought before hanging up.

"Yeah, let it go." Susie concurs tonight. "Nothing is set in stone."

But of course it is. Of course my flash-forward has already shown me what's going to become of us. It turns out that so many things are set in stone—just not the promises that my husband once made me.

"So anyway," I say, waving my hand. "How did Austin take the news that you were leaving?"

"Not well." Susie shakes her head. "Cried and cried, and I guess I cried a little too." She pauses. "He begged me to forgive him. Wailed on and on about how much he loved me." She takes a long sip of her drink. "Why does he think I can just forgive him?" She motions to Tina Sacrow for another round.

"Because he still loves you?" I make one last pitiful plea for her to reconsider.

"That doesn't have anything to do with this." She stares at me. "What does love have to do with any of this?"

"Something." I shrug. "It has to have something to do with this." I think of Tyler and how much I have loved him since I was just sixteen, how I have loved him more than I have ever loved anything. And then I mull how much I need to believe that love can salvage some part of what he's about to shatter. "I mean, maybe I love Tyler enough to move, even though it's the last thing on the planet I want to do."

Yes, maybe. Maybe love needs to have a little something more to do with this than just my panic at the thought of leaving the town that is my everything, of the pattern of my life that provides so much comfort. Maybe this is how we end up leaving: not because he makes me, but because I decide I'm willing to make that sacrifice.

"Love does not lead a husband to make out with his assistant. I'm sorry, but it doesn't," she replies.

I start to defend him but find that I am out of words. That as much as that part of me—the part that uses the camera flash even on a clear day to illuminate her life—would like to shine that very flash on Susie's marriage, perhaps there's no brightness to be found here. Perhaps some things just go dark, even when we've used all our tricks to make it otherwise.

"You're not going to talk me out of it? Tell me to change my mind and take him back? That's all you've been doing these past few months." She looks at me, then Lulu, with surprise.

"Maybe you're right," I say. "What do I know?"

"Usually everything," she says, her astonishment morphing to sadness.

Before I can answer, I hear the squeak of metal chair legs edging on the floor and look up to see Eli Matthews sliding up to the table with fistfuls of longneck beers.

"Hey, I hope you don't mind." He places the four bottles on the table, then leans down and pecks my cheek, catching me off guard and with no time to reciprocate. "I saw you over here and figured beers were the least I could do for inviting me out."

"I don't know who you are, but I like you already," Susie says, extending her hand and making introductions.

"And before I forget," he says, unraveling his messenger bag from across his chest, "I brought you this. For that test drive." He offers a Nikon, shiny and expensive, and places it in my open palm.

"I can't take this." I nudge it back to him, a halfhearted gesture at best.

"Just as a loaner. To regain your sea legs," he says. "Digital is a whole new world."

Lulu knees me under the table, and then I feel Susie eyeing me, also unsure of anyone's motives, unsure why Eli and I might be semi-flirting, and since I am similarly unsure, I am grateful when the dimmed lights shutter to darkness, and then a spotlight homes in on Dante up on the stage. He taps the microphone three times and wipes his brow.

"Uh, hey, everyone. I want to thank everyone for coming, for showing up to support Murphy's Law tonight." He pauses for a smattering of applause. "But I'm not going to kid myself. I know you're all here to witness the incomparable Darcy Everett, making a special appearance all the way from Los Angeles."

The crowd, full of old friends and people she left behind, claps wildly, and Susie catcalls out a loud whoop. Eli, and then Lulu, follow her lead, and soon, as Dante lumbers stage left and the spotlight fades to black, the four of us are whoop-whoop-whooping, with ridiculous, loopy smiles painted across our faces, a little levity when it feels like the life outside of this moment might be too much to bear.

Finally, the curtain draws back, and there is my darling baby sister, centered, sitting behind the keyboard, and in autofocus for the hundred-plus of us who have gathered on this Wednesday night to watch. Murphy's Law has set up behind her, Dante fading into the shadows over Darcy's shoulder.

She exhales, a tiny motion that perhaps only I would notice, and just like that, I am nauseatingly nervous for her. I haven't seen her perform since Berklee, when we all flew to Boston for her graduation. I've never even headed to Los Angeles to visit, let alone to see her tear up a gig at a club. *Jesus.* Surprise at my passivity swells inside of me.

I swallow down a gulp of nerves just as she starts in on a quiet, lilting melody, her fingers leading the way, her haunting voice soon following. Everyone at Oliver's is hushed, entranced by the emotion of the moment, by the passion behind every key that she touches.

I see Eli remove the lens cap from the camera on the table and push the Nikon toward me.

"Here," he says, leaning over to whisper in my ear. "Start now. She's perfect." I smell his vanilla shampoo.

I nod and give him a grateful smile, so thankful for the small pleasure he has brought me, for his consideration to even think of me in the first place, when it feels like on the hierarchy of anyone's list, I don't even make the first page. So I raise the camera to my right eye and scoot around Lulu and Susie for a better angle. I know Eli is watching me now, so I turn back and mouth, *Thank you.*

I hold the lens up and peer through the window, and then, *snap, snap, snap.* I capture the evening knowing full well that these images won't just serve as a reminder of the past, that they might just be my ticket into the future as well.

thirteen

I wake early to discover Darcy next to me in bed. The ill-advised fourth beer I gulped just as she and Murphy's Law closed down their set yaps at my temples, a hangover headache to mask the real reason I drank too much in the first place. Because that third beer turned everything around me to mush, pressed away my fears about Tyler, and made Susie and Luanne and Eli so much funnier, so much more buoyant, that the fourth seemed like a good idea when Eli offered another round on him. It was easy to see, I think, as I watch the gentle wheeze of Darcy's slumbering breath, why my father did it. Why he drank his way out of, but then back into, despair.

Dante must have dropped Darcy off after I kissed her good-bye, and Luanne, who of course wasn't drinking, ushered me out of there, steadying me at the elbow. Darcy had fans beckoning her; they swallowed her up, eager to congratulate this superstar who had made it out of Westlake and returned bigger than all of us. Even though, of course, in Los Angeles, she was bigger than no one.

And while I lay unconscious, cloaked in an alcoholic fog, she must have crawled into bed with me, her black, smoky clothes still on, and closed her eyes in the crook of my arm, exactly where Tyler used to lay before he took to passing out on the couch in front of the TV.

It is still early, so I tiptoe to the bathroom, draw a steaming shower, and ready myself for my day, thinking of Tyler and how *he doesn't know who he is without me, without this town,* as if that's any reason to blow our lives in two opposing directions. *"Is this really the life that you want?"*

I realize now, as I wash the conditioner out of my hair, the water spilling down over my forehead, my shoulders, embracing me, that I likely can't change his mind, change the future. Our empty phone calls have proven that—he held firm on this new opportunity, no longer hedging that a week might just be a week. No, a week might actually be a lifetime. What I saw while I was passed out on my father's basement floor is happening, *like it or not,* so I'd better find a way to like it or the move to Seattle will be the first in a series of ways that we undo ourselves.

Dressed and dried, I grab an apple from the fruit bowl on the kitchen counter, then down two Tylenol to combat the steady pulse of blood behind my ears and slip out the door toward school. Eli's camera is tucked in my purse from last night, stuffed full of memories—good ones, for a change. I dig my hand into the side pocket and feel for it, the spare key he made me, and *yes, there it is.*

The parking lot is desolate when I pull in. Three beaten cars sit near the gym: athletes, no doubt, who have pried themselves from their beds for an early weight-lifting session. I make my way through the vacant halls, running my hands over the iron lockers, listening to their clanging echo behind me. The key snaps open the door to the art room effortlessly. I wind my way past splattered easels, past half-built sculptures, until I find what I'm looking for.

Back in the corner, where my beloved darkroom used to be, is a
half-open door to a cramped cube where two computerized work-
stations now hum, waiting patiently for me to catch up with mod-
ern technology.

I plug the camera into the computer cord, and the machine
whirs alive, as if its brain is back from a coma. The pictures from
the Nikon are crystalline, sharp, vivid in a way that my old lens
could never replicate, bursting with details that a disposable
camera—the kind I use these days, if at all—could never capture.

I flip past each of the images, which get freer, less constrained
as they go on, thanks, no doubt, to the liquid gold pulsing through
me with every beer. There is one that catches Susie in a reflective,
quiet moment, staring into her margarita, when her bravado has
fallen away. There is one of Eli making a distorted, silly face at me,
his tongue thrust out, his smile nevertheless intact. There is one of
the crowd—I crouched in front of the stage and shot outward—
mesmerized by Darcy and her talent; you can see it washed across
them, in their eyes, the size of globes.

But of course, most of the pictures are of Darcy. Darcy with
her mouth open wider than I thought possible, belting out a high
note, wailing out the misery that might seem almost overdramatic,
though if you know her, you know that this misery is as much a
part of her as oxygen. Darcy hunched over the keys, her fingers
electric, though in the image they are still, frozen, as each note
shoots through her, like IV meds for her ailing insides. There is
Darcy smiling, finally smiling, when she dedicates her encore song
to Luanne and me; I catch her profile just as she turns her head
toward our table, her dimple, too often flattened in her sorrowful
cheeks, revealing itself.

I am so lost in the maze of images that I must not hear the
door open, then shut, behind me.

"Hey, early morning for you too, I see." I turn to see Eli behind me, holding an aluminum coffee cup, his messenger bag slung back over his shoulder.

"Couldn't sleep," I say.

"I never sleep," he says, pulling a chair up to the desk and eyeing the photos. "But hey, last night was so much fun. Thanks for inviting me. The most fun I've had since I've gotten here."

"From the way you say that, it doesn't sound like there was much competition." I smile at him.

"It's growing on me." He shrugs, not unkindly. "So do you need any help here? There are so many ways you can manipulate these digital shots."

"I still miss the darkroom," I reply, turning back to the screen, noticing his two-day-old stubble and how it makes his eyes seem greener. I almost feel disloyal until I remember Tyler and his own disloyalty, so I just flick my guilt aside. *Tit for tat, Tyler Farmer! Takes two to tango and all of that.*

"These times they are a-changin'," he says, standing and touching my shoulder. "I have to head down to the supply room to restock for today, but if you need me, you know where to find me. I'll show you a thing or two to do with these."

The door nudges shut and his footsteps fade to nothingness. I stare closer at a new shot, one of Darcy right as she's standing to bow, to inhale her glory that she deserves so very, very much, even if it's not the grand lights of Los Angeles that she's still hoping will shine upon her. She has just noticed me shooting her, and her eyes pop open just enough for the camera to catch them, a sly smile curling on the edges of her mouth. Because I know her well, I can tell what she is thinking. She is thinking, *Welcome back, Tilly*; that she is as proud of me for trying to regain the love of something that I once lost as I am of her for slaying her set tonight. I stare at the picture and know that it isn't much, me reclaiming my passion for photography, but I also know that it feels a little bit like something, a little return to the self that was taken from me when my mother died.

I flip my fingers over the mouse, cruising through the lot of the pictures, freezing on the image of Eli with his ridiculous tongue pointing out at me. He looks inane, goofy, but I can't help it, *don't want to help it.* I smile anyway. And then I think, *Well, what the hell, why not see what I can see? What's the harm in that?* So I focus in harder, firmer now, willing myself backward, or forward, or really, I'm not even sure where, just willing myself into his existence, and then, yes, there it is, that rumbling, foreboding thunder of a spark that is about to shoot through me. The cramp weasels up through my calf and then past my knee, coursing straight through my heart, and because I know it's coming, because I *will not let it own me,* I clutch the armrests of my chair, exhale my breath, and steady myself for the ride. *If I'm going to be taken,* I think, right before the room goes black, *I may as well sit back, hold on tight, and go where it takes me.*

<hr>

The Arc de Triomphe looks as wondrous as I had anticipated. Regal, towering, and sure, a tiny bit plasticized with its faux-stone exterior and its painted-on details, but still, parked up against the back wall of the gym, buffering the drinks table and the buffet, which is replete with mini-éclairs, it is a showstopper. Perhaps the best prom theme and execution in years, *I consider from my spot on the bleachers. I grin, in spite of the current circumstances that have landed me outside the time-space continuum.*

Below me, the strobe lights gyrate at a dizzying pace,

and the juniors and seniors, most of whom are salivating to graduate even though their diplomas won't change much— they'll still be moseying through Westlake with their beat-up trucks, working construction jobs or, at best, aspiring to middle management—have turned the dance floor into a giant throb of muscle. Up, down, up, down, they jump in unison to a hip-hop song that I'm too old to recognize.

CJ is huddled in the corner, her face washed with a disgruntled mix of sadness and boredom that marks at least half of all teenage years, gabbing with her best friend, Lindsay Connors. Yellow flowers spring from the cleavage of her cream-colored dress, though her breasts pour out all the same, and her strappy gown hugs her a little too tightly, reminding me of a swaddled baby, a mummy, a buttery blintz.

I scan around for Susanna, but either she's concealed behind the mass of pulsing teenagers or she's opted out of the evening, maybe at home, nursing a glass of wine or maybe, I realize—surprised at my happiness for her—out on a date.

I spot Eli near the DJ station. The lights are spinning over his face, illuminating his cheekbones, then his nose, then his chin, and then his features are cast in relative darkness, and he is rubbing the arm of a woman whose back is toward me. She is skinny, skinnier than I am, and her hair is choppy on her neck, a blunt cut of a bob that shows off her bare nape. From my place on the bleachers, I feel an unfamiliar sentiment: jealousy. Really? Jealousy?

With Tyler, there was never any reason to be envious: he was always mine, for as long as I could remember. It occurs to me just now, watching Eli run his finger down his date's forearm, surreptitiously almost, that there is something to be

said for longing, for needing, for not taking the other person
for granted such that there is rarely a spark of emotion,
other than contentedness, between you two. Not that the
trust I have with Tyler isn't comforting. Isn't wonderful. But
now, with this threat of Seattle, even that, the trust we built
our foundation on, might be gone or at least seriously
warped, and as the rigid metal from the bleachers slowly
lulls my butt to sleep, I wonder if maybe being too satisfied
with your life and becoming numb to it aren't somehow in-
tertwined. Like there isn't something just as dangerous
about playing it safe.

The beat of the music eases, and the DJ blends in a new
song, a slow dance. The dance floor is immediately vacated,
gangly kids staring at their hands, congregating to the side
of the gym to eye the brave few who remain. Slowly, guys
find the guts to ask their dates to dance, and the pairs sway
back and forth, some pressing too close, some holding each
other at a distance that can be described as awkward at
best. I laugh to myself, because some things never change,
even as everything else does.

I look back to Eli, who is whispering in the woman's ear,
and they collectively giggle, an intimate gesture with their
heads angling toward one another. Then he takes her hand
and leads her to the dance floor. He pulls her into his shoul-
der, and she rests her head against it, and they start to
move, slowly, back and forth, reminding me of a ripple of a
wave. Eventually, the song peters to its end, and she lifts her
chin, kisses him on the cheek.

As I watch them stroll toward the shadows, he rubs the
small of her back, then links his fingers into hers, and even-
tually, near the refreshments table, they are swallowed up in

the crowd of rented tuxedos and clingy dresses. I refocus my eyes and search in vain, desperate for one last glimpse of him, of her, perplexed by this heat of envy swarming over me—dateless in the shadow of my own Arc de Triomphe— but no, they are gone, and soon enough, so too am I.

I come to instantly this time, gasping for oxygen, my blood tick-tocking in my neck. My hands still clutch the chair, palms clammy, knuckles white. Slowly, I find my breath—in, out, in, out—and steady my vision, tweaking my vertigo until the floor is flat and the walls aren't rolling like funhouse mirrors. I have to concentrate to stand, but eventually I do find my way upright, though my legs still feel brittle, breakable almost. As I turn to leave, I hear rustling in the next room.

"You okay?" Eli says, appearing before me, his arms over-loaded with drafting paper, his hands stuffed with pencils and brushes.

My face flushes to what I am certain is cherry tomato, the deepest of sunburn red.

"Fine, *fine!*" I say a little too hysterically.

He cocks an eyebrow.

"You don't look fine," he says.

"Just hungover," I respond, waving a hand in front of me, hoping I don't betray my anxiety. *Who are you dating??* I want to scream. *Why do I care??* I want to scream louder.

"The camera, don't forget it." He drops the supplies and tugs the Nikon free from the computer cord. "From what I could see last night, you still have the touch."

I nod, my throat too dry to answer.

"So come back," he says, taking my hand and placing the camera in it. "Shoot some more and come back."

"I will," I finally say, then turn to go, suddenly too shy to meet his eyes. *You bet your ass I'll be back,* my inner voice yells, though a wiser part of me knows that Ty is coming home on Saturday and when he does, he's taking me with him, and that I might never find my way back again.

fourteen

Tyler's flight is twenty minutes late, thanks to a passing thunderstorm, proving the weather forecasters only partially right—it has turned cooler, but the sweeping rains are too stubborn to push west. I've forgotten to call ahead, so I'm stuck at Westlake's tiny commuter airport with nothing but stale coffee and Muzak overhead to keep me company. The blue pleather chair at his gate is stiff but comfortable, and I prop my feet up in front of me, watching the sporadic flights come and go, shooting off into the sky, soaring through the dusk, and then growing smaller until they disappear entirely.

I have rehearsed what I will say to him. I will tell him that we can compromise: that I can't leave until my father is healthy, until I am pregnant, but when we have tackled both of those hurdles, then yes, I will uncover the strength to vacate the only home I have ever truly known. I'll look at him, and I'll find the courage to say these things, even though every cell, every instinct in me will revolt. But I don't know what else to do. *I can't change the future; I may as well change my perception of it.*

I mentioned it to Susanna yesterday, during our first rehearsal/working lunch with CJ, which went about as well as could be expected, with Midge Miller, who is about one hundred years old and has been teaching piano for seven decades, filling in for Darcy, who had decided that she might be too good for this "high school musical shit."

"Do you even have a choice about it?" Susanna said quietly, as CJ or Midge, it was tough to tell, stumbled over the melody for "Hopelessly Devoted to You." "I mean, listen, I can't tell you how relieved I am to have made a decision about Austin, but still . . . you and Tyler? I mean, really, there's no other option. You guys can't split up. You have to go with him."

I looked at her, chewing my tuna sandwich, forcing it down, and realized that I never knew that maybe Susanna wasn't happy with Austin, with her lot. I knew she was sarcastic and biting and maybe a little jagged around the edges, but relieved that her marriage was over? No, I'd never have expected that. And then I also realized with certainty that I couldn't be like her, that she was right: I simply didn't have the stomach to start something new, because Tyler was all I'd ever known and that was something worth fighting for. Yes, the heat of my jealousy over Eli and his girlfriend has been worming through me, like a parasite eating away my intestines, like an illness I can't eradicate, but *that is fleeting, that will pass,* I tell myself; it's just a shard of misplaced emotion from a lonely wife whose bedrock is cracking beneath her. And yeah, maybe I don't know who I am without Tyler, but maybe I don't want to know, either.

He asked me if this is the life that I want. *"Yes. Of course, this is the life that I want,"* I replied, and still, it holds true. So I will tell Tyler today, as I told Susanna yesterday, that we'll find a compromise, even though it's not really a compromise if you're the only one giving something up.

I am practicing my speech in the airport, watching a prop plane hover for a landing, when the loudspeaker overhead tweets with feedback. His plane is here, the woman announces above me. Arrival of flight 284 from Seattle. Tyler is back.

My speech echoes through my mind as I toss the sour coffee in the garbage, press the wrinkles from my shirt, and wait for Tyler to stroll through the gate. I will look at him, at the only man whom I have ever loved, and I will defy my better judgment of who I am and what I can handle, and I will tell him that someday soon, we will make this work, make that coaching job a reality.

My stomach roils, and my heartbeat accelerates, and then, the door opens and the passengers make their way off. It is a small plane, a commuter, so there are no more than a dozen wayward travelers—not many people find the need to stop in Westlake.

I see a harried mother and her balled-fisted, sweaty toddler, and then I see a pork-bellied man whose polo doesn't cover his paunch. They amble through the gate door, followed by an assortment of Westlake's own: I wave to Teddy Carver, who makes weekly trips to Seattle to visit his sick mother in her nursing home because Westlake's couldn't provide her adequate care, and nod hello to a woman I always see at Albertson's yet have never actually spoken with.

Eventually the flow of passengers slows, and the solitary flight attendant disembarks, rolling her suitcase behind her, headed to a local motel until she can turn around and get the hell out of here.

"Excuse me," I say, stepping in front of her. "My husband was supposed to be on this flight. Is there anyone else still on board?"

"No, sweetie," she says, though she looks about my age, only swathed in too much foundation and excessive blush. "That's it. We did have one cancelation at the last minute, though." She shrugs. "Maybe you should call him and see."

She waves her fuchsia nails and heads off, the wheels of her bag scraping against the linoleum floor. My pulse flares in my forehead as I turn to stare out the picture window, out into the wide open steel-colored sky, simultaneously empty and layered with a blanket of dull clouds, and though I should pick up my phone and call Tyler, instead I stand there frozen, as desolate as the sky, struck with immediate clarity. *Clarity!*

Damn you, Ashley Simmons.

Tyler is gone, I now realize, and he's not coming back. He is building his life—a new life—without me, without this town, and without the past that I was certain would carry us on its shoulders into the sunset of the our future. We aren't moving. He is.

fifteen

Ashley Simmons has agreed to meet me for breakfast on Monday morning. I have told Susanna that she and Darcy—who, after a supposed spectacularly wretched rehearsal with Murphy's Law, is willing to lower herself to playing high school piano once again—can handle the "Summer Lovin'" choreography today, its side-to-side shuffles and its snap, snap, snapping beat, and I've e-mailed the prom committee that I'll be taking the week off. The Eiffel Tower, the freaking idiotic Arc de Triomphe can wait.

I've spent the better part of the weekend burrowed underneath the covers of our bed, *my* bed, as the plural no longer seems to apply, mourning the vestiges of my marriage. Susanna came by with rum and varied triumphant epitaphs about how men are mostly synonymous with assholes and how women could certainly survive without them, were it not for their sperm, but her rantings, accurate as they might have been in my specific situation, couldn't lift me from my cocoon of despair. Darcy joined us in bed, our trio pressed against my headboard, as we watched season one of *Alias*, which Susie had rented to try to give me a shock of estrogen-boosted adrenaline. Needless to say, it didn't.

Tyler sent me an e-mail late Friday night, a perfect capper to this whole fucking debacle.

From: Farmer, Tyler
To: Farmer, Tilly
Subject: I'm sorry
Dear Tilly,

    I know that there isn't any way to make up for what I'm doing to you. I know that I need to call and explain everything to you, and that e-mail is a really crappy way to say what I need to say. But I wanted to put this down on paper to get it right, so I apologize for a lot of things, including the fact that I'm e-mailing you.

    Look, I know that I'm a coward. I know that I owe you more than this, but I also know that I don't know what else to do: I don't want to take you from Westlake, and I also don't know that you should come with me anyway. I just need to figure out who I am without you. I hope that you won't hate me for this. And I hope that you know that I never wanted things to go down this way, but right now, this makes sense for me.

    I'm sorry. I'll call soon.

                          Ty

"An e-mail!" Susie huffed from behind my computer as we reread it together. "A piece-of-shit e-mail!" she scoffed, her anger palpable for the both of us.

I was too shocked to be angry, too numb to have the energy for rage. So Susie and Darcy made up for me, plotting vengeance, smearing his constitution, threatening him at every turn, as if they'd ever go through with any of it.

"Let's chop his balls off," Darcy sneered.

"Maim his throwing arm," Susie suggested while they both nursed tumblers of rum.

True to his word, he did call me three times on Sunday, and on the third, I nearly picked up, but instead, Darcy intervened and tossed my cell straight across the room.

"I will not have you begging him to come back or telling him that your suitcase is packed to join him!" she said, refilling her glass and then mine. I nodded because I knew that she knew that this was exactly what I would do: scrape the true bottom of my dignity—*pleading with a man who announced his decision to likely vacate our marriage in an e-mail*—and so I let her hold my backbone sturdy when I wasn't able to do so myself.

But by the time I woke on Monday morning, I was angry; I was very, very angry. That seed of venom, planted on that day at the fairgrounds, spreading within me. I'd left Tyler a long, expansive, expletive-filled voice mail the night before, full of words I didn't realize I even knew—*"You are such a motherfucking shitbag, a goddamn cocksucker!"*—bursting with rage that had slowly been brewing. And the truth was, it felt strangely out-of-body good—this fiery ball of anger, the release of it out into the world. But it wasn't enough—getting so pissed off that my ears burned. I needed more: more answers, more control, more understanding of what the hell was happening to me. And best I figured, like it or not, I needed Ashley Simmons' help.

She wanders into the Back Street Diner looking like she's just tumbled out of bed, a look that isn't so different from mine, with my eyes marshmallow puffy and my hair unwashed since Saturday. Darcy had implored me to take a shower, but my tiny act of rebellion—*No, I will not tend to my personal hygiene, and eff you,*

Tyler!—provided some sort of intangible satisfaction, and as I swirl my black coffee while Ashley orders her own, I consider how long I might be able to go without bathing. *What sort of record could I set to let Tyler know that he has totally pilloried me, to understand the destruction that he has caused?*

The air smells like refried grease, a side effect of the sloppy omelets they serve, and the scent, in combination with my coffee, turns my stomach into a twisting siphon, as if my digestive tract is attempting to physically purge my angst.

"No offense," Ashley says after she requests a stack of pancakes and a side of eggs over easy, "but you look like death."

"Tyler left me," I say plainly. "Which I suppose you already know."

"I didn't know," she responds, her face filled with genuine astonishment. "How would I have known?"

"Because of what you can do!" I whisper. *"Because of what you did to me!"*

Ashley giggles, an annoying trait left over from childhood that I suddenly remember. Her way of filling the quiet while she composes her thoughts.

"Tilly, I told you the other day. I didn't really do much. *You're* the one who is doing everything."

"Cut the shit, Ashley," I bark, then sip my coffee to calm myself, because she's not the one who betrayed me by leaving. She's just the one who showed me that he would. "Listen, whatever you did to me . . . I'm *seeing* things that are going to happen . . ." I pause, because I'm not quite sure what I'm asking.

"Can I ask you a question?" she says, as a non-answer.

"Why not," I snap, steadying myself for yet another one of her long-winded, cagey probes on why I ever believed that marriage, that Tyler, should be my salvation. The bell at the front counter dings continuously, a sign of a ready order, and the clanging is worming its way under my sinuses, back behind my eyes, a fleck of an oncoming migraine.

"Back in middle school, why did we stop being friends?"

"What? I don't know," I answer, and then consider it. "Didn't we just outgrow each other? You went one way, and I went the other. Why? What difference does it make?"

"I guess none." She shrugs. "But back then, it made a difference to me. I thought we were like sisters, and then . . . then I guess things got hard for me, and I looked up, and you were gone."

"I wasn't gone! I never got the sense that you wanted me there in the first place," I say. "I remember you mocking us, thinking that we were inconsequential. Cheerleaders. You hated us."

"It wasn't like that." She shakes her head. "I just thought you were capable of so much more. I always thought that you were smarter than you gave yourself credit for." She pauses. "But then again, you were never so good at reading what was right in front of you."

"What's that supposed to mean?"

"It's nothing," she says, though I sense that it is much more than nothing. She waves the hand that isn't attached to the coffee mug. "Besides, it was a long time ago. Maybe it doesn't have anything to do with who we are now."

We sit there for a quiet moment, a delicate truce drawn between us, and Hootie and the Blowfish pours out from the overhead speaker. An anthem of my youth. A reminder of Tyler and me in his truck—*Hold my hand! Want you to hold my hand!*—the wind rushing through the windows, the sun warming our cheeks. God, we were perfect.

No, no, *I will not remember him like this*, I think. I am too angry, too *fucking furious* at my husband and who he promised he'd be to me and what he's now done, to look back on that time through a golden filter. And just then, as if I'm not close enough to the cusp of a mental breakdown, Darcy and my father walk through the diner's front door. My face must register my surprise, because Ashley swivels her neck to glance toward the counter.

"Is that your little sister?" she asks, turning back and scooting her eggs around her plate. "I haven't seen her in years. Thought she got out of here."

"She did," I say, my eyes still on the mismatched pair who I'd thought were sworn enemies. "She came back for a quick visit but is sticking around until I sort this out."

Poor Darcy, I think, an earthquake of pity moving through me. I pleaded with her this weekend to take her return ticket and head for sunnier skies, away from the insanity that was swallowing my life, what with my off-the-wagon father, my deadbeat husband, and my ability to see into the future, but she shook her head, like a stubborn toddler, and refused to abandon me. After all of these years of begging her not to go, it turned out that the only thing that could actually pin her down was me asking her to leave.

My father fishes into his pocket to pay the counter lady, and Darcy glances around, her eyes finding their way to me. She offers a perplexed wave, then shuffles to our table.

"What are you doing here?" she says, noticing Ashley, whom I can tell she recognizes, though she doesn't know how.

"I told you I had a breakfast."

"I see you cleaned yourself up," she says, her sarcasm ringing clear.

I stare at her coolly as a response and then say, "You remember Ashley Simmons. From middle school."

"Hey," they say in unison, each bobbing her head upward as a hello.

"What are *you* doing here?" I ask.

"Dad hasn't left the house in four days. I felt sorry for him, so I told him we could take a quick drive for breakfast." She flops her hands, an empathetic admission from my hardened sister. "I thought he did okay with you this weekend, so I don't know. Just trying to make the effort, you know."

I nod because I do know how difficult it might be for her to acknowledge my father's recent kindness; upon hearing the news of Tyler's abandonment, he had turned up at my bedroom, stood in the door frame until Susanna assured him that I was asleep, and then slept in the hallway just outside, in case I woke up and needed him, though he knew, all too clearly, that I wouldn't. That I didn't. But it was his way of saying, "Hey, I am a gargantuan screwup, but I'm still your dad," and we all were the wiser, we all were the *kinder*, for recognizing that.

My father suddenly announces himself at our table and leans down to kiss me.

"Didn't know we'd be seeing you here," he says.

"Ditto," I say back, not because I'm trying to be curt but because I'm so drained from the past two and a half days that I have to choose where to expend my energy.

"Hi, Mr. Everett." Ashley extends her right hand. "Ashley Simmons. It's been a while." She squints her eyes and waits for him to remember her. When he does, he thrusts his head back just a sliver, a manifestation of his surprise at seeing her, at how much she's changed since she was twelve.

"Wow." He runs his hand over his chin. "Ashley. Nice to see you. It has indeed been a while. How are your parents?"

Ashley giggles, that hyena yelp, betraying her discomfort.

"My mom is sick, unfortunately," she says, watching my father as she speaks. "My dad passed a few years back."

"I'm sorry to hear that," he says. "He was a very good man. We lost touch, but I remember him being a very good man." What my father doesn't say is that they lost touch when my dad alienated nearly everyone he knew with his drinking, and some people never came back to him, even when he had atoned for his sins.

"He was." Ashley nods.

The counter lady calls out, "Darcy, hon, order's done," and she and dad say their good-byes. Ashley's eyes follow them as they head toward the parking lot, then she looks back at me and sighs.

"I see your dad has straightened himself out."

"Sort of," I say, but then remember his perch just outside my door and decide to give him more credit. "He had a little relapse, but we're working through it."

She laughs. "That's you, Tilly. The glass is always half-full until the bitter end." She pushes away her plate, and I take a bite of her buttered toast, the first thing I've eaten since yesterday afternoon.

"Enough about that. I know how you feel about me," I say.

"Not really." She shrugs.

"Listen, Ashley, I just need some answers. I asked you to meet me because I need you to make it stop."

"Do you want it to?" she asks.

"Yes!" I hiss after a beat. I'd thought—just for one woebegone second last week—that it could be fun, whimsical, that wild ride that I so rarely hitched myself to. But Tyler and his abandonment have shown me that it isn't, it can't be, it can only bring more havoc, damage, because all I am is a helpless observer, a witness to a future that *I want no part of*! These visions aren't going to bring Tyler back, aren't going to make me pregnant, make me happy, make me anything other than a haunted shell. *Yes, God damn it, I want it to stop!*

"I wish I could help, but I already told you," she says, plunking down her coffee, which spills over the rim and onto the

Formica table. "I can't do anything about it. You're the one in control."

"But I'm not! I'm *not*!" I say. "I can't speak, I can't move, I can't change anything! I *tried* to change what happened with Tyler, and I can't, I couldn't!"

I slap my hands down on the table, sloshing my own coffee, which I mop up with my elbow.

"You're thinking about this all wrong," she says before nudging the check toward me. "It really is a gift. If you give yourself a little more time, I bet you'll find a way to see it that way too."

A week later, the bursting August air is even more humid than any living creature thought possible, and despite all odds, I have mustered the dignity to crawl into the shower, step into a mostly wrinkle-free pair of khaki capris, and drive in to work. Darcy has offered to accompany me, but I shake her off. She and Dante have booked another gig at Oliver's, so I tell her to spend the day with him instead, honing their act—a small deflection of the fact that I'm a little embarrassed at the role reversal, at how, with one abrupt detour of my life's plan, I've devolved into a total basket case. *I was the one who took care of people's messes! I was the one who always had an actionable solution.* No, I assured her this morning, I could hold my head up fine without her.

Of course, this isn't true. This isn't true at all. I can barely lift my head off the floor, where I want to splatter out my intestines to make my asshole of a husband feel worse about himself than I do, but alas, I have a prom committee meeting that I simply cannot avoid, and by God, if these kids can find a way to spare a few minutes between their summer jobs and their second summer jobs, then I can put that bastard aside and get over myself, if only for twenty minutes.

I close my office door behind me, lean up against it, and exhale.

"Hey!" CJ says from my couch, and I jump six inches, nearly ramming my head against the coat hook.

"Oh, good lord, CJ! What are you doing here?"

"You told me to stop by a few minutes before the prom meeting," she says. "You e-mailed me about it last week." *Last week*, I think. *A lifetime ago. Who can even remember what I was thinking of last week?*

"I told you to stop by?" I have no recollection of doing so, though I have no recollection of the life I had when something like *prom* actually mattered, so I take her at her word. "Okay," I say, dropping my bag by my desk and sidling up beside her on the love seat. "What did we need to go over?"

"How would I know?" she says. "You're the one with the lists."

"Well, I don't have my list today!" I say, indignant. *Why can't anyone else around here take care of these stupid lists?* "So please, tell me, what did we need to go over?!" My chin quivers, and it's obvious to the both of us that I am not ready for this, that I am in no way prepared to either guide or counsel, much less perform the two of those acts together, but CJ's eyes just widen, while mine fill with obese tears, which somersault down my face before I can command them to stop.

"I'm sorry," I say, batting my hands in front of my cheeks. "I'm sorry. I'm a bit of a mess this morning."

"I heard what happened," she says, wincing.

"Who hasn't?" I say, dropping my chin into my palms.

"Probably no one." She concedes, then smiles wistfully. "It sort of makes my point."

"About what?" I grunt.

"About this town." She shrugs. "About how it takes everything from you: your privacy, your identity . . . hell, just the fact that I can't stand it here makes me an outcast."

"You're not an outcast, CJ," I say. "You're the senior class vice president and social chair. And star of the musical. And about a million other things." *Just like I was*, I think. Like being appointed to some silly position in your school government actually matters in the scheme of your life. Like being anointed as something, as someone special, *back in high school* really promises a spectacular future. Back then, of course, I thought it did. Now, it feels like CJ might be a much wiser version of my old self.

"Well, whatever," she says, which feels like a reasonable enough argument for me right now. *Yeah, well, whatever, Tyler, you asshole!* "No one here has any aspirations other than to live here, die here, and long hail the Westlake Wizards." She flops back on the couch.

Suddenly, I realize that I can't be here, in my office, with this child who is wiser than I am. *I cannot deal with this right now!*

"The Arc de Triomphe," I say.

"What?"

"The Arc de Triomphe. That was on our to-do list—bring it up at the meeting. You're in charge for today. I found one online, and I want you guys to order it and be sure that it can be here on time." My mind flashes with a vision of Eli at prom, with that willowy girl swaying by his side, and my perpetual nausea resurfaces.

"I can't stay," I say, rising abruptly.

"Um, okay, but also, I hate to ask, but community service?" CJ says.

"Community service?" I ask back, wondering if she's suggesting that I need mental help, which, actually, I might.

"For Wesleyan," she says. "You said I needed it. I applied for an after-school position at the hospital, if you think that's okay. I'll just mostly be restocking supplies and shuffling paperwork, but they were the only ones who could give me something between school and my shift at the restaurant." *Oh, yes, this is what I wanted to talk to her about in the first place.*

"Oh, yeah, this is why I told you to come in, but yes, yes, I'm sure that's fine. To be honest, it's puff work. Just something for your resume. Who really cares?"

She cocks her head at me, at my unusual brittle candor, as I fling myself out the door, then down the hallways, past the judgment and the whispers and the shattered comfort of place that once hugged me like a life vest. Now that the outside world has weaseled its way in, nothing will ever be the same, *can* ever be the same, and the question becomes, without that life preserver, do I sink or do I swim? At this point, as Tyler might say, it's anyone's game.

sixteen

The bottle of tequila is half-empty on my nightstand when I finally force my eyes open. They're crusty, and I slap the back of my hand against my lashes, but still, the hardened goo remains. My mouth is like flypaper, sticky with condensed saliva, and my tongue tastes like rotten tuna fish. My pupils slowly focus on a figure hovering above me, and I squint to make it out.

"Get up," his voice says. "Come on, get up. You've been this way since Wednesday. Enough."

My dad strips my sheet from me in one billowing swoop, but rather than acquiesce, I yank a pillow over my head, fending off the headache that is threatening to overtake my brain.

"Go away," I say, muddled, from beneath the pillow. My voice is a scratch, like it has gotten comfortable not being used in a while.

"No. Get up. You need to shower, get out of this house, and do something with yourself."

I pull the pillow back from my face.

"Ironic, coming from you." I meet his eyes. "Come on, join me. Have a drink. The bottle's right there."

If he's surprised at my retort, at my heartlessness, he doesn't show it. Maybe he thinks he deserves it, or maybe, more likely, he's just used to the way that alcohol draws out our family's less enticing attributes. His was mindlessness, absence when we needed him. Mine appears to be unfiltered, raw honesty.

He wiggles his hands underneath my armpits and hauls me into a seated position, folding me like a Raggedy Ann doll on the bed. The mattress bounces beneath me, and I'm surprised at his strength, how easily he lifts me. My father crouches onto his knees, his old joints cracking.

"Listen," he says. "You can't do this. Getting drunk and sleeping through your life is not an option. Not for you."

"It was good enough for you."

"You're not me," he says, placing his hands over mine.

"I need Tyler to come back," I say. "I can't do this if Tyler doesn't come back."

"Well, he's not coming back," my dad offers. "At least not right now."

I vaguely remember calling Ty just after I peeled out of the school parking lot on Wednesday, already on my way to the liquor store before heading home. He picked it up on the second ring.

"Really?" I started with. "This is what you're going to do to me? Really?"

He sighed. "Hi, Till." I heard him suck in his breath. "I'm sorry."

"You said that already in your e-mail. In your *e-mail*."

"I can't come home." He said it so softly I had to mentally replay it to be sure that I'd heard it correctly.

"You certainly *can* come home! You're choosing not to come home! But *I'm* here! Your wife! Your marriage! Your life!"

"I need to do this, Tilly. I tried to tell you that." He paused.

"And I'm truly sorry that I'm hurting you. I wish you could under-stand it, how I feel, how I've felt."

"This is our marriage, Tyler!" I flew into the strip mall park-ing lot, the tires squeaking on the pavement below, and dove into a spot, hitting the brakes too late, so the SUV bounced off the con-crete sidewalk.

"You think I don't know that?" he yelled back. "You think this was easy for me? You think that I wouldn't choose to go back and figure out a different life?"

"A different life?" I asked, my breath spinning away from me, my heart expanding, exploding in my chest cavity.

"That's not what I meant," he said, more gently.

I didn't answer, because I could tell that this wasn't going to end well, that the more he confessed, the more I'd understand the extent of his discontent, and I'd already heard more than my psy-che could bear.

"That's not what I meant," he repeated. "I just meant . . . I do wish I'd gotten a handle on this sooner. I should have told you. I guess I should have told you, but now it feels too late. I feel better here, clearer here."

"Shut up!" I screamed. "Just shut up! Just stop fucking talking!"

So he did, and then I did, and then I stuffed the phone into the glove compartment, walked into the liquor store, and proceeded to buy the extra-extra-large tequila bottle.

And now, my father is crouched on my bedroom floor, trying to implore me to reconstruct a life that I don't recognize, a life that I have no interest in inhabiting.

"Tilly, here's the thing," my dad says, lifting my chin so I have no choice but to meet him square on. "It's easy to become like me. It's a lot harder not to. But this? This isn't you, this isn't who you want to be. You know that."

I nod, exhausted, drunk tears spilling forward.

"Come on," he says, rising and offering me his open palm. "Let's get you showered, and then let's get you some food, and then let's figure out a plan."

Every cell in my being wants to shove itself back under the comforter, wants to numb itself with more tequila. *More tequila, please!* I can practically hear them begging in my ear. But my dad's hand is outstretched, so I grab it and stand with him, then shuffle slowly to the bath.

"I don't know who I am without you," Tyler told me. Yes, well, sometimes, I guess you've got no other option than to find out.

A month slips by in a haze that feels both nascent and never-ending. I wake up, I find some way to wade through my day, some way not to fall over under the weight of my exhaustion, under the oppressive sadness that tails me like a black shadow, then drive straight home and dive into bed. *Grease* has come together better than I could have hoped for, the prom is cruising along effortlessly, and yet, I can't get myself to care, can't convince myself that any of this *matters*, which would be funny, if it weren't so unfunny, because that's all that mattered before. Before.

Tyler and I have spoken twice, once when he asked me to send him some clothes, again when he called to thank me for the care package and announce that he'd be back around the end of October to collect the rest of his things.

So there it was. Permanent. He mentioned this casually, like it wasn't the most catastrophic chasm to ever carve itself into his life, and I listened to him and wondered how the same act could define two people so differently.

But I did as he asked. I flung open his closet door while Darcy muttered behind me, parked on the bed, and told me to set the bulk of his clothes ablaze in a bonfire in the front yard instead of honoring his request. I gently picked out his polos, his khakis, lovingly folded a few sweatshirts, rolled up his oxfords so they wouldn't wrinkle. I was still angry, to be sure, but I was so tired, just so goddamn tired, that the fight had been vaporized right out of me.

School kicks off after Labor Day, and what is usually my favorite time of year—those early days before the delinquents have proven that they once again can't keep their smart-ass mouths shut, before the panicked skirmish to finalize college applications or community college plans, when everything is still tinged with hope and newness and possibility—offers nothing but gloom.

"I know I'm not normally one to say it," Susanna says while we approve wardrobe fittings after school on the third day back. "But you need to buck up."

"Touché," I answer, fingering Wally's a-little-too-Elvis-y-to-be-Danny-Zuko-but-we-have-to-settle-for-what-we-can-get leather jacket. I'm wondering if there's any way I can find something less, I don't know, cabaret club, until I realize that he wears this *in my vision*, whether I like it or not, so I just let my hands fall limp and squat onto a nearby folding chair.

"Hey, at least I'm trying," she says, and I nod because at least she is. She and Austin are working with a mediator to settle things as amicably as possible, which isn't so possible when one party is still beside herself that the other disappointed her to such depths, but she's right, she's trying. "To be honest, though," Susie continues, grabbing a needle and thread to sew the hem of CJ's impossibly snug pleather pants for the finale, for when Sandra Dee has made her full transformation, "I do sort of wonder if I'm going to be alone forever."

I remember her quiet corner on opening night, her hands a
bow around someone else's waist, and smile at her with as much
love as I can muster, and assure her that she won't be.

"Me, on the other hand . . ." I trail off.

"Hey, no one has said a word about divorce between you two
yet," she tuts. Which is true. But no one hasn't said a word about
it either. And I suspect that one day soon, Tyler will, and then I'll
crumble like a shoreline being washed out to sea. "You know
what?" she continues. "You should go grab that fancy camera the
cute art boy gave you."

"Not happening," I interject.

"Whatever, you still should," she says, ripping the hem out
now with her teeth. "Document this, you know?"

"What? Our sad-sack selves trying to put up a musical?"

"No, our sad-sack selves making a comeback from the assholes we were probably too good for in the first place."

"I admire your positivity," I say before I skulk down the left
stage stairs. *("Stage left!" Wally corrected me yesterday. "That's
stage left, not left stage, Ms. Farmer, which I'd expect you to know
by now.")* "But I'd rather stick to my own brand of self-pity."

"That's not the Tilly Farmer I know," she calls out to me.
Which is true, I think, as I exit the auditorium, *but maybe this one
was biding its time inside of me the whole time, a cancer waiting to
spring.*

Susanna was right, of course, that I'd probably get a boost out
of documenting our work, but I've put aside the camera for now. I
avoid Eli in the hallways, though he always waves with the jovial-
ity that makes him so likable, occasionally knocks on my door and
pokes his head through to say hello, and I inevitably feign busywork. His was my last flash-forward, intentionally so. After I met
with Ashley, and then after it was clear that Tyler wasn't coming

back, it became all the more clear that whatever it was that I was seeing was written in indelible ink, and it felt like too much of a burden, to know what the future would bring and not be able to do one damn thing about it. I returned the camera two weeks ago when he was out on his lunch break.

The next day, the fourth morning of the new school year, the radio alarm bounces me alert, and I listen to the DJs spar back and forth, and then the traffic guy comes on, and then the news, and then I hear the date, September 7: it has been two months exactly since Tyler left me. Because even though he didn't leave me back on his fishing trip when he announced that Jamie Rosato just wanted to feel things out, well, let's be honest, yes, that's when he left me. July 7. That's when it all started to unspool. An entire two months have slid by while I've been swimming underwater, rendering myself nearly sightless, almost deaf. It's been easier this way, anesthetizing myself to the world.

I flip off the radio, the too-cheery DJs fraying my nerves. I try to remember my to-do list for today: prom . . . maybe? CJ's application . . . perhaps? There really is nothing. Just a muddy fuzz that comes when you plunge your head underneath the deep end and sink toward the bottom.

But it's not just that—there's more, on this date. *Oh yeah.* It's also the anniversary of my mother's death. Darcy will implore me to visit the cemetery today, and I will go, of course, and I will remember, despite everything, that I still have a life, that actually, Tyler or not, I can continue to spiral until I suffocate under my own misery, or I can find a way, impossible as that might seem, to hack off the anchors that are holding me hostage and swim toward shore.

The house is at rest as I pad through. it toward the kitchen. My father moved back home, when? Yesterday? The day before? Last week? I shake my head because it's all jumbled together. He has been sober for more than sixty days now, a small milestone but a milestone nevertheless, and though he stayed here three weeks longer than necessary, Darcy finally drove him back to our childhood house after I begged off of it, too exhausted after a day of toiling with other people's problems to celebrate my father's attempt to wrestle his own. Darcy did it without complaint, while I lingered at my bedroom window and watched them go. Without me as a buffer between the two of them, they'd somehow managed to wave white flags. She begrudgingly sat with him at dinners long after I'd pleaded fatigue, and later, if I got up to use the bathroom, I'd hear an occasional guffaw from the den where they were watching some godforsaken reality show that they both seemed to delight in.

I start up the coffeepot, and it hisses in reply. It has been two months, *two months*! And still, I am here, spinning in circles, drowning in my grief.

Two months is nothing, it's a blip, a passing cloud, certainly not enough time to mourn the vestiges of a lifetime— that is what I'd tell Susanna if she were me. But she's not, and I am. Whatever Ashley Simmons unlocked in me, and certainly, it was something—rage, fearlessness, honesty—I'm still Tilly Farmer, God damn it! I watch the drip-drip-drip of the browned water slipping into the pot, and I can almost feel those things— that rage, that honesty—awakened again, broiling inside of my intestines. *Shit or get off the pot, Tilly Farmer! Pull your act together! Get over your self-pity, whatever else Tyler eff-ing Farmer has destroyed in you! You've wasted enough time on that.* If I listen closely enough, I could swear that I'm hearing Ashley, even though, quite obviously, I'm not.

I reach for a mug, lift its steaming contents to my lips, and swallow grandly, the coffee awakening my senses. It is time for a change, for a new path, a new way of thinking. Yes, maybe it's finally now time.

seventeen

As it turned out, the date, September 7, was familiar for more than just marking the two-month anniversary of the implosion of my marriage and because of my mother. *Oooh yeah*, I remember, as I pull into the WHS parking lot and spy a large trailer with the Westlake Hospital icon painted on the side. The blood drive. I'd chosen the day intentionally, a way to memorialize my mom.

It was actually Luanne's idea, last May: she thought, what better way to kick off the year, to get the kids involved in their own health and in responsibility for our fellow citizens, than to ask them to donate a pint and receive a chocolate chip cookie in return. Tyler, too, had encouraged the idea before he left me. When I told him about it way back when, he smiled and kissed my palm before turning back to his cereal and ESPN.

"You do make this world a better place," he said. "That school is lucky to have you."

At the time, I watched him shovel in his Frosted Flakes and thought that I could say the same of him, how lucky I felt to call him mine. Now, I flip off the engine to the SUV and stride toward the blood drive trailer, and I can't help but wonder if Tyler was already planning his exit back then, tossing out generic compliments but never turning to look me square in the eye as he said them. Maybe I should have seen it, I consider, because Tyler was many things, but a good liar was never one of them.

The breeze kicks up, one of those last-gasp-of-summer embraces, and it warms my shoulders, my collarbone, my core. Two months into this maze of loneliness, and yes, it dawns on me that perhaps I could have seen it, not just in my premonition, but in Tyler's distance, in the way he was slowly creeping away from me, the ant who discovered a way out of the farm when he saw the light up above.

The trailer door is ajar, so I step inside. Every chair is full; no surprise, really. Students are given a pass from class if they opt to donate, and I spot CJ in the last seat, closest to the cookie station. Johnny Hutchinson is next to her, and they're giggling back and forth, the pulsing red tubes at their inner elbows no deterrent to teenage hormones. She sees me and smiles wide, sunshine in her eyes, and I suppose that one of the many things I missed over the past two months was that they'd gotten back together, despite her protests that he was too small-town, that anything about Westlake was too small-town for her.

A nurse motions for me to have a seat, so I do. The door hinges squeak, and two sophomores amble in, cameras swinging from their necks. Eli, *oh, God, Eli*, tails them, shooing them inside farther, until they are a compact huddle in the nose of the trailer, reminding me of a cluster of cells, pressed together, looking for room to expand.

I swivel toward the nurse, eyeing her, hoping she'll usher me toward the back *so I do not have to face him and have him ask me about the rumors that run rampant through the halls like last winter's flu, so I do not have to consider that even now, two months later, I'm irked at the thought of his girlfriend, even while knowing that I can't care, shouldn't care, because I'm still married, God damn it!* But the nurse is focused on finding the vein in Reggie Valdez's left arm and pays me no mind.

"Hey, Tilly!" Eli says over the shoulders of one of his students. "You donating blood?" I nod and press the apples of my cheeks upward, too fatigued for a real smile. He returns my nod. "We're taking pictures for the yearbook."

"You're dedicating an entire page in the yearbook to the blood drive?"

"For the community service page. We'll see what we get and then decide. Better to have taken it now than wish that we had it when the time comes."

I nod again and think, as I always do these days, of Tyler. Two years into our marriage, I asked him if maybe we could start trying for kids. Susie's twins were nudging toward their first birthday, and I began to feel that itch, the tug toward motherhood, even though I was going to night school to earn my master's degree and the two of us were barely eking by on Tyler's sales commissions from the store and my day job as the assistant to the principal. I raised the subject one Sunday morning when we had the whole day in front of us, nowhere to be, no one to answer to. We stretched out in bed, and Tyler read the paper, and I rested on his shoulder, and suddenly, the words flew out of me, that I was ready to be a mother.

"If not now, then when?" I still remember saying to Tyler when he glanced down at me, crumpling the paper into his lap, his face already an answer.

"We're so young," he replied, and he was right, we were. But I didn't want to be like his mother, aching and creaky by the time our children were in high school, and I told him I'd always wanted a daughter, whom I would name Margaret, after my mom.

He smiled at me when I said that. Even now, as I sit in the blood drive trailer, I can remember that smile—tender, kind, complacent. He wasn't ready, he told me, but he would be soon. He leaned over and kissed the top of my head, and I knew that he meant it—well, I thought that he meant it, anyway.

I watch the crimson sludge drain from Reggie Valdez's inner arm and understand fully why Eli is here. He is covering his bases, just like I should have done, rather than loiter around assuming someone else, my husband, would step up to the plate.

"Have you shot anything lately?" Eli asks me now, scooting around his yearbook staff. The trailer isn't meant to accommodate the lot of us, so he is squished too closely to me, and I feel like the spider in my office who has run out of crevices in which to hide when the sole of my shoe hovers above.

I tilt my face, unsure of his question, wishing I could ease back a few extra inches. *Have I shot anything lately? Only my husband if he'd ever get his ass back in town!*

"Photos," he clarifies, jabbing a finger toward his Nikon and then emitting an easy laugh. "Have you shot any photos lately?"

"Oh. No." *My life has fallen off a cliff, and snapping pictures is hardly the first thing on my mind. Much less the stories that those photos might lay out for me and only me to see.*

"Here." He whisks the camera strap over his head, grabs my hand, and shoves the camera in. "Your turn."

"Thanks anyway," I say, shoving it back toward him.

"Nope," he says, shaking his head. "It's yours for the day. I don't need it; you do."

I jut my chin out in protest because *I don't want anyone taking care of me, Eli Matthews!* But before I can make this clear, he steps back, past his students, and shuffles down the steps.

"Here's your assignment," he calls to me. "I want documentation of the blood drive, and then I want candids from around the school. You can have them on my desk by end of day next Friday."

The door slams shut, and his yearbook staff stand there awkwardly, eyeing me, wondering just what the hell that was about. They toss glances between them, trying to assess what has transpired between the substitute art teacher and the guidance counselor who looks like she hasn't slept in three weeks (she hasn't), hasn't eaten a green vegetable in a month (ditto), and might be on the cusp of a mental breakdown (entirely likely).

I am too tired to chase after him and set him straight, even though I know I should, even though it is the anniversary of my mother's death, and she'd never want me to wilt, to cower as I have so easily, too easily. Even though I have resolved, this very morning, to buck up, pull myself together. Maybe tomorrow. Yes, maybe then. But for today, I slump in my chair, sigh, and simply wait my turn. Soon enough, the nurse hails me over and tells me to sit back, exhale, and relax. This will only hurt a pinch, she assures me, so I close my eyes, breathe, and let her drain me of one pint more.

Susanna turns thirty-three three days later, and we convene for a potluck dinner at her house once the twins have gone down. Darcy tags along, and I've called Ashley to see if she, too, would like to join us, because I am tired of the misplaced, judgmental compassion and the whispers and the glances at CVS, those *"Poor Tilly Farmer"* sidelong glares, like my entire existence should depend on my husband, even though, yes, let's be honest, most of my existence did, whether I realized it at the time or not.

So I have invited Ashley along tonight because she is certainly one who will cast me no pity, and besides, she's also the only one who knows my secret: that I can see things, even if I no longer opt to see them. And yeah, she's the very person who did this to me, but now, it's done, and part of me feels grateful to have her ear, her confidence.

She arrives with a box of Dunkin' Donuts, the best she could do, she says, after her mother had a bad spell. Ashley's mom is dying. She told me this two weeks ago when she dropped by the house to ensure that I wasn't slitting my wrists in the bathtub. I wasn't. I had instead crawled home from work early, stared at the empty answering machine, considered tequila but opted merely to flatten myself against the kitchen floor and gaze at the ceiling. Ashley found me there forty minutes later.

"My mother is dying," she said that night, an attempt to shock me out of this, to figuratively shake me by the shoulders and say, *"Your husband is not everything, you dolt."* But all she did was remind me of my own mother dying, and that life is short and you should surround yourself with the people who love you. Which circled me right back to Tyler. Whom I'd have called if I didn't hate him so much.

Susanna uncorks a bottle of wine, pouring full, sparkling glasses for each of us. We down them nearly whole, too quickly, and Darcy, in a turtleneck and burgundy corduroy jumper, just like she used to wear when she was little, circles around Susie's kitchen island for refills.

Susie raises her glass.

"To thirty-three," she says. "God help me, may it be a better year than thirty-two."

"I'll drink to that," I say as the four of us clink our glasses together and swallow deeply again, the merlot already softening us.

"Well, I have news!" I wave my free hand in the air.

"Tyler's coming back in a few weeks to get his stuff. He texted me today."

"He *texted* you?" Ashley says.

"Indeed." I nod. "He *texted* me. Welcome to the twenty-first century, in which your asshole husband doesn't have to actually speak with you for months on end."

Susie's shoulders begin to shake, her back toward me as she slices thick pieces of lasagna on the counter. When she turns, her face is distorted with the sick humor of it all.

"You have to got be kidding me," she says. "He seriously sent you a fucking text?"

I giggle because we all know that I'm not kidding her, that there's nothing to joke about when your husband sends you a two-line, hackneyed text declaring, essentially, that your marriage will be over when he returns in October to retrieve all of his crap, but the alcohol is like armor now, and what the hell, anyway.

"I know, what a prick," I say.

"To pricks!" Darcy interjects, so we clink our glasses together again and drain them once more.

"Now *there's* something I can certainly drink to," Susanna says, gesturing us toward the table. "So you know what? Come stay with me for that weekend when he comes back," she says, dishing a tong-full of salad onto our plates. "Don't give him the satisfaction of being there."

"You should give him something," Ashley says, "though, yeah, satisfaction is definitely not it."

"A pole up his ass," Darcy offers helpfully.

"I'll think about it," I say.

"About the pole?" Darcy asks.

"About staying here."

"Too bad. He could really use that pole," she answers.

"The pole not withstanding, I think that he should have to look me in the eye and tell me it's over," I say, testing out a piece of lettuce, the likes of which my digestive tract hasn't seen in weeks. "I want him to at least have to do that."

"He's such a weasel, that brother-in-law of mine, ex-brother-in-law of mine," Darcy says. "What a douche. All I know is he better not show up here and beg for you back."

For a fleeting second, I almost pipe up and say that *of course I want him to show up and beg for me back*, but I can read their faces—even in my slightly murky two-glasses-of-wine state, I can tell there will be hell from them if I so much as utter this sentiment, so I stuff down some lasagna and bob my head in agreement.

"I say that all men are assholes," Ashley declares, rising to open another bottle.

"I always thought you were a lesbian," Darcy says. "It now seems to be confirmed."

Susie laughs so unexpectedly that tiny pieces of tomato-covered pasta fly out of her mouth onto her arm.

"I'm not a lesbian!" Ashley says, struggling with the cork. "Though trust me, I've long considered it. Like it wouldn't be easier to be in a relationship with one of you guys."

"No offense," I say. "But I wouldn't date you. Too brooding."

"Me neither," says Susanna. "But then again, I actually might have a prospect with a penis, so I'll take him by default."

"I might date you," Darcy adds. "Check back later."

Ashley wins her battle with the cork and tops off our glasses.

"Um, rewind, missy," I say to Susanna. "Who is this prospect and why am I just hearing about it now?"

"Because it just happened. This afternoon in the teacher's lounge. Scotty Hughes came up to me and asked if I want to get coffee sometime."

"Scotty Hughes, the lunchroom guy?" I ask, confused, then consider it. I suppose that could have been him, the man backstage in my vision.

"Yup, I know, random," she says, wiping the corner of her lips with the butt of her hand, too loose now to care about a napkin. "I said no. Too soon."

"It's not too soon!" I say, now more sure of what I've seen, piecing it together—his build, his hair. *Yes, that was probably Scotty Hughes.*

"Seriously, get back on that horse," Ashley says.

"I thought all men were assholes?" Susie asks.

"Not if they're cute and asking you out," she explains, like this makes sense, which, to us, in our current state, it sort of does, so we nod as if she's offering the wisdom of a Zen master. We chew our lasagna, mulling the possibility.

Later, we've lost track of the refills and the room is wobbly. For the first time in months, surrounded by their generosity, their fury on my behalf, I can feel it—that power that Ashley let loose in me, the strength, the truthfulness in my guts. We park on Susie's living room floor, our heads resting on couch pillows, and we cast our eyes up toward the ceiling as if we were kids again, staring at the stars. Ashley opens the doughnuts, and I lay on my back, sucking on a chocolate Munchkin, its crunchy sweetness blending better than expected with the residue of merlot still on my tongue.

"Do you remember our sixth-grade soccer team?" Ashley asks, sitting up abruptly, then steadying herself when she starts to lean over, a human Tower of Pisa. "Do you remember that fight that your dad got into with the ref during the playoffs?" I prop myself up on my elbows, watching her giggle, and I realize that underneath her overdone eyeliner, she's softly pretty, if she'd only allow herself to be.

"What? No," I say, looking to Darcy for confirmation, then remember that she'd have been only a toddler. "I don't remember that at all."

"Oh yeah," Ashley says, standing now to reenact the scene. "He rushed the field when the ref retracted a goal that you'd scored. *'You don't know what the hell you're talking about!'* " She shook her finger wildly, her neck turning pink, just as my dad's would have. " *'You are a goddamn moron if I've ever seen one! And blind too! You're a little piece of shit! A blind little piece of shit!'* " She plops back down and laughs. "After all of that, we didn't win the game, didn't make it to the championship."

Darcy laughs along with her, though who knows why, whether it's the alcohol or the irony of my father playing the classic role of papa bear.

"How do you remember that?" I ask, trying to focus, recollect. "I seriously have no recollection. Susie, do you?"

Susie shakes her head, then reaches for another doughnut.

"I just do," Ashley says simply. "Actually, I remember it because my dad talked about it the whole ride home. Thought your dad deserved a medal or something. And my mom told him he was setting a bad example for sportsmanship and to please be quiet." Her voice stalls, almost sober now. "Then they had a huge fight about it."

"I know it was ages ago, but I can't remember your parents ever fighting," Susanna interjects. "Which, hello! Welcome to marriage!" She starts to pull herself upright but opts not to expend the effort and flops back down to the floor.

"They did," Ashley says, her head bobbing just slightly. "They definitely did." She looks over at me. "And besides, just because you don't see something, doesn't mean it's not there."

"I forgot!" I say, jumping too quickly to my feet, the blood pushing into my head like a pinwheel. "My camera!"

"Cute art guy's camera," Susie corrects, her eyes closed now.

"Cute art guy's camera," I concede, pulling it from my purse. I flip off the lens cap and steady the viewfinder toward my eye.

"Say cheese!"

"Cheese," they all say in unison.

Click. Click, click, click.

I stand beside my friends and capture this time. So that one day, I can look back on it and say, *I might have felt broken, but at the end of it all, I didn't allow myself to break.*

eighteen

The taxi drops Darcy first at Dante's, the wine warm in her stomach, easing her inhibitions. I haven't inquired as to their status of late, but even in my fog of self-absorption, I've noticed him occasionally loitering around the house, exchanging easy banter with my dad when he's over, toting in fried chicken for dinner while Darcy hums some new melody behind him.

"We're just working on some songs together," she says. "A collection."

I raise an eyebrow, because Darcy has never been one for collaboration, but I don't pry.

The streetlight has blown out in front of our house, so as the taxi pulls into the driveway, the gravel spinning out beneath its tires, it's almost as if the house isn't there. Just a pocket of dead September air. I flick on the porch switch as I climb the stairs, sift for my keys, and lumber inside.

The house is as black as the night outside, which suits me in a way it wouldn't have before, before all of this. I'm still not used to finding it so empty. With the exception of my sophomore year, when I had a single at college, I've never actually lived alone. I moved into my sorority house as a junior and then, of course, bunked with Tyler upon graduation. I navigate my way through the hall, my hand sliding up the stairwell, my fingers finding the brass knob to the bedroom.

I fall onto my bed, a belly flop, reaching in the darkness for a pillow to smush over my head and shut out even the tiny slivers of light. It's funny how I couldn't envision that incident on the soccer field, I think. Funny how paralyzingly clear the memory was to Ashley, but for me—nothing. I shake my head, trying to suss out the scene, but I can barely remember playing soccer, much less the playoff game in which my dad was red-carded. Hazily, in the corner of my memory, I recall a picture of the team, lined up in golden yellow jerseys, a Tony's Pizzeria icon patched on our sleeve, our knee socks pulled high under our shin guards. Our ponytails flapped in the fall air; our smiles were ensnared in the finest metal Westlake's orthodontists could provide.

Frantically, I flip on the bedside light and am on my knees, plowing through my bottom dresser drawer in search of confirmation of what Ashley recollects so easily. I surf past my wedding photos, those reminders of when life promised to be perfect, and press on. Tyler is suddenly so distant, so unimportant, because what matters, *what I need to see this very second*, is that moment in time before we were all broken. When I had a dad who hadn't started drinking and instead stood in the bleachers and catcalled the other team. When my mom was still flourishing, alive, robust. When Darcy was round and innocent and gazed saucer-eyed at the world, ready for all that it could offer.

But there is nothing here. All of these photos were taken after the years that my friendship with Ashley splintered apart. I lean against the bureau, the spot between my shoulder blades pressed into the circular wooden handle, and I implore myself to remember. *Remember, God damn it!*

The doorbell suddenly echoes in the downstairs foyer and my

veins seize. It is well past 10:30, and news at night is never good news. Still ensconced in the blackness, I shuffle down the steps and steel myself for something else unimaginable: what, really, could it be? My father is drinking again? My husband is leaving me?

The hallway tiles are cold, even through my socks, and I pull my sweatshirt tighter over me. I exhale and prepare myself, then fling the door open wide, waiting for the flood, the plague, the grim reaper.

But there, hovering on the porch, is only Ashley. The overhead bulb behind her turns her ethereal, almost angelic, and her weary face draws a kind smile when she sees me.

"Here," she says, thrusting forth her hand. She still reeks of alcohol. I suppose that I do too. "I thought you could use this."

"What's this?" I ask, relieved, surprised, confused. I draw the Polaroid closer to me, angling it toward the light.

"It's from back then," she says simply. "I thought it might be important." She pauses, her voice quieter. "It seemed like you needed it."

The evening air is quiet around us, the scent of burning leaves, of damp mulch blowing through. I stare at the shot and try to remember, and slowly, I do. It is a shiny, buoyant picture of Ashley, in her sunshine-colored jersey with the number 12 hanging off of her still girlish body. She is cross-legged on the grass, beaming up at me, holding her index finger aloft, curled at the tip. A bystander might think she is anointing our team number one, but no, I can remember clearly now, she instead meant that we were sizzling. We would lick the tips of our fingers, touch each others' waists, and pretend that we were frying like bacon, cooked eggs on a sidewalk.

"That was the day your dad went ape-shit," Ashley says. "That's probably why I kept it."

"I took this, didn't I?" I peel my eyes away and look toward hers.

She nods.

"I can't believe I didn't remember this. I can't believe you kept it." We're both suddenly sober, the veil of wine no match for our emotion.

"It meant something at the time." She looks toward the porch planks.

I want to ask her to elaborate, but then I see something else in her, something that tells me this is more than just a courtesy call.

"You want me to do it, don't you?" I ask.

She shrugs, her eyes round with damp emotion.

I shake my head, thrusting the picture back toward her. "I don't do it anymore. I don't want to see anything else. I told you, I stopped."

"Please," she says, her voice nothing more than a whisper. "Please, my mom is dying, and I need to know that I'll be okay, that I'll make it through this."

"I can't even tell you that! I have no idea what I'll see . . . I just see!"

"I don't even care," she says now, crying for real, and because Ashley Simmons has never, ever cried in front of me, not even when she broke her arm in third grade when she fell from the monkey bars, a sliver of sympathy opens inside of me.

"Oh, Jesus, fine," I say, grabbing her elbow, pulling her inside.

We sit, the two of us, at the kitchen table, and I stare, and I stare, and then, there it is. My brain loses control of my muscles, the pain, the cramping winding through. Ashley clutches my hand as the spark soars through my blood, through my veins, through my very soul. I squeeze her fingers because I know that she'll stay beside me until the blackness lifts its cloak, until I find a way to swim back up.

The hospital smells like sanitation, that distinct blend of fruity cleaner and embalming fluid that every medical facility has. The halogen lights glare overhead, illuminating the dark circles and the wrinkles that have seeped into the various faces littering the halls. Wrinkles that come with the gravity of life-and-death circumstances. Nurses in pink scrubs push past one another, friendly enough but not really all that friendly, each of them scurrying about, all carrying clipboards holding life-altering information.

I am standing just to the right of the vending machines toward the end of the hall and facing two adjacent patient rooms. Their glass windows offer little privacy, though a cheap fabric shade is pulled over the one to my left. A frazzled-looking doctor wanders past me, really brushes right up against me, and drops three quarters into one of the machines, which spits out a Twix. He uncrinkles the wrapper and leans against the wall, his sigh a sputter of exhaustion.

I eye him, wondering if he is the reason that I'm here, but he just chews on his Twix, savoring the quiet moment of his break time, until I notice Ashley emerge from the room with the open shade. How I didn't see her before, I'm not sure, because now, as I look through the glass, I realize that the patient inside is her mother. She's got tubes in every possible orifice, a heart monitor beeping a steady beep, an IV drip cutting into the crook of her flaccid, aged arm. A fraction of the woman she once was.

The doctor finishes his Twix, crumples the wrapper and tosses it into the garbage can, gives Ashley a quick nod, and bolts off, reminding me of a startled rabbit. Ashley tugs a wrinkled dollar bill from her pocket and shoves it into the *dollar slot of one of the machines, which refuses to accept it. She tries again, and then again, and then one more time, but each time—whhhirrrrrr—the machine spits it back.*

"God damn it, I want a fucking Snickers!" she screams, her fists now balls, pounding on the glass. "Is that too much to ask? A goddamn Snickers?"

Her tears come like a flood, a broken dam, covering her face in an instant, and she leans against the machine, as if a flimsy vending machine in a so-so hospital in our small town can actually prop her up, be her salvation. Her body shakes, and her moans are guttural, and more than anything, I want to fix her, because this is what I do. Or what I did, at least for most of my life. But I know that I can't, that my legs won't move and my voice won't resonate, so all I can do is whisper, over and over again, "It's gonna be alright, Ashley. It's gonna be alright." Because, though her pain feels unbearable, I know that eventually, it will be alright. After all, I lived it too.

Steps approach to my left, and I swivel around to see my father. My father! My father? He doesn't take notice of Ashley, a mound on the floor, and instead stops just outside her mother's room. His shoulders sag. I can see this from behind him, his body growing smaller. His head drops to his chest, and his back rises in a giant inhale.

"Is she going to be okay?" Ashley's eyes are still closed, her question directed at my dad, as if she was expecting him, as if she knew he'd be there.

He turns to face her, his features aged a decade since I've seen him last, since he moved back into his house and assured me he'd wrestled the beast of his insobriety. His skin is ragged, the pouches beneath his eyes sallow and bleak.

"They don't know everything yet," he replies, his voice breaking.

Ashley's head plunges down, an anchor, when suddenly a high-pitched siren—an alarm—sounds from her mother's room. She bounds to her feet and throws herself inside, and three pink-clad nurses, now stripped of their clipboards, rush past my father to her mother's bedside.

My dad slaps his hands against the glass, a silent wail, and just before I am gone, left with more questions than I came with, he slides his fingers down the window, and the last thing I see, the last thing I will remember, is the steam, the heat left from the imprints of his palms, at first clear, concise, and then evaporated, gone, just like me.

My spit tastes like sour grapefruit, and my jaw throbs like it's been sucker-punched, like I've been grinding my teeth over and back on themselves. My eyes twirl into focus, and Ashley's pensive face hovers above me.

"How long was I out?" I ask, pressing myself up on the couch, my palms behind me, my elbows bending like protractors.

"An hour or so," she says, helping to steer me upward. "I dragged you over here when your head knocked down against the table."

"I'm not doing this again, you know. I'm retired after this. It's too much, too hard." She nods, understanding and anxious all at once. "But I did it because I get it," I say. Our eyes meet now, both too sad for two people so young. "I mean, I guess I always wondered what could have been different if I'd known what would happen in the future. How many times did I wish for that after my mother was sick and then died?"

"I know," Ashley says. "I sensed that in the tent that day."

"So you also know that I can't change anything anyway. That I can only see what happens, that what happens is going to happen regardless."

She nods.

"I saw your mother." I sigh. "She is very ill."

"I already know that," Ashley says quietly.

"But my dad was there too. What was my dad doing there too?"

nineteen

A week coasts forward, and summer has flitted out as quickly as it came in. Already, the fall winds are nipping all around us; there will be no extended summer this year, no last gasp of lingering days by the lake, late-evening barbecues during those final minutes of sunset.

In years past, I have loved fall, much like I have loved the first few days of the school year, but now, the season only reminds me of how change rushes in too fast—one day you're weeding in your garden in a tank top, the next, you're hauling through your closet in search of an extra sweater. But, because I am trying, at the very least, to distract myself now, and, at the very best, to pull myself out of the muck, I set out to complete Eli's assignment, to document the ins and outs of Westlake High from the view of his Nikon.

"You're totally trying to please him," Susanna said yesterday during our first dress rehearsal when she noticed the lens dangling from my neck.

"Oh, give me a break," I said, then shouted to Wally to *ease up on the jazz hands already!*

"Wally, dude, this is the fifties, and you're the resident stud,"

Darcy said from the piano bench. "We're not doing *A Chorus Line* here." The kids in the ensemble laughed, and Darcy sat up a little straighter. Darcy had recently told Midge Miller that she would take over full-time, and Midge just cracked her knobby arthritic fingers, shrugged, and shuffled out of the auditorium.

"Anyway, I'm not doing this to impress him," I said, turning back to Susanna. "I enjoy this; you know I do."

"Who says it can't be both?" she answered, keeping time with her foot. "And hey, I'm not criticizing. You were always good with what other people asked of you."

True, I thought, watching the teenagers attempt to master the hand jive sequence, which for most of them seemed about as natural as speaking Cantonese. Elbows were askew, knees were out of sync, a mishmash of misinterpreted rhythms and too-complicated choreography.

But yes, I have milled through the halls for the past five days, popping into classrooms, loitering in the gym, stealing candid frames of my students' lives. The prom committee convened in my office on Wednesday, and rather than dictate the remainder of the to-dos—the invitations needed to be printed, the chaperones needed to be confirmed, the éclairs, which they had all readily agreed on, ordered in bulk from the bakery in Tarryville—I simply handed the list to CJ and clicked, clicked, clicked while they hashed over the details themselves. It was almost exquisite, I thought after they headed out of my office, their faces flushed, their words running over each other—*berets, canapés!*—that when I stepped aside, took my hands off the wheel, they somehow managed to steer it just fine without me.

Oddly enough, the same can also be said of my father and Darcy. It's not that Darcy has totally absolved him, but just that there's less rancor when she speaks of him, less rage when she speaks *to* him, which they've been doing regularly now, mostly about me and my mental health. I hear them sometimes, whispering when they think I've fallen asleep or zoned out in front of the TV.

"I don't know what to do with her," my dad said the other night when he thought I was out of earshot. "I can't stand to see her like this! I'm going to kill that kid."

"Let her be," Darcy replied, as she always does. "She'll pull through. She's more capable than you realize."

I listen to them go back and forth, too exhausted to go out there and say, *"Hello! I can hear you!"* but it hasn't escaped me, how much credit Darcy's been giving me, how much faith she's placing in me, when maybe I've never done the same for her. When, frankly, it's been hard enough to imagine doing the same for myself.

And as I stole through the school this past week, I couldn't help but be awed by these kids, with their naked sense of invincibility. Just like I once had. How Tyler and I had linked arms our senior year, and just like CJ and Johnny Hutchinson, or Gloria Rodriguez and Alexander Parsons, or any number of the couples who pocked the hallways and the parking lot and the make-out spot behind the gym, we felt shinier, braver, more human than we had been without each other. I lifted the camera to my eye and marked their bravado not just for the yearbook, but for me, to remind myself that once upon a time, I, too, was untouchable.

Eli is staring out the back window of the art room when I swing the door open and plunk the camera down on his desk. I don't want to look at him, don't want to loiter, because even though it's been two months since my premonition, and even though I have done *everything I can to stop thinking about it*, and even though my husband has abandoned me and broken my spirit and then infuriated that spirit more than I thought possible, I am still un-nerved at my jealousy over his girlfriend.

"Here," I say, not meeting his eyes, though he has turned toward me. "I'm returning this. But I did what you asked, and I'm pretty sure you'll find good stuff for the yearbook."

"And what did you think?" he asks, taking three steps and sit-ting on a stool at one of the painting tables. He shuffles it closer, and it squeaks against the tiled floor.

"I thought it was fine," I say, the blood in my cheeks defying my ambivalence.

"Fine?" He laughs, a disbelieving but kind laugh. "This from a former art nerd? You simply thought it was fine?" He pushes out an adjacent stool, an invitation.

"Okay, it was pretty great," I acknowledge, still standing. I wonder if he knows that my husband has left me, though I then re-member that of course he knows that my husband has left me—it may as well have been the headline in the *Westlake Courier*.

"Sit," he says. "I'm tired. And you look tired too."

I *am* tired, so rather than argue, I obey.

"What was your favorite thing you used to photograph? Back when you used to do it a lot?" He weaves his fingers together, his hands on the table, his nails a collage of purple and blue paint that has stubbornly refused to come off.

"Oh, God, I can't even remember," I say, though of course I can remember. I remember it instantly. In the last two months of my mother's life, she was mostly bedridden, incapacitated, tor-tured by being housebound. My mother's zeal was boundless, pas-sion that poured into her music, informed her love of all earthly things. In the summers, she tended to her garden; in the winters, she would layer long underwear and disappear for an hour through the dense forests in the neighboring woods. She would re-turn with crisp cheeks and a bright Rudolph nose, and pour us hot chocolate before we all piled on the couch to watch a movie. I was never one for the cold, so I'd always beg off joining her. Luanne sometimes went, and once Darcy was old enough, especially that last year, she tagged along without hesitation.

When my mother grew too sick to inhale anything other than stale bedroom air and later suffocating hospital air, I decided to bring it to her instead. Darcy and I would amble outside, through those same woods, and I would click, click, click. It was summer then, so Darcy would run through the stream near the fallen, hollowed-out oak tree, and *click*, my mother wouldn't miss out. Or we'd stumble on a patch of errant wildflowers, willfully growing in the lone patch of sun, and *click*. I'd hurry to the darkroom shortly thereafter and then, *"Here, Mom, look what we brought back for you."*

Those were my favorite moments, of course, my favorite images to lock down forever.

"My favorite is probably children," Eli says. "Probably in Kenya."

"You've been to Kenya?" I say. I haven't even been to L.A.

"Last March." He nods. "It was hot as hell, and I couldn't stop sweating, but still, it was amazing. Just their appreciation for what they had, which was basically nothing. But these kids, oh man, they didn't stop smiling. They'd play soccer in these dirt roads, singing and clapping, and even though I went there to get away from some things, I felt centered, balanced, you know?"

I don't, but I bob my head anyway. "What were you getting away from?"

"Oh, you know, relationship crap. Bad breakup. That boring old stuff." He waves his purple-and-blue-spotted hands. He looks at me, and I know that he knows, that he is well aware that I'm a stray dog milling about, feeding on emotional scraps. But he doesn't articulate this, and for one gushing moment, I am so grateful that he refuses to pity me, that he doesn't ask me *"What hap-pened?"* and say *"Oh my gosh, Tilly, I simply cannot believe that Tyler up and left!"* which is exactly what Gracie Jorgenson said three days ago in the cereal aisle at the Albertson's.

"I guess I've always wanted to go to Paris," I hear myself say-ing, though I didn't even realize this to be true.

"Well, that explains prom." Eli laughs.

"I guess it does." I laugh along with him, a cramp building in my belly like in a muscle that hasn't been used in far too long.

"So go," he says simply.

"Nah, maybe one day. But not now." I dismiss it with a flop of my hands.

"Paris is amazing," he says. "My parents took us there when I was ten. My dad worked for the government, so we were always traveling around. We lived there for six months, and my sisters—I have four older ones—used to take me out to cafés and storefronts and roaming about the streets . . ." He pauses, his thought a mem-ory. "Anyway, you should go, you'd love it."

"Why aren't you married?" I say suddenly, and then realize my candor, a look of utter horror illuminating my face. I burst into staccato nervous laughter. "Oh my God, I'm sorry! I'm going a lit-tle crazy right now."

He laughs with me. "No, no, fair question. I think my parents would like an explanation too. All of my sisters are, though one is getting divorced." He winces. "I'm an uncle five times over . . . but, I don't know, I guess I'm always moving around, looking for the next big adventure. It's just never suited me well for relationships."

"Hence Kenya," I say.

"Well, actually, Kenya was a reaction to the one relationship I'd decided to stick around for. Turns out she didn't want me to."

We fall silent, a mutual understanding of the pain of being so disposable.

"Anyway, you'll like those pictures," I say finally, pushing back the stool, heading for the door.

"Take a look at them with me," he says.

"I have to run," I answer, which isn't true at all, but I feel like I've already exposed too much.

"Well, then, hang on." He unsnaps the tiny door on the bottom of the camera and pulls out the memory card, then reaches for another in his desk and slides it right in. "This is yours for now. Take it. Bring it back when you're ready." He pushes the Nikon over to my side of the table.

"I can't," I say, though certainly, I know that I can, that I'd even like to.

"You can," he answers, as if he can read my mind.

I stop by my father's store on the way home from work. Darcy has opted to pick up a shift or two each week as a means for extra cash; when she finally dialed her boss at the bar she waitressed at in L.A. last week to inform him that her return date was indefinite, he promptly also informed her that he'd fired her back in August.

The store is deserted in this dead time of late September to early November, the before-Christmas shopping moratorium that too many households impose on their budgets. Not cold enough to replace heating systems, not warm enough to overwork a freezer. Come November, the door will be in nonstop motion: DVD players for wives who intend to learn yoga at home (though they never will); big-screen TVs for husbands who already spend too much time watching ESPN and big bass fishing on Saturday mornings; Wiis for teenagers who should be studying instead. *Jesus, Christmas.* I wonder whether or not I can shove a metaphorical bag of coal right down Tyler's figurative stocking. *Possibly.*

As I get deeper inside, I hear them arguing near the stock-room, in my father's office. I wind my way back there, through the mini-fridges, and the boxed-up microwaves, and the digital cameras. It smells like stale coffee here, in the bowels of the store, which, I consider, is better than smelling like old beer, which it once did.

When I pop into my dad's office, they both freeze, creating a vacuum of noise. Their eyes are wide orbs, and quickly, though they clearly hope that I won't notice, they glance over to each other.

"Hi, love bug," my dad says. "What brings you here?"

"What's going on?" I'm deflecting. "Why were you guys fighting?" *Why weren't they fighting?* I think, only to realize I hadn't heard Darcy snap at him in the better part of the last few weeks.

"It's nothing, doll," my dad says, leaning back in his rickety office chair, which emits a squeak in reply.

Darcy glares at him—her look of a thousand scorched suns—and her neck turns stiff.

"It's nothing," he repeats, deflecting her gaze, shutting her down.

"Are you okay, Darcy?" I ask. "Is something going on with you?"

"This isn't about me! Why don't you ask him?"

"Um, are *you* okay, Dad? Is there something going on with *you*?" I consider the past month, whether anything has been particularly askew, whether or not my dad still seems sober, whether or not I can even remember monitoring him, keeping track. *No, not really, I can't.* I eyeball him up and down.

"I'm fine; there's nothing going on with me," he answers, and I nod because, well, he seems fine, and I have enough problems of my own.

"Oh, give me a goddamned break," Darcy says before stomping out of the room. A few seconds later, the chime of the front door rattles as she makes her escape. I'll find her waiting for me, stewing in the car, right back where we began before the whole mess unloaded itself on me: before my dad, before Tyler, before the visions of my royally screwed future.

"You should go after her," my dad says, sighing, his fingers pinching the bridge of his nose, a habit I inherited. "But it's just our usual stuff. Nothing more. Don't worry about it."

"Okay," I say, turning to leave. "Hey, by the way, are you friends with Valerie Simmons? Ashley's mom?" I'm certain I'd have known if he was, but I can't stop thinking about him at the hospital, his hands pressed against the glass, a prostrate position of mourning.

"Who?" he asks, already lost in some papers on his desk. Likely September inventory with the month nearly to a close.

"No one," I answer before heading out the door to my thunderstorm of a sister. "Forget I even mentioned it at all."

twenty

The Westlake grand premiere of *Grease* is slated for homecoming, the second weekend in October, during which time the town virtually spins itself into a self-parodying snow globe, filled with red and white streamers, red and white banners, Wizard hats, Wizard wands, Wizard glitter that lays sprinkled in the streets long after the Westlake Wizard parade has wound its way through town. Old players return and sit atop convertibles, waving to their friends and family, who cheer and shout and screech like there isn't something a little weird about the subtle acknowledgment that maybe these grown men, at twenty-five or thirty-five or sixty-five, reached their peak at seventeen. I'd never actually thought of it that way until just now, now that I don't have my husband to hoot for, to get a little misty for, as he and his classmates are wheeled around, kings on their rusted thrones.

I texted him three days ago, *"Will u be back for homecoming?"* thinking he'd never miss a chance to have his own horn tooted—this, after all, was what these men lived for. But he replied six hours later, *"No, might have to delay some more. Maybe end of Oct. WLYK."*

I spent the better part of an hour trying to decipher *WLYK*—

Will love you k? Would like your knees?—until Luanne peeked over my shoulder and said, "Will let you know," and then under her breath added, "A-hole." To which I said, not at all under my breath, "Amen." I then resisted the urge to respond with a short and succinct, *"FU"* (*"Even he could interpret that meaning,"* Luanne noted), and instead simply left it at, *"LMK."*

Three days later, on homecoming morning, he still hasn't—hasn't *LMK*—though I know that his silence lets me know everything all the same. That one day soon, the winds will push in a cold rain from the west, and he and Austin will lug his belongings—all of the material items he's collected as he built his life with me—out of our house, out of this town, out of my life entirely. I consider for a fleeting moment, as I run a blush brush over my cheeks, calling the Salvation Army, dumping all of his crap—the sweaters I bought for him, the prized ball he caught at a Mariners game, the golf clubs I gave him two Christmases ago—right into their truck. *Ha! Yes! Ha ha!* I flourish the brush over my left cheek, a smile worming its way over me. *Would that be rich, wouldn't that be just the perfect capper for him to return to—coming back to pack and discovering there's nothing here to pack at all!* I wrap myself into the fantasy, knowing I'll never have the guts to do it but reveling in it all the same. I can at least revel in that.

The homecoming parade is set to kick off at eleven, and Darcy and Murphy's Law have been invited to play at the staging site. I wouldn't be going at all if not to support her: I tried to convince Susanna to let me deal with the last-minute *Grease* snafus—someone had spilled gallons of water, God knows how, over our "Beauty School Dropout" backdrop, which left it looking more like a blurry sea of tacky, glittery blues, golds, and silvers; and the chorus (aka, the kids who really, *really* couldn't sing but needed to fulfill a music elective and thus were relegated to the ensemble) *still* couldn't master the hand jive, but she tsk-tsked me and shooed me away.

"Scotty volunteered, anyway," she said, the corners of her mouth upturning. "He's bringing me coffee, and we'll repaint the sets."

"Nice." I smiled back.

"Whatever," she said, though neither of us believed her.

So while it is quite possible that the last place on the planet that I wanted to be right now was out and mingling with the very people who had pinned their hopes on Tyler's right arm a decade and a half ago at the state championship or gifted us with hams or cheap knife sets for our wedding, or who, I know, burned up the phone lines when he left, I'm here regardless. To cheer on my baby sister, who has tried to cheer me on during these past few desolate months.

The parade begins in the same parking lot that I careened into way back in July, swerving in for a fix of tequila when I simply couldn't take another second of clarity. *Clarity.* The word clangs around in my brain, and I nearly laugh, because whatever Ashley hoped to impart to me, she has done just the opposite. I have tried to shut down my brain, stop it from wondering about the unresolved questions the visions have raised, or why they matter in the first place. *It all happens anyway!* What, really, is the point? Enough with everyone's issues—Ashley and my father and Darcy—and their hiccups and their problems! I've had enough of everyone else's crap, and God help me, I'm not about to see any more of it. Not when all it proves is that more crap is ahead on the horizon.

I watch as one of the reporters from the newspaper staff interviews Principal Anderson, and I spot Principal McWilliams from my own years at Westlake, grinning beside him. His face now looks like a worn cowhide, and his dentures are still one size too big for his mouth. *Good God, some things never do change.*

A hearty crowd of several hundred, most adorned with red and white face paint or ridiculous wizard hats or some sort of school pride paraphernalia, has gathered by now. A platform is set up toward the side, nearly in front of the liquor store, bordered with two large speakers, already emitting tiny, grating waves of feedback into the crowd. It is one of those quintessentially perfect fall days, with apple crisp air, ruby red leaves, and bursts of sun we'll all be longing for in another few weeks. I glance around, wondering if Ashley will show today. I haven't seen her in half a week, since she showed up at my office unannounced right when I was busy procrastinating, doing nothing.

"She seized," she said, her hands cradling her face. "Her eyes rolled back into her head, and I called nine-one-one . . ." She paused for breath. "So this is probably it. She's going into hospice. She's never coming back home." She looked up at my wall of Polaroids and tried to smile. "I wish I could be sixteen again."

"No you don't," I reminded her. "You hated being sixteen."

"Probably." She shrugged. "But I'm not loving thirty-two either."

I knew that she wanted me to offer to tell her more, to try to flash forward and tell her when she—when we all—could be put out of this misery. But she didn't ask, and I wasn't about to offer, because, as I'd learned already, who knew if we'd *ever* be put out of our misery, and really, who needs to know that it might never end?

I swivel my neck skyward: there are no signs of the incoming storm that will mark Tyler's arrival, only, in the distance, my dad flapping his arm at me across the way, moving closer. He is wearing his Elks Club jacket, ready to march through the town with his compatriots, waving at neighbors and friends like he doesn't see them every other day at the gas station or the drugstore.

I've walked in the parade three times, all in high school, all as a cheerleader for the Westlake Wizards. Each year, we'd spin ourselves mad, tossing legs high into the air, punching pom-poms with gusto that only fifteen-year-olds can possess, screaming our little hormonal lungs out for our baseball-playing, football-playing, basketball-playing boyfriends, who had captured the championship crown earlier that fall. My senior year, just after we crossed the end line, with the Wizard band blaring behind us, Tyler whisked me up, tossed me over his shoulder, and plopped me down in his truck, where we proceeded to make out to a particularly off-key version of "La Bamba," in which the tuba players needed neutering.

Last year, though, for the first time since graduation, Ty begged off. Said he wasn't feeling well, though now I'm sure it was just another red flag, another alarm bell that I overlooked. I came home with flushed cheeks and *"You won't believe it"* stories pouring out of me, but the house was silent. When he got home thirty minutes later, I was knee-deep in editing college applications, and I remember noticing that he was sweaty and seemingly recovered.

"Feeling better," he said before he ducked up the stairs toward the shower. "So I went out for a run." I nodded and hadn't thought of it again until now. Your memory does that sometimes, plays that trick on you, rewinding passing seconds of your life, and you realize you overlooked the most important details of that bygone moment.

"I don't know who I am without you." Tyler's words vibrate through me. Slowly, I am understanding that indeed, every part of who I have become in Westlake is pinned to him in some way as well. The problem is, I don't know how to *unpin* myself. Maybe it

was always this way, I contemplate, as I kiss my dad hello and Dante jumps on the stage to kick off the festivities. Maybe it was just that I never thought there'd be a time when defining myself outside of Tyler would actually matter. But now, I can't go any-where—*anywhere!*—and not see him, even though, of course, I recognize the irony in this, that I'm only seeing him everywhere because he is gone.

The thought of this, of him, of this ridiculous shebang—the Westlake glitter flitting through the air, the crowd gathered to cheer on these men choking on their glory days—makes me want to heave my insides out. Who throws these men these stupid pa-rades? Why do we give one stinking shit about what they did three goddamn decades ago? I *do* wish Tyler was here, I realize, but only so I could smack him clear across the face. *God, wouldn't that feel good.*

I am sinking into that vision, of his skin against the palm of my hand, of me letting him know just how much he has *fucking disappointed me*, when I feel a tap on my shoulder. I spin around, violence still on my brain, and there is Eli.

He is out of breath, the edge of his forehead dotted with sweat, so when he runs his hand through his hair and says hello, his bangs sort of stick there, aloft, jutting out toward nowhere.

"I knew I'd find you here," he says, then adds, by way of ex-planation, "I ran here, had to double check that the yearbook staff was on time and set up to photograph everything." He cocks his head. "You okay?"

I start to respond, but Darcy's voice reverberates over the speakers, and the crowd emits a supportive cheer as she thanks them for coming out, which I find sort of endearing, considering these folks would show up for a Westlake Wizards prostate exam, but Darcy has never been one not to embrace an audience. I push Tyler away—*poof*—yes, I can eradicate you just like you did me.

The drum plays a steady percussion and the guitar kicks in with a searing wail, and Darcy is off, both pulling us in and pushing us away as she enters her frenetic, transcendent state onstage. I thrust my hands into my purse and pull out the Nikon. *Click.* Darcy leaning out toward the crowd like she is a superstar. *Click.* Darcy's eyes folded shut, lost in the meaning of a lyric. *Click.* Darcy nearly smiling now, absorbing the approval and applause of the crowd.

"She's mesmerizing," Eli leans in and says over my shoulder into my ear. He smells like minty toothpaste.

"Too bad Tyler isn't here," someone says into my other ear, and I look over to find Ginny Bowles parked next to me. Ginny graduated beside me, was a fellow cheerleader for the duration of high school. She also harbored a crush on Tyler well into our college years, and now, despite marrying Chuck "the Chicken" Stanley, who now runs the local auto repair shop, she still makes googly eyes and pushes her breasts higher toward her neck and at Ty every time she has the opportunity. "I hear he's moving out of here for good."

I shrug, hoping that will shut her up. *Just shut up!* I raise the camera back to my eye.

"So it's true that he left you?" Her breath is too close to me and smells like old Juicy Fruit, her fuchsia lipstick smeared on her front teeth, reminding me of a crazy, drunken clown.

"Oh, shut up, Ginny," I say, and her penciled-on eyebrows pop.

"I was just asking, for God's sake," she sniffs.

"You've never been just asking." The camera is down now, and I turn and size her up, wondering if I can take her in a fistfight if I need to.

"Don't shoot the messenger," she says, open palmed, faux-innocently.

"What does that mean?" I yell. "Do you have any goddamn

idea what that even means, because it doesn't mean what you think it means! You're not the fucking messenger, Ginny! If you can't learn to put on your lipstick properly, at least learn to use your clichés properly for Christ's sake!"

Even with the din of Darcy's music, people have turned to stare.

"Hey, hey," Eli says beside me. "Come on now." He clutches my elbow and drags me two steps away. "Want to get out of here?"

The crowd is throbbing now, red and white all blending together to create a flashing, snaking vision of my rage.

"Yes," I say, my pulse racing so furiously I can feel its echo in my neck. "Yes, let's go. Please, get me as far away from here as possible."

I suggest lunch, but neither of us is really hungry, and besides, Eli notes, he has a better idea. He drives for about fifteen minutes, not saying much, mostly listening to the country music station that whinnies out of the radio of his old BMW. "I can tell you're not from here," I say, "because no one around here would drive a BMW." He laughs and asks if it counts, since it's from 1992.

"Darcy always wanted a BMW," I say. "Which is sort of fitting. She never undersold herself."

"Is everything okay from back there?" he asks. "I mean, we don't have to talk about it, but I thought I'd be sure."

"It's just crap from the past. You know, high school." *Ginny Bowles. Like she hasn't wanted Tyler forever.* I stare out the window at the rush of the jewel tones blending together as we coast by. The leaves have already turned with the colder-than-normal fall air, and soon, they'll be plunging from their perches, eventually renewing themselves, but not until they deem it safe enough to bloom.

"Ah, the proverbial crap from the past. Is there any other kind of thing from your past?"

"Oh, I don't know, I'd like to think so." *Maybe I should just let her have him. Or go narc on her that she's still trying to get into my husband's pants. Yes, maybe tomorrow I will suddenly need an emergency oil change and pay a visit to the Chicken.*

"I admire your optimism." He bobs his head and turns up the radio just a smidge. I lean my head back into the crook of the seat and close my eyes, grateful for Eli's ability not to need anything more from me, for his appreciation of silence when someone else might yammer on through, for his understanding that everyone needs to come unraveled every once in a while, even the people who seemingly have it totally held together.

"We're here," he says after we cycle through another song that I recognize but can't identify. He kills the engine, and I push my heavy eyes open from the brink of sleep.

"What is this?" I ask. An abandoned rest stop that I've driven by before on my way to Seattle sits a hundred yards down, and a few broken beer bottles are crumbled near our tires.

"An old hiking trail I found a few weeks back." We slam the car doors shut in unison. "I wanted to get away for the day, so I asked Scotty Hughes for some off-the-beaten-path places. He actually mapped out something down the road, but I found this instead."

"Scotty Hughes? Who runs the lunchroom?" Who's sitting in the auditorium right now painting sets with Susanna?

"Yeah, he just does the lunchroom thing for the paycheck," Eli answers, stepping off the pavement curb and onto the knobby dirt ground. "He's into extreme sports on the weekend. Competitive stuff."

My forehead wrinkles as I digest this, that people have unanticipated layers even when you've stared at their surface for years, that happiness—Susanna's, mine, who knows who else's—can be uncovered even when you're sure it's lost its way to you, even via a detour to the dingy school cafeteria.

"Come on," Eli says. "Take out the camera."

I scoot around a tumbleweed of fallen branches and do as he says. As we start to ascend the leaf-littered path, barely discernible amid the overgrown nature, I'm overwhelmed with what a relief it is to have someone else lead the way. I unsnap the lens cap and slide it into the pocket of my bag, my breath keeping time with my pulse. Truth told, my muscles have atrophied these past few weeks, and I can already feel the burn in my glutes, my thighs mocking me. Oh, God, am I going to pay for this over the weekend.

Eli wanders ahead of me, looking back occasionally to make sure that I haven't keeled over, but mostly leaning and crouching, snapping and clicking, tilting his head at various angles to capture just the right moment with his camera. I manage to get hold of my breath, and then I do the same—lose myself behind the lens—and it's impossible, as we make our way through this untouched acre of forest, not to think of those days when my mom was sick and Darcy and I fled to the woods in an effort to bring back a piece of it for her.

I don't know how long we've been hiking when Eli whispers down to me, frantically flagging his arms in my direction, beckoning me up.

"Look!" he says almost inaudibly, pointing toward a depression in the vegetation to our left. My eyes adjust through the camouflage of leaves and branches, such that at first, I see nothing but a wild mass of woods. And then, my brain sorts it out, like one of those IQ puzzles that kids take for college prep, and the picture is so clear I can't believe I couldn't see it in the first place.

A baby deer is curled amidst a pile of broken sticks and flaky mud, its eyes closed, its gawky legs angled inward as it rests.

Eli moves in slow motion, silently raising the camera and snapping.

"Where's the mom?" I whisper, like Eli would have any idea.

He shrugs a tiny shrug, as if even moving his shoulders could mar the serenity of the moment.

I want to get closer for a better shot. So I inch forward, slowly, slowly, the deer undisturbed, still quiet. But then I get a little braver, a little more bold, and move faster, mesmerized by this marvelous stolen glimpse of nature, trespasser that I am.

My eyes are fixed on the animal, and so, when my feet give way beneath me, my nervous system takes a good three seconds to catch up with my body. I am tripping, my hands flailing outward, my camera already on the ground, sucked down by gravity. I land on my side with a bruising thud, a jagged branch scraping against my cheek.

"Are you okay?" Eli rushes over, his camera swinging around his neck like a pendulum.

I glance behind me and see it now, a giant pocket of earth that had been masked by broken twigs, scattered foliage.

"That hole," I say, out of breath and terrified and embarrassed all at once. "I didn't see it." I look ahead and notice that the baby deer is gone, fled, shot into the woods. My cheek burns, and I press my hand against it, pulling back my fingers to discover ripe, red blood.

"Jesus," Eli says, crouching down. "You're bleeding."

"It's nothing," I say, pressing myself into a seated position. My left ankle throbs, and my knee feels twisted.

"It's not nothing," he says, and reaches into his backpack, rooting around for something until he pulls out a napkin. "It's all I have." He smiles, offering a lame little thrust of his shoulders.

"You probably weren't expecting a casualty." I smile back, taking the wadded napkin and holding it against my wound.

"Eh, I've seen worse." He scoots away some leaves with his hands and plunks down.

"Me too," I answer, then pause. "Sorry about the deer."

He waves a hand. "You saw a shot you wanted and went after it."

We sit there in silence as the woods settle into themselves, the branches occasionally cracking, the remaining few birds occasion- ally calling out to each other, the squirrels occasionally scurrying near, but not too near, to us.

Finally, I signal that I am up to walking, so Eli stands, offers me a capable, firm hand, and lifts me to my feet. From there, we navigate toward home.

The auditorium is full—as I knew it would be—and the show has sailed by nearly without a hitch. Well, there was a small hitch or two—the curtain that twice got stuck halfway open; the wayward light that crashed down stage left, nearly beheading one of the Pink Ladies during "Look at Me, I'm Sandra Dee"; Wally's ever-present, emasculating, overzealous jazz hands—but still, as I hover backstage for the penultimate number, I can't help but be a little elated, a little high on life at what we've pulled off.

Onstage, CJ struts front and center, inhaling her clove ciga-rette, tossing it to the floor, snuffing it out with her toe. She's made that transformation that we all know is coming but that is shock-ing all the same—from good girl to good girl gone wild, with her painted-on pleather pants, her cleavage-enhancing tank top.

"Sandy!" Wally exclaims.

"Tell me about it, stud," she says back.

Darcy and her merry gang of music makers start in with the intro, my toe tapping along, my joy spread wide across my face.

"I've got chills, they're multiplying! And I'm losing control!"

Wally croons, falling to his knees, exactly like Phillip McKinley did way back when for Susie, back when we were still unscarred by everything that the future would bring. " *'Cause the power, you're supplying, it's electrifying!* "

The crowd starts to cheer now, loudly, an echo of our thoughts, that for these two glorious hours, these kids were nearly goddamn perfect. I see Susie, opposite me on the other side of the stage, and she gives me a thumbs-up, biting her bottom lip in an attempt to disguise just how *goddamn perfect* this was, just how right I might have been about this whole shindig all along. Even though I lost my way, left the details to her and Darcy, discovered that a high school musical—or a high school prom—can't change the tenor of the soundtrack of your life. Still, though. It can change something, even for a moment, for these two passing hours.

"*You're the one that I want, the one that I want.*" CJ shimmies and Wally shimmies back. "*Ooh-ooh-ooh. The one I need, oh yes indeed.*"

I mirror Susanna's grin, and then watch them, the two of them, Wally and CJ, ripe and glorious and deserving to bask in the reverence for every last second that it's offered. And then the audience claps louder, and louder still, and I applaud along with them, and then the lights go dark, the curtain shutters for the finale, and they bring the house down.

twenty-one

The rain begins slow and steady on Tuesday morning. It feels cold enough for snow, but no, it just drip-drop, drip-drops endlessly, a whitewash of water outside my office window. The windows are firmly shut now, keeping the spiders at bay.

Tyler will be back in three days; he finally texted, *"Back this wkend, sorry 4 late notice."* I was still on a high from *Grease*, but then Tyler's text came in, and *pfft*, there went all that bravado, all of that golden, blissful pride I'd reveled in since Sunday. The pizza I'd stuffed myself with at the after-party made a riotous appearance through my bowels, and yes, despite my bluster, despite my roiling anger—that fireball from the past few months—as the hours counted nearer to his arrival, I found myself not so much furious, but just gut-wrenchingly, heave-over-the-toilet panicked.

"You should just flash to see what happens," Ashley said when she called from the hospital yesterday. "Just, you know, flash on him, because maybe you'll find a way to make it work."

I didn't tell her that I'd tried to already, that I was so desperate that I'd given up my pact to stop messing with these visions, but that I couldn't see anything. *Nothing!* That two nights ago, I'd stumbled upon a self-portrait from my senior year and stared at it for the better part of an hour until my eyes went fuzzy and a bleating headache forced me to quit. It was only then that I realized that this portal had so far only been possible looking into someone else's life, not my own. *That simply looking at my own life was cheating.* So if I really did want to know what was going to happen, which I'd long decided I didn't, but if that weakness struck, I had to buck up and piece together the mysteries of the other visions, the puzzle parts that I refused to unite. *No thanks,* I thought, setting aside the picture. *No thank you at all.*

Tyler called last night with his flight arrangements, and though Austin will be the one picking him up and housing him, he asked if it wouldn't be too big of an inconvenience for me to steal a few boxes from the storage room at school to save him a few bucks in packing. I hung up the phone and wanted to murder him for asking—*Good God, haven't you asked for enough?* I should have said, but curtly agreed because it seemed like the easiest option.

And today, three days from Tyler's arrival, with the rain pitter-patting outside my office window, the prom invitation is lying on my desk atop three bursting folders of college applications, all due in less than two weeks. *"Westlake Does Paris!"* the creamy paper sings in a gold cursive font. I still haven't adjusted to the fact that I will likely be attending prom alone, for the first time since, well, ever. I'd be happy to go with Eli simply for the companionship, but I suspect his allegiances, despite our friendship, are elsewhere. When I finally worked up the nerve to ask him about a girlfriend on the drive back from our hike in the woods, he offered a vague "It's complicated," and I promptly lost said nerve to press him.

My door creaks open and CJ pops her head in, her vibe still glowing from the rave reviews and the mad applause when she brought the house down. *"You're the one that I want!"* This girl does indeed know what it is that she wants. Screw her circumstances,

202 / ALLISON WINN SCOTCH

screw her broken town, screw the fact that the deck has been stacked against her. She's always known what she wanted, and I look at her now and smile at her guts, her integrity, her unwillingness to accept what her future might have had planned when she planned otherwise.

"Ms. F, I'm sorry to bother you," she says, leaning in but not stepping fully toward me. "But I wanted to remind you to swing by the hospital."

"The hospital," I say, though it is more of a question. I drop the invitation into my desk drawer and close it firmly.

"Yeah, I asked you last week," she says. "Wesleyan requires a signature from my guidance counselor that you've verified that I'm actually doing work there, not just sitting around filing my nails. Now that the musical is over, I'm there full-time after school." She shrugs. "I switched to weekend shifts at work."

"Oh, sure, yes, that," I say, nodding my head, as if that makes me any more authoritative, as if that doesn't belie the fact that I have no memory of our previous discussion. "Okay, sure. I'll come by tonight."

"Great, see you then," she says, swooping back into the hallway, leaving the door ajar. Only two seconds later, Eli nudges it open.

"Hey, are you in charge of this?" He holds up the cream invitation and laughs. "Because I had a few questions about the dress requirements: beret, *oui* or *non*?"

"*Non,*" I say. "Very much a *non.*"

"Cool," he answers. "Because I don't even know where I'd get one of those around here." He falls onto the purple couch. "So have you checked out those pictures yet? From homecoming?"

I shake my head no. After that night I'd spent honing in on my self-portrait, I didn't trust myself anymore—it felt too reckless, too much like I was testing fate, testing myself.

"Okay, well, sometime, when you're ready, come find me," Eli says, rising from the couch as quickly as he sat. "I'd love to see them."

"Sure," I reply, after he's already moved out the door, down the hall, a spiral that can't be pinned down. "When I'm ready. I'll come find you."

The hospital has that eerie quietness that all hospitals have. Nurses speak in hushed tones, waiting families lean into each other and whisper closely, as if talking aloud would disrupt the placid overtone of calm that silence brings, even though in reality, the silence is more unnerving than anything. Whenever a doctor rushes by, barking in full voice, everyone swivels to see who is marring the quiet, like that bark might mean that someone else's loved one is dying, while yours, who is only spoken about in those soothing tones, is holding steady.

I am standing at the nurses' station, waiting on CJ. Luanne is working this shift, so she has paged CJ, and I am picking at a defeated-looking fruit salad that she got at the cafeteria. I pop a purple grape into my mouth and puncture it with my back teeth.

The phone rings at the station, and Lulu pulls it to her ear. "Be right back," she says, then darts down a fluorescent-lit hallway, the soles of her sneakers squeaking like a dry-erase board against the tiled floor, her expanding stomach pressing against her scrubs.

"Tilly!" I hear a voice behind me and expect to see CJ but find Ashley instead. "What are you doing here?" She smiles wearily, and though it's only been a few weeks since I've seen her, her cheeks hang more gauntly, her jeans sag on her hips.

"Oh, I had to sign a form for a student. Make sure she was actually working here for her college application." I sigh because there are about a million places I'd rather be than here, though if I were to actually consider it, I couldn't name one of them. Is there such a thing as wanting to be elsewhere without being anywhere at all? Perhaps invisible. Yes, maybe I would like to be invisible. "How's your mom?" I ask finally.

"More or less the same." Her waffle-sleeved T-shirt drowns her frail frame. She's a different person entirely than when I mistakenly found my way into her tent, when she altered everything for me, maybe even for the both of us.

Ashley lowers her voice, her eyes aflood. "When you saw . . . what you saw, do you know, well, *when* you saw it? How much longer we have? How much longer *she* has?"

I shake my head no. "I'm sorry, I wish I did. I've been trying to make sense of it . . ." I don't finish the thought, because looking at her now, I can't bear to lie to her. I haven't been trying to make sense of it, because nothing about anything makes sense anymore.

"Eh, it's okay. I figured. But I wanted to ask anyway." Her face is a mask of hollow grief.

"Ashley?" a familiar voice calls from around the corner. She and I turn in unison. "Ashley?"

My father rounds into the hallway, and even though I knew it, *knew that he'd present himself,* I'm still stunned, shell-shocked. That's the slippery thing about seeing the future and then finding yourself in it: you never really know when you've caught up, when exactly you're *there.* Only that one day, you will be.

"What are you doing here?" we say to each other simultaneously, then sputter with explanations, talking over each other.

"She's asking for you," he says finally, to Ashley, not me, and she gives me a little apologetic shrug, averts her eyes from my dad, and scampers away, gone.

"I know what I'm doing here," I say after I can no longer hear her footsteps. "But what the hell are *you* here for?" Because even though I know that *of course* he's at the hospital in the future—which is now the present—I still don't understand why.

"We were friends a long time ago," my dad says, his words catching. "I started coming by to keep her company."

"Keep Ashley company?" I ask.

"Valerie. Ashley's mother."

My eyes form a squint. "You come down here and keep Valerie company?"

He flicks his head to one side, my father's typical nonexplanation explanation, his metaphorical way of saying, *Let's just let that go.* The pieces of my vision start to fall into place, even though I haven't asked them to: my dad, ghostly, shaken, hands on the glass of the hospital room window as Ashley rushes toward her mother's bedside. She was asking him, my father—not the doctor with the Twix—about the prognosis. About her own mother's prognosis? The more the puzzle starts to click, the more it comes undone.

"I never knew you were friendly, at least beyond the usual neighborly stuff," I say, my doubts hanging on like static cling.

"I know this comes as a surprise to you, Tilly, but there are a lot of things that you never knew."

Clarity. Ashley's prophecy echoes throughout me.

I start to reply, but just then CJ circles into the hallway, waving her hand in my direction, flagging me back toward the nurses' station, where I will sign her last form and grant her freedom, freedom so far away from Westlake. My father turns and disappears around a corner.

"Did you know that Dad was here?" I ask Luanne at the desk, where she is perusing charts and entering information on the computer.

"Hmmm, what?" she asks, not really listening.

"Dad, did you know that he comes by to keep Ashley's mom company?"

She looks up at me, still typing, a bluffer's tell.

"Uh." She pauses as her thoughts catch up with her fingers. "Um, yes." The clicking on the keyboard ends. "Yeah, he's come by a few times."

"Don't you think that's weird?" I hand the signed forms back to CJ, who has been staring at the wall, trying to pretend she's not intruding, trying to pretend that while I came down here under the guise of being her guidance counselor, I seem like the one who could use an outstretched hand right about now. "See ya tomorrow," she whispers, and saunters off.

"Look, I don't know," Luanne says, and I think, *Of course you don't, because you never do!* then immediately regret my spitefulness. "But I have a lot of work here, Till, so . . ."

I nod and blow her a kiss good-bye, then start toward the elevator, but am pulled instead toward Valerie. I know where to find her, of course, because I have already seen it, and just as anticipated, her room is tucked in the shadows of the vending machines. Ashley is sitting by her mother's bedside, her mom asleep after just a fleeting few minutes of consciousness, so when I appear in front of the glass, Ashley hops up and joins me outside.

"I know you think it's strange." She circumvents me. The circles under her eyes are no longer circles; they're carved-out half moons that completely alter the structure of her face. She reminds me of one of the dementors from Harry Potter, which seems like a particularly cruel judgment, but there it is all the same. "B-but . . . I know this is weird. . . ," she stutters. "Look, I'm alone here, doing my best, so when he came down and offered some support, I took it."

"I don't think it's strange that you accepted it," I say softly, empathetically, because, after all, despite everything that has happened to me lately, I still understand human nature, still grasp how despair and pain and anger and failure can help define a person. "I just think it's strange that he offered at all."

"I know that too," she says, her words a sigh. "It's complicated."

"How?" A simple question.

"It's too much to get into right now," she says, rubbing her temples as if I'm giving her a migraine, as if this whole thing is causing her mind to implode, when I think, spiteful again, *I have a right to have a migraine of my own!* "You're a smart girl, Tilly. You'll figure it out, you'll see. You have everything you need to figure it out."

Before I can ask her what that can possibly mean, a nurse pops up from behind me and murmurs something about blood pressure and medicine and IVs to Ashley, who absorbs this information like a medical student and, without even so much as a good-bye, retreats to her mother's room to oversee the process.

I stand there, for how long I don't know, watching them tend to her mom, Ashley's hand resting on her mother's forehead, a tender sign of devotion. I could stay there forever, the passive observer, watching as a life literally unfolds in front of me. But then, the paging system blares out an emergency, and I turn to head on my way, down the darkened corridor, back to the parking lot, wondering just what the hell it is that Ashley thinks I have the power to see.

twenty-two

Tyler arrived on Friday but doesn't make his way to our house until late this morning. I have changed the locks on the front door at Susanna's suggestion—unnecessary, perhaps, but just vengeful enough to send a message—so he rings the bell twice before I grant him entry inside. I have taken the time this morning to pull myself together, like a needle stitching up a ripped, jagged seam. A lingering shower, a squirt of perfume, a puff of blush, and a jade turtleneck that Tyler once told me made my eyes look like Easter eggs, bright and shiny and welcoming. I stare in the mirror as I blow-dry my hair until it lays flat against itself, spun golden thread, and try to resolve why I'm working myself into immaculate perfection: whether I want him to plead with me to allow him back or whether I want him to die of regret, right there on the front porch. Probably a little of both, I decide, before dropping my wedding band in my jewelry box. I still wear it every day, but today, no, I wouldn't today.

It is still raining when he arrives, though the forecasters have called for the first snow of the season once the afternoon skies darken, and when I open the door, my stomach is a pit of fiery nerves, my sweat glands marching forward like a mutinous army.

"Hey," he says, and swallows.

"Hey," I hear myself reply, though I feel as if I'm having an out-of-body experience. Tyler has cut his hair short, shorter than it's been since college, and it makes him look both younger and older at the same time, like the kid he used to be and a retired military officer who spends his days barking at his poor wife because he has no one else to order around.

We stand there flanking each other, me, mostly paralyzed, him, I don't know what because I no longer know him, until he finally steps across the divide and hugs me. I want to reciprocate; I can hear my brain willing me to lift my arms and throw them around him, hug him close and smell his neck and convince him that he has made *the biggest mistake of his life!* But instead I feel frozen, so he hugs my limp body, until he releases me, and I slide aside so he can come in.

"Austin is coming over in a few." He makes his way to the kitchen. This is the first real thing my estranged husband says to me after three months apart. *"Austin is coming over in a few."*

"Okay," I answer, trailing him. His boots leave wet spots on the wood floor, and I slide my socked feet over them, sopping up the imprints with each step.

He opens the fridge, like this is still his home.

"Where's all the beer?"

"It's eleven thirty in the morning," I say. "And I threw it all out, remember?" *Of course you don't remember, because you were never present in the first place!*

He closes the fridge and sighs, leaning his back against the stove. His hands grip the top, just by the cusp of the burners, and his knuckles turn white. "Tilly, look, I know that I'm an asshole. I'm sorry for how I did this." He can't find the guts to look at me, so instead, he focuses on the floor.

"Are you happier now?" I ask, pressing back tears of terror, of loneliness, of a million other things that I doubt I could ever look back on and articulate.

His eyes make their way toward mine, slowly, but eventually, as he takes in the question.

"I think so." He pauses. "I'm figuring it out. I'm not sure I really know what happiness is, anyway."

"That's ridiculous," I snap, my rage overtaking my grief. "You know damn well what happiness is. You're just choosing to complicate it for yourself!"

"I know you find this hard to believe, Tilly," he says flatly, "but I don't. We don't all just walk around with this intuitive idea that the world is shiny."

Fury soars through me at his presumptuousness, my heartbeat a mirror for my anger. *None of this is intuitive! I have waited for happiness to come to me because I know that it is out there; I know that it is something I have earned! Every cell has wanted to quit, to say, "Well, screw you, happiness, you've certainly worked your lot on me," but I have forced myself not to crumble when faced with bleakness! I have forced myself to believe that happiness isn't in permanent remission for me!* How does he not get this?

I take three steps toward him, raise my open hand, and slap him across the face. His head jerks to the side, and when he turns back toward me, I can make out the red finger marks from his chin to his cheekbone. There is life in there yet.

"You're right," I say, my voice dead, my pulse throbbing. "You don't know anything about happiness."

The doorbell rings, and Tyler whispers, "Austin," just as I say, "Susanna," and because he doesn't move, because he looks as if he's been nailed to the stove like a crucifix, I stomp through the foyer and fling open the door to find Austin standing there like a matted dog, his hands thrust in his pockets, his forlorn face already telling the story of how little any of us want to embark down this path, how little any of us anticipated that our lives would spin so far out of our control.

He strolls inside with a little nod, just as I see Susanna pull up in her minivan. She has passed the twins to her parents for the day so I can get out of the house, so I am not forced to bear witness as my husband dismembers our life. She slams her door shut, scampers in from the rain, and embraces me without even a word. Then together, side by side, we walk toward the kitchen, where we will face the men we have loved since we were teenagers and who betrayed us both equally, giving us unwanted freedom, but freedom all the same, freedom we might just hand back to them if given the choice. But we're not. Not given that choice, so we roll it around in our palms and try to see how we can mold it, to shape it to fit our lives.

"We're going to the movies," I announce. They're each standing there like teenagers, waiting for punishment for stealing their dad's car, and for a tiny flicker of a second, I remember that before all of this, I loved Tyler so very, very much. That when he *did* steal his father's car, before he had his license, before we were even dating, but back when we were friends and back before I fell into a heady whirlwind for him, he picked me up one early summer night, and we all went skinny-dipping in the lake. The mosquitoes were out, and the water hadn't quite crossed over from frigid to refreshing, but it was before my mother got sick and before my father got drunk and before my life disintegrated into dust, and so, in this moment, even though he has destroyed nearly everything that I've rebuilt for myself and for my life, I can still remember how I loved him.

For just a second, I can't help myself, and I say, "I separated your winter and summer clothes. You'll see on the bureau." I try to smile but my face refuses.

Susanna looks toward me like she wants to wring my neck, but last night, when I couldn't sleep, this ritual somehow brought me comfort. Tyler and I used to do it twice a year—swap in and out our seasonal clothes—and even though I knew it was a remote chance, at two o'clock in the morning, I convinced myself that if Tyler managed to leave his summer clothes behind, maybe he'd come back, maybe he wouldn't leave me behind as well. Now, in the glare of daylight, it seems infantile.

"Okay, thanks," Tyler says with no commitment, no understanding of the meaning behind my act of kindness. His hand is still massaging his jaw.

"We'll be back in a few hours," I say, grabbing my purse, my anger deflated. What I really want him to do is beg me to stay and help, which, I admit as Susie ushers me toward her car, is the last thing I'd really like to do, but I'd like him to ask all the same.

"What assholes," Susie says when we've strapped ourselves in and she's careening toward the movie theater. "Can you believe we married those guys?" She starts to giggle, in spite of the circumstances.

"I slapped him," I say, my laugh overtaking my words. "This morning in the kitchen, I slapped him. I just couldn't look at his goddamn face for one more second without inflicting some honest-to-God pain."

Susie laughs harder, and so do I. Until we finally calm ourselves, and she reaches over and squeezes my hand.

"Well," she says. "At least you know that you left your mark."

When we get back home, Tyler and Austin have begun to load up the U-Haul, which he'll attach to the SUV. He and I have agreed that he'll take the SUV back to Seattle, one of the few logistical details we've actually discussed, and I'll buy a sedan with some of our savings, coupled with the thousand-dollar signing bonus he received. I don't need the extra space anymore, now that it's clear there won't be baby seats in the back, playdates to rush to, and the car just reminds me of that void—one void among too many—so I'd rather get rid of it anyway.

I feel a flash of déjà vu as I watch them lug his boxes outside, the steady rain already soaking them, their baseball caps bobbing down the path toward the driveway.

There are voices shouting in my kitchen, so I drop my umbrella by the door, shake off my coat, and pad inside to find Darcy, who has dyed her hair purple since I last saw her, and my father at full throttle.

"What is going on?" I yell to get their attention.

"Oh, Tilly," my dad says, startled. "I came by for moral support. Wanted to be here in case you needed me."

"Thank you." I nod. "But what's the screaming about?"

"I found this!" Darcy yells. "This piece of bullshit in your pantry!" She shakes a half-empty bottle of vodka in her right hand.

"Calm down," I say. "Whose is that? It's not mine." I try to assert my guidance counselor voice but discover that it has nearly left me entirely, like that was just a part I used to play that I no longer remember how to embody.

"It's a bottle Dad stashed here!" Darcy's face is pomegranate red, the rounds of her cheeks pronounced, her eyes popping out ever so conspicuously, like a wasp's.

"Why did you keep a bottle here, Dad?" I turn toward him. "I cleaned this house out. And you're not drinking."

"Because he's not really sober!" Darcy says. "I knew it! I knew this would goddamn happen!"

"Now, listen." My dad's rage erupts. "I am certainly sober! You are still my daughter, and you don't have the right to talk to me like this!"

"Will you two just shut up?" I yell above their din. "And somebody please start telling me what is going on here?"

"Fine." Darcy pouts, throwing herself into a dining chair, her hand still clutching the bottle. "I got home from Dante's this morning and wanted some cranberry juice, so I started going through the pantry. And I found *this.*" She shakes the bottle like she wants to strangle it. "I knew it wasn't yours—I remember that you threw everything out—and then Dad showed up and I asked him, and he denied it, and then he didn't deny it, and now it's just more of the same bullshit, bullshit, bullshit!"

"Dad?"

"So look," he says sheepishly. "I admit that I kept one bottle hidden here, in the back of the pantry, just in case."

"Just in case of what?" I ask, both stunned and furious at once.

"I don't know," he answers. "Just in case." I glance at Darcy, but she just flares her eyes wider, as if to say, *Don't ask me, oh, and by the way, I told you so!*

"Just in case of *what*?" I demand again.

"Just in case he decides that one day, he wants to go off and be a gigantic fuckup just like he's always been!" Darcy interjects, because she can't help herself. "And just to be sure—to be very, very clear that you have zero, *zero* chance of ever drinking this again, I'll take care of it myself." And then, to really make her point, she swivels off the top, pours the remaining vodka down her open mouth, and swallows. She misses the last ounce, which flies onto her sweatshirt and slowly spreads out to a messy, wide stain. Just as I knew it would if I'd really thought about it—my vision and the Rorschach blob. It takes her at least five giant-sized gulps to polish off the bottle, and I can tell that she is so desperate to prove herself here that she is willfully fighting the urge to gag it all back up.

"Jesus Christ, Darcy," my dad says, defeated.

"Go fuck yourself," she answers, her words already flying behind her as she flees out the front door, into the frozen rain, past Tyler and Austin, who are loading up the remnants of my former life. From the driveway, she yells, "I'm tired of keeping your secrets only to have you fail me every time you have the chance to prove yourself."

"What's that about?" I ask, a triage nurse, unsure which wound to stitch up first.

"I'm not drinking again, Tilly," my dad says, unanswering, his face open with the fear of unknown repercussions. "Please believe me."

I stare at my dad for a beat, then another, and am suddenly as angry as I've ever been. At him, at Darcy, at Tyler, for bringing this fucking mess into my house, into my life, in the one moment when I have asked nothing from anyone but hoped, without even recognizing it, that they'd be selfless enough to offer themselves for everything that I had once given them.

"Just stop it," I say, disgust showering my voice. "Just stop it! Clean yourself up. Get treatment. Not the kind of treatment where you need a bottle around 'just in case.' Be there for me. Be there for your daughters. Start being a goddamn father. Because I can't be your daughter until you start acting your part too."

"That's not fair," he starts to protest. "These past two months . . ." But his words fade along with his nerve, because he knows that two months of competent parenting cannot compensate for the years of failure. Tears swell and then roll down his face, but I don't stay to comfort him. Instead, I stride up the stairs two by two, slam my door, and fall flat on my bed, tugging the pillows over my head, trying to shut it out, all of it, every last bit. It's only when I pull myself up and set the pillows back in their proper place that I realize that Tyler has packed up everything—his winter clothes, his summer clothes, his shoes, his ties, his belts, his baseball hat collection that he's been amassing since before we even wrapped ourselves up with each other.

I look over at his closet, and it is empty, open, a coffin without a body. I rise and then throw myself inside, folding my limbs onto themselves on the dusty hardwood floor. Above me, the silver poles are naked; beside me, the shelves are lined with nothing but air. A tangle of lonely wire hangers swing from what was once his shirt rack. I lean back and exhale, broken, barren, the quiet overtaking me now. I nudge the door nearly closed with my right foot and then close my eyes, wishing this slice of darkness could swallow me up forever, wishing it could actually swallow me whole.

twenty-three

Darcy hasn't returned by the time my pizza arrives. Susanna has vowed to stay the night, just like we used to when we were ten and Ashley was still part of our triangle, and we'd titter until the early hours when our bodies would lull themselves to sleep despite our best efforts. Back when the only thing we had to worry about was learning how to French kiss or how far to roll up our jeans. In fact, I invited Ashley tonight, but she begged off. Her mother was now barely lucid, and she couldn't leave her now, not in these last waning moments. I understood more than I wished to and tried to block out the memories of my mother's final haunting moments when we hung up the phone.

My mom's death was quick, though not painless. The cruelest part of it all, if I could ever pinpoint the cruelest part, was that at the last hour, we thought she'd been granted a reprieve. The chemotherapy was working, even though the doctors were sure that it wouldn't. But her tumors were shrinking, and our hope was swelling like a rising wave, and the doctors murmured things like, "It's too early to say for certain, but things are looking cautiously optimistic," or, "She might be one of those long odds; she certainly has the spirit for it," as if spirit counts for anything, as if spirit is enough to beat back cancer's call. But her tumors were indeed shrinking, and her white blood cell count was steering itself back toward normal, and though we were told not to be too hopeful, that was, of course, impossible, because when you are nine or fifteen or seventeen and your mother is a shrunken shell of herself in a hospital bed, the only thing that you have left to buoy you is hope. Because you don't yet know that the world can be cold and illogical and operate without any reason or compassion. These are lessons that would come later, *should* come later, though not for us. They came too soon.

But my mother was on the upswing. The doctors had stymied the cancer in her abdomen, slowed it in her bones, eviscerated it in the original spot: her ovaries, the very place she nurtured us to life. We heard the news, and though my father was down at the store, the four of us, all girls, cheered in our wallpapered kitchen, raising mugs of chamomile tea and clinking them, tiny chimes of triumph. No one in our house was a tea drinker before my mom got sick, but then it became one of the few things she could stomach without vomiting back up, so we learned to love it.

We had a good week, then another, and then my mom collapsed one Sunday afternoon on the front porch. My dad was still working—it was Labor Day sale season—so I screamed to Darcy, *"Get into the station wagon!"* and Luanne and I heaved up my mother, curling her limp arms around our shoulders, and raced to the hospital. It wasn't long after that. The cancer had swerved into her brain, and there was no stopping it from there. It ate up her cells, ate up her mind, and soon, ate her up entirely. We all were there when she went, and I like to think she let herself go because she knew that we'd be okay. That I'd insist that we'd be okay, because I understood that this was the weight of my inheritance. I'd promised her late one night when she was sleeping, still in our house, not yet at the hospital. I crawled into bed with her, warmed myself under the comforter, stroked her hair, and whispered that I'd make it all okay. I wanted so badly to end her pain that I figured I'd do anything, *say anything*, to make it right, even if it meant giving her up, giving up the only thing I never wanted to part with.

Until now. Now I didn't want to part with Tyler either, but life lessons stick, even if I tried to cast them off, tried to pretend that they didn't. Life can be cruel and bitter and nonsensical. And as I try to stuff down a slice of pepperoni with my oldest friend, while my other oldest friend whom I've found my way back to prepares to bury her mother, I realize that lessons are meant to be learned, honored even, or else you can spend your life running so far from them that you erect a false existence around the very thing you should be embracing.

"Life sucks," I say to Susie.

"It can," she agrees, wiping the grease from her chin with the back of her hand. "But it won't forever."

"I'm not sure I believe you."

"You're the optimist among us." Susie laughs. "If you don't believe me, then we're really screwed." She pauses. "I sort of really like Scotty Hughes. I know, well, I know that you weren't always so thrilled about me leaving Austin . . ."

I wave a hand. "That was my own crap. About Tyler and me. You know, about how maybe I didn't want things to ever change, and if you and Austin could . . ." I shrug, and she nods, the both of us getting it.

"Do you think you should check up on Darcy? Make sure she's alright?" Susanna says finally.

I'm still too angry to chase after her, though a niggling part of me knows that I should. Knows that I'm just as guilty for establishing my caretaker role as she is for accepting it, and now, rather than blame her for not putting me first, I should surrender to the fact that she is mad and vengeful and probably needs her big sister more than ever.

"I'm sure she's at Dante's," I say, the crust of the pizza lodging in my throat. I reach for a Coke to wash it down.

Just as I say this, the phone rings. "Her." I roll my eyes and hand the receiver to Susanna. "Answer it. I don't want to deal."

"Hello?" Susie crunches the phone between her neck and her shoulder so she can reach for another slice. "Yeah, hey." Her eyebrows dart, making sharp angles toward her nose. "No . . . no . . . we haven't seen her." She looks at me, her face flashing with concern. "Okay, yeah . . . I'll tell her. Yeah, we'll let you know. We'll give you a call back."

"What's that about?" I say, picking at the errant cheese specks on my plate.

"Dante. He wanted to know if we knew where Darcy was. She was supposed to show up for an audition and didn't. I guess the manager at Oliver's arranged for some sort of potential opening tour act."

"Did he try her cell?" I ask. "She pulls this shit all the time, you know."

"He sounded concerned," Susie says. "Tried her cell, tried everyone they know. No one's seen her. And he said she was really excited about this, that she wouldn't have missed it."

"Well, I don't know," I say, rising to dump my paper plate in the garbage. "Her battery's probably dead and she probably doesn't give a crap anyway, that she stood people up, that people are running around looking for her."

"Till," Susie says softly, the legs of her chair squeaking as she swivels to face me. "That's not fair. That's not who Darcy is now."

"Well that's how I see her," I answer, even though I know this isn't entirely true.

"She's been good to you. She stayed here to make sure that

you had someone. She didn't have to do that. The *old* Darcy wouldn't have done that."

I consider this for a moment, and it resonates. She's right. Whether or not I am furious over today, and I am, Darcy isn't the little sister she was when she showed up on my porch steps in July, willful and self-righteous and pissed off that the world had inevitably failed her. She has helped protect me, though, as I stare at our kitchen floor, at *my* kitchen floor now that Tyler is nearly gone, I am surprised to realize that we can only protect each other from so much.

Darcy, my little baby sister, has shed her skin and grown into something more. Now I am the one who needs to do the same.

"Okay," I say to Susanna with a nod. "I might know where she is. Come on, let's go."

I grab the keys from the counter, leaving the pizza box open, the contents half-eaten, already fermenting. Because there are burdens that we bear together, and then there are burdens that we have to bear alone, but even those, the ones that we must forge ourselves, are easier to shoulder when we can sense the firm assuredness of our sister, of our friends, standing right beside us, holding us up in case we falter.

The snow is coming down now, the cooler air swarming over Westlake, turning those rain pellets into something more treacherous.

"I can't remember it snowing like this in October," Susie says. "It's not even winter yet! Christ."

"It'll be a long one," I concur, focused on the road.

I've never liked winter, never been one for snowfall, even though it's Tyler's favorite time of year. He finds the snow peaceful, comforting, while I always wonder if I'll slip and fall, suffocating myself underneath a blanket of whiteness. I didn't tell him this: it would belie my sunnier nature, so instead, I just complained about the frigid temperatures of the season. But if I had been honest, I would have said this: that winter frightens me, that it can eat up and spit out the more fragile among us, leaving only the strong to survive.

I drive slowly, the windshield wipers whipping furiously to bat back the fat flakes that are pounding the front window. In the trunk, a litter of Tyler's belongings, which he has left behind this afternoon, occasionally rattle as I coast over a speed bump or ease to a halt, reminding me of the literal and metaphorical heft of what I'm carrying around.

"You think she's here?" Susanna says, breaking the quiet.

"I don't know where else she would be," I answer, hoping that I am both right and wrong. Right, because I want to pull her tight, apologize, and bring her home. Wrong, because it is perilous outside, and no one should be left out in the elements now, much less my sister in her flimsy, vodka-covered sweatshirt and leggings.

The city around us has virtually shut down, a ghost town. The forecasters, for once, were correct, and Westlake's residents had been wise to heed their warnings. At least six inches, maybe up to a foot, depending on which way the winds blew, they said. We coast past darkened storefronts and quieted taverns, and I wonder if I can get Tyler to shovel the walkway before he leaves tomorrow, but quickly flush the idea. *No, I will shovel it myself,* I think, flicking on my blinker to make the turn down the long road that will take us there. A small victory, but a victory nevertheless. This I can handle. This I can do.

I abort the engine in the empty parking lot. There are no tire tracks, no footprints. The snow is already piling on the windshield, and as we step down to the ground, our feet sink in, the flakes covering the noses of our boots. Soon, we'll be ankle deep.

"It's freezing out here," Susanna says, her breath a cloud shooting out, then disappearing, in front of her. "Come on, let's hustle."

We shuffle down the path as fast as the slippery foot bed allows. The lights are on, glaring as always, but with the snow falling nearly sideways, visibility is almost nil. We hold our gloved hands in front of our faces for protection, like we're blocking out the sunshine of a glorious day instead of just the opposite.

The headstones, too, are amassing inches, teetering untouched mini-mountains of flakes. If the snow pours hard enough, some of the words, the dedications, the names and dates and meanings, will be swallowed up, concealed so one headstone will resemble the other, each of them anonymous symbols of loss.

"Down here," I pant, pointing the way, the snow exhausting my thighs, taxing my concentration lest I lose my footing.

We descend the hill, the trees looming above us with their heavy, deadened branches, the sky a blanket of tumbling white. I see my mother's gravestone and break into a run, despite knowing better, despite the ground that might slay me at any moment.

"Darcy!" I yell. "Darcy?" I yell louder.

My blood courses through every limb, every digit, every extremity. I run fast, faster, and the snow gives way, such that just before I reach my mother's resting place, I am sliding, careening toward her headstone, which I collide into with a thump.

Susanna tails me, catching up from behind.

"Shit," she says, succinct, accurate, the epitome.

We both cast around for Darcy, for any signs of life, but we are in a graveyard, after all, and if flesh and blood is what we're looking for, we certainly won't find it here. I push my hand against my mom's headstone and wearily rise.

"Darcy!" I scream one last time, because I don't know what

else to do. This is the only place I thought she might be, the only safe haven I could think of.

I sigh and without warning, purging, violent tears appear, tears for this whole thing, this whole shitbag of a mess. They streak down my frozen face, and though I can't feel them, I know that they are there. I wipe them away with the back of my glove, snot congealing in my nostrils, my lashes sticking together like iced meringues. Susanna huddles close to me and rubs my back until finally the tears abate.

"I'm numb," I say, starting back toward the car loaded up with the remnants of my marriage.

"Who isn't?" she responds.

"Good point," I say.

"So what now?"

Now there's a question to which, for once in my life, I have no answer.

twenty-four

There is no word from Darcy by the time Susanna leaves the next morning to retrieve the twins from Austin. Dante has rung me twice by 7:15 A.M., after making a second wave of calls to their friends, to the bars that stayed open last night despite the storm, to anyone he can think of. I checked with school security and she wasn't in the music room, protecting herself behind the safety of piano keys. The bus station has closed because of the weather, and I'd already thought to confirm with the airport, which also shuttered its doors at the first prediction of the storm. I had to be sure, though, because it would be like Darcy, like the old Darcy, to flee straight out of town, a caged bird set free, at the first—well, maybe not first, but certainly at the most arduous—signs of trouble. I have phoned Luanne, who checked the hospital, and spoken with my father, who sounded questionably sober but swore not only that he had not heard from her but that he hadn't touched a drink, which I asked him in passing, not because it was my primary concern of the moment.

I am on my third cup of coffee when Ashley dials me, on a break from her mother's deathbed, to lighten my mood about Tyler's return and unleash a rash of man-hating insults. I stop her midsentence to explain what has happened. That Darcy is gone, and no one knows where to find her.

She falls silent, and I say, "Hello, hello, Ashley, are you still there?"

"I'm here," she answers, her voice simultaneously more hollow and yet more firm.

"Anyway, sorry, I'm just venting. How's your mom?"

"You know where she is." I can hear the hospital paging system announce itself in the background.

"Your mom? Yes, I know where she is. I'm sorry for that," I say, embarrassed at myself for pouring out my problems to someone who already has them by the barrelful.

"No. *Darcy*. You know where she is."

"I don't. I wish I did, but I don't!" My voice catches.

"You do. Think about it hard enough, and you do." Someone says something to her, and she muffles the phone, then returns. "Look, I have to go. Call me later. Think about it. Trust me. *Trust yourself*. You'll find her."

The phone goes dead, static electricity in my ear, and I sink into the couch and contemplate her words. *"Think about it. Trust me. Trust yourself."* My eyes scan my broken living room, littered with debris from Tyler's packing. Discarded balls of shipping tape, scattered broken bits of cardboard boxes, a few errant coins. I move to the mantel, covered with pictures of my old life that I haven't had the heart or the stomach to take down. Tyler and I at our wedding; Tyler and I at Susanna's wedding; Tyler and I at his championship game our senior year. I pick that one up, run my fingers over our faces—collectively so innocent, so wrapped up in the possibility of life—and then I promptly chuck it with every last ounce of strength I have, with every bit of muscle mass in my frail, tired body, toward the fireplace.

It shatters with a crack and then slips to the floor, shards every which way, fragments shooting clear toward the rug.

The picture, though, remains intact. It stares up at me upside down, leaning askew against the bricks. I can barely recognize either of us from this angle, though there we are, smiling giddily at the camera.

"Think about it. Trust me. Trust yourself.*"*

"Oh my God," I say aloud. "Oh my God, oh my God." I race out of the room, bound up the stairs, and burst into my bedroom in search of my bag. Eli's camera is hidden in the depths, cast aside since homecoming and our day in the woods. My fingers vibrate as I tug it out from below my checkbook, below my breath mints, below the prom invitation, below a few wadded-up memos from school that I barely bothered to read.

I power up my laptop, plug in the Nikon, and wait for it to whirl to life.

Yes, I will trust myself, I think as I start to scan through the photos, scan for any signs of where Darcy might be and how I might save her, even though I've given up on saving anyone as of late.

I pause on my last shot from the homecoming concert. Darcy is taking a curtsy, the sunlight radiating down on her, her cheeks pressed so high in her wide, beckoning smile that I fall in love with my baby sister all over again. I turned on the flash, unnecessary but all the more illuminating, so the picture is golden, shiny, perfect. I stare and stare and wait for it to come, to come take me, to come rescue me so that I can rescue her.

I feel it now. That pain in my toe, the seizing cramping that overtakes my calves, then my thighs, then my abdomen, then the clutch around my heart, then the breath that seems to press against my lungs, and then, finally, my mind, my brain, my synapses.

"Trust me. Trust yourself.*"* Yes, maybe I can.

The first difference I notice is that I am not frozen, that my legs aren't paralyzed as they have been in the past. That somehow, I am controlling it, instead of it controlling me, and so, my feet are weaving in and out of fallen branches, over frozen snow. It is cold—I know this from the puffs of breath that cloud around me as I hike—though I am not cold. Because I am not really here, I am simply moving through space, moving through time, moving through someone else's life.

These woods are familiar. I stop, planting my boots into the newly fallen snow, and glance around, searching for signs, for bearings. For a moment, I believe that I am back in the same woods as on that day with Eli, but the slope of the hill is less steep, the thicket of trees more dense. Then it comes to me, rushing back to me, with surprise. Surprise that I hadn't thought of it before, surprise that she would still remember this, because, after all, she was so young. Just nine.

These are the woods, of course, that we used to try to save my mother. As if snapping stolen moments of nature could nurse her back to life. Back when you are nine or even seventeen, you believe in magic, in a healing balm that can make your family complete. Because you don't know what else to do. And you don't know yet what else life can do.

But Darcy knows now, and even so, she has wound her way back here. Back to the hidden path that we used to take, up to the tree by the running stream that will now be both dry and frozen, where one day we unwrapped our sandwiches, and guzzled lemonade from thermoses that I'd packed, and in a fit of illicit abandon, carved our initials into a tree. She asked me if Mom would get better, and I told *her that I had hope that she would, and then she asked me, in a tiny voice, what would happen if she didn't. And I didn't answer, though even now, I remember that I told myself, but didn't dare to say it aloud,* I will take care of her. *But I distracted her with the knife, and then the carving, and she didn't bring it up again. And just a few hours later, before we'd even had time to develop our pictures, my mother collapsed on the front porch, and that was the end of that. That was the end of all of it. I hadn't been back since.*

My legs pick up speed, moving below me, jumping over brush, flying over broken logs. I know where she is. Of course, I know where she is. I am the only one who would, and I am the only one who can find her now, who can save her.

Though it has been years, the trees look the same, the paths weaving a familiar pattern, and soon, there she is—I can see a trickle of her purple sweatshirt the same hue as her hair, and then her face, too pale, nearly blue, leaning against the tree, against that very tree. Our initials have been overgrown; the tree's bark has shed and renewed itself in the last dozen years, and even though we once etched something indelible there, it turns out that you can never be sure what is permanent, what will stick, and what will fade even when you are so certain that it won't.

"Darcy!" I scream, tears thundering down. "Darcy!" I yell again, arriving in front of her, assessing the damage. Her legs buried in snow, her hands plunged in her pockets as though that might keep her warm.

I scream again and again, but of course she can't hear me, either because I am a ghost or because she is too far gone, so I find a way to focus back into myself, to force myself into lucidness, into the present day—Trust me, trust yourself—*and then, because* I am controlling it; it is not controlling me, *I snap out of this alternate world and back into my own. Back into my own world, where I might have a chance to save her.*

~~~~

I jolt awake in front of my computer. I check the clock and have lost only fifteen minutes, though I'm so spent that I feel like I've been sucked into a time warp that has shaved off months, years even. I want to rescue her myself, but I know that even I have limits. I will need someone strong, someone capable, someone who can haul her out of the woods without hurting us both.

I reach for the phone and frantically dial Austin's apartment, but it rings four times and clicks onto his answering machine. I try again—*Wake up!*—but am met with the same result. "Uh, hey, this is Austin. You know what to do." *Beep!*

"Tyler! Austin! Wake up! Darcy's in trouble, and I need your help. *Wake the hell up!*" I scream into the phone, then linger to see if they do indeed pick up, but no one clicks on the line, so I slam the receiver down and call Tyler's cell. I'm shot straight into voice mail and am instantly pissed, ragingly pissed, because I know that they are dead weight on the couch, recovering from a three-beers-too-many night while my baby sister withers away in the woods behind my house.

I pause and regroup. Reliable. Capable. My list of men with these characteristics has shrunk to just about zero. But then I think of one more. Yes, there is still one, and he will be awake because, like me, he never sleeps, and he will come because, like me, he wants to matter. I reach for the phone and call the only other person I can think of who might make a difference. Eli.

twenty-five

We find her exactly where I knew we would find her. Eli has thought to call an ambulance that is minutes behind us, and he has also thought to bring blankets. I am toting her winter jacket, which I found balled up at the foot of the guest room bed, and though she is not conscious, she is breathing steadily, and that, Eli says—and I believe him, because he says it like he knows about this sort of thing—can make all the difference. He deems her strong enough to go, then he lifts her in his arms, reminding me of a painting of a savior I once had to study in Sunday school.

As we descend through the woods, toward his old BMW, which he has parked in such haste that it is abutting the curb, and toward the waiting medics, I feel the veil of my guilt descend. If only I'd taken the time to try to uncover the pieces, to glue the puzzle back together. If only I hadn't been too selfish—and skittish—to look at those pictures, to know what the fates might hold for her. But I didn't, and I hadn't, and now, it had come to this.

We trail the ambulance and race to the hospital, where Lu-anne runs up and pulls me tight, then retreats to call my father. Ashley appears from a side corridor to give me a strong embrace, a sign of confidence that I've found a way to finally seek clarity, to use the gift she's bestowed.

Eli retrieves coffee from the cafeteria and we sit in a cocoon of silence, amidst the blaring cacophony of the emergency room. Doctors are yelling, sirens occasionally whirl outside, angry family members bitch at the administrative staff for not yet admitting their loved ones, for making them wait out their pain in the indignity of these stupid maroon plastic chairs, even though they are mostly in a terrified panic that their husbands or fathers or wives ignored the newscasters' reports to stay home and take refuge, and instead insisted on driving in this treacherous weather and eventually landed themselves here. *None of us ever really stop to consider that the worst can actually happen to us,* I think. We always assume that it will be this guy or the other guy, but never us. And then your tires give way on the patchy back road, and an hour later, they find your car flipped in a pasture. This is how life works. Why don't any of us ever learn?

The doctors have rushed Darcy back behind flapping doors that bear a red sign reading HOSPITAL STAFF ONLY! so the only thing left to do is wait. I made out words like "acute hypothermia" and "severe frostbite," and Eli told me that they were probably trying to raise her body temperature, to cook her from the inside out, though he used kinder words than those.

"How do you know all of this?" I ask.

"A vacation in the Andes a few years ago with my best friend." His head drops just a nudge. "It . . . well, there were some problems." He starts to say more but catches himself when he gets to the part about a small avalanche. I can see him watching me, watching my fear rise, so he aborts his story and instead rubs my hand. "Better told another time," he says. "We have enough sad stories for now. Let's think of better ones."

I rest my head on his shoulder because I feel like it might

teeter off of my neck under its own weight, and I close my eyes and try to think of better ones but come up blank. I am slipping into that transcendent state, somewhere between wakefulness and sleep, when I hear my name shouted from across the room.

I snap open my eyes to see Tyler, trailed by Austin, rushing toward me. They are wearing the same clothes as yesterday, and when he kneels down to hug me, he reeks of old hops and cigarettes. His Westlake Wizards baseball hat covers his matted, in-need-of-a-shower hair, and when he rises, standing in front of me, he reminds me so much, too much, of one of my students. A kid who never grew up. A man-child who never rose to the occasion of adulthood, of everything that adulthood asks of you. Four months ago, this is what I might have loved about him. Now, I cock my head and wonder.

Eli clears his throat and introductions are made: Eli squinting his eyes and assessing; Tyler oblivious to it all, to the undercurrent, the innuendo, the strange man who helped rescue my sister when my husband could not.

"Listen, I should go," Eli says, kissing my cheek. "I have a houseguest, and she doesn't know anyone in town." His words falter. *The girlfriend*, I think, though I don't ask. It doesn't matter; it doesn't matter enough to ask, because whoever she is, I called him, and he came, and that was enough to ask of him for now.

"Thank you, *thank you*," I say again and again because I cannot think of a better way to say it. Tears build and then spill over.

"I'll check in later, once my friend gets a flight out of here," he says. The snow had let up by the time we found Darcy, so maybe the town, the airport, the roads, the stores would open back up. Or maybe not. Maybe his guest would be stuck here along with the rest of us. *We're all a little stuck*, I think, giving Eli a final hug, watching him lope down the hall to the exit, his lanky torso, his confident stride.

Tyler takes Eli's place on the row of chairs, my actual husband, who has failed me, swapping in for my surrogate one, who has not. He links his hand into mine, and turns my face to meet his own, and runs his fingers over my long blond strands, and then presses his lips to the tip of my nose, which is what he used to do way back when, before everything.

"I'm sorry," he whispers, and I fight to hold his gaze, to not look away, because I'm not even sure that I want to hear this, not even sure what he's sorry for. There is so much.

"Okay." I nod, the easiest answer. I am too exhausted for any other complications.

"I'll stay," he says, after I have broken our stare and am focused on the ER doors in front of me, willing a doctor to emerge and promise us that she will be fine, that I didn't get there too late, that my selfishness wasn't her undoing. "I'll stay," he repeats when I don't respond.

"Thanks. My dad should be here soon. So the company would be nice. At least until he's here." My eyes are frozen on those damn doors. *Please open and bring us good news!*

"No, listen, look at me." Something in his voice forces me from my trance. "*I'll stay*. Here. With you. In Westlake." He hesitates, aware of the weight of his words, of how they are flying against everything that he has done, and undone, in the past four months. "At least until Darcy is better. They don't need me back right away anyway for the off-season. How about that? Let's start with that."

I nod. *Okay*. I don't really want to think about it now. But yes, at least until Darcy is better. Yes, let's start with that.

My father and Luanne insist that I head home at dusk.

"Go shower, go get some sleep," he says, acting like the parent he is. "I'll stay here for now. She probably won't wake up tonight anyway." His throat catches, his eyes instantly glistening. I know that the only person perhaps more eviscerated by this than I am is he, so he tries to absorb some of my pain, my guilt, sopping it up like a sponge, and for once, I let him. We are both complicit in this. And we both know it to be true.

The doctors have informed us that Darcy is in a coma, which sounds more severe than it really is, they said.

"We have every reason to believe that she will recover," they said. "That she will wake up in the next twenty-four to forty-eight hours, and we'll take it from there."

"Take it from there—what does that mean?" I asked one of them, the one who looked the oldest, the most experienced, the one who might have the answers.

"It means that sometimes there are lingering effects from hypothermia—memory loss and such—that we can't predict until she wakes," he said, and I felt my insides crumble at the idea that Darcy might not return to us the same way she went. "There was also severe frostbite," the doctor added, as if this was an afterthought. "Her fingers and toes sustained some damage, her toes more so. When she wakes up, we'll see if she has the full span of movement. She may need therapy to regain it all. Stay here in the rehab wing for a while."

I let out a little scream, an anguished cry, because of all the things to strip Darcy of, her hands, her lifeblood, would be the cruelest. Luanne shushed me and told me not to worry, that she sees things like this all the time, but I couldn't tell if she was just being her usual clueless self or if, for once, I should actually take heed and believe her.

My dad smushes me into a taxi, and soon after I've made it home, Tyler shows up with a duffel bag. I've already changed into my pajamas, and I let him in wordlessly, then pad upstairs to the bedroom, so drained that my legs nearly give way halfway up the steps. I sink under my sheets, hoping that sleep will heed my call.

The door creaks open just as I am slipping away, and the mattress shakes beside me. I turn to find Tyler in my bed—our bed—as though he didn't vacate it three, nearly four, months ago, and really, many months before that.

"Hey," he says. "Is this okay?"

I press my lips together to form something of a smile, though I have no idea if it's okay, no idea what to think at all. But my husband is back, and he wants to sleep in our bed, so I accept it and try not to think too much. I am so very, very tired, but he moves on top of me, and then kisses me, tenderly, softly, like he has missed me as much as I've missed him, so I muster some strength to kiss him in return. His lips come toward me faster, more desperately, and soon, the movements come naturally. We've been doing this, after all, since we were nearly children.

Afterward, Tyler rolls over and slips quickly into a steady, sound slumber. But me, no. I can't sleep, though all logic dictates that I should, that with my husband back beside me and the two of us tucked so securely in our bed, just like the old days, that surely, sleep should beckon. But it doesn't. So I just stare at the ceiling, listening to the rise and fall of Tyler's breath, waiting for morning, waiting for tomorrow, waiting for what it will bring.

twenty-six

There is good news and bad news the next morning at the hospital when Tyler drops me off. He'll join me after making a rash of calls to the UW, explaining the circumstances, working out the details, details that we haven't discussed, but he'll assess them first with his bosses, then assess them with me. "Fine," I tell him when he suggests this tactic. "Whatever works," I say, closing the car door in the hospital's drop-off zone, already flushing the conversation, ready to move on to something more critical. The good news is that Darcy is showing signs of waking up; the bad news is that Ashley's mother is slipping away.

I check in on Darcy but am quickly scooted out of the room by a hovering nurse, so I meander the halls until I find my father, staring into the glass to Valerie's room, Ashley crumpled on the floor by the vending machines. Just as I knew I would, though I'm still never quite sure how these visions will unfold. Only that they will. I overhear Ashley asking, "How is she?" just as I approach and watch my father's limp shoulders flop, his face turning toward her, an empty voice answering, "They don't know everything yet." *Darcy, he was talking about Darcy.*

Machines blare suddenly from inside the room, and Ashley

bolts up and through the door, letting it slam behind her. My father, as I'd seen him do once before, slaps his hands up against the window in a naked display of grief.

The beeping stops as quickly as it started, and I move toward my dad, rubbing his back as a way of hello. He turns and clutches me so tightly that I am nearly smothered, his shirt scented with sweaty fatigue, his breath the odor of the hospital's egg sandwich.

"I'll go sit with your sister for a while," he says, releasing me. It's obvious that he doesn't know what to do with himself, that if he goes home, he may drink himself into an unconscious stupor, so he stays here and tries to make himself useful. I agree that he should go sit with her, even though I know the nurses will probably turn him away at her door, but I want a moment with Ashley.

She emerges from her mother's room—the doctors have taken over, trying to give her mom a few more days, though the hours are growing shorter—and falls into me, a hug of sorts, really more of a cry to be held up.

"So you figured it out," she says after a moment, pushing back and reaching my eyes. "Figured out what I meant."

"I did," I say. "Though it took me too long. I should have gotten there sooner."

"You were never the fastest learner," she says, ribbing me, which feels both so inappropriate given the circumstances and so utterly Ashley that I can't help but laugh. To know that despite everything, despite *all of this*, she can still shovel it out at me. She pauses, more words on her tongue. "And the rest of it? Did you figure that out too?"

"What rest of it?" I ask. "Isn't this it?" *What the hell else could there be?*

She shrugs. "There's always a little more."

"Stop being so damn cryptic," I snap, my raw edges breaking through.

"Fine," she huffs. "I'll help." She turns to gaze at her mother, all wires and tubes and machines now. "Don't you ever wonder why we stopped being friends?"

"You asked me this before," I say. "At the diner. It's because you went all weird, and I became a cheerleader." I try not to think back on that time, even though for the better part of my adulthood, it was the only time I wanted to think of. But now, no, not now. Not when I've discovered how easily it can all shatter, like the glass frame against my fireplace.

"That's not why," she scoffs, and then reconsiders. "Though there's that too. I never did like cheerleaders." She smiles. "Look, this is for you to figure out. I was pissed at you back then for not getting it, but I'm not pissed now. Because I know that you didn't know. That you didn't want to see it back then because it was so much easier. I get that. I wish in some ways that I hadn't seen it either."

"Honestly, Ashley," I interrupt. "I'm so tired. Can you just enlighten me?"

She starts to say something, but then a voice calls my name from down the hallway. I spin around and see my father, then turn back toward Ashley, and something clicks into focus. But before I can even fathom what is sliding into place, my father shouts for me again.

"Tilly, come on," he cries. "Darcy's awake. She's asking for you."

Darcy and I start sobbing simultaneously when I enter her room. Her hands are bandaged, wrapped tight to ward off the damage, and her limbs are ensconced in blankets. I wonder if she'll ever warm up, ever be the same, but those questions won't be answered for some time now.

"I'm sorry," I say to her, sitting at her bedside, between my sputtered gasps, between my tears. I don't know if she can ever forgive me for this. Less important, or perhaps more important, I don't know if I can ever forgive myself for this.

"I'm sorry too," she says, and it's clear that she doesn't hold me responsible, though of course, how could she know that I could have seen this coming, that if I'd thought harder, been less selfish, maybe I could have stopped it?

We sit there in comforting quiet, kept company by the beating monitors, the drip of the IV, two sisters, taking care of each other, maybe what we should have been doing from the start. Darcy's eyes droop, and I study her face. She's no longer a child now. The layer of baby fat has long since dripped off her, the smooth luster of adolescent skin somewhat dulled. But she is still breathtaking; her cheekbones are sharp protrusions, her hair with its sheeny gloss despite purple dye and a diet of pizza and Coke.

Her lashes flutter, and she looks up at me.

"What?" she says, self-conscious but happy to be admired all the same. The perfect contradiction, as always. That, at least, hasn't changed.

"Nothing." I shake my head. "I'm just thinking about everything. Everything we've been through, you know?"

"I do."

My dad raps on the window and gives a little wave, a flimsy peace offering that I hope she'll latch onto. I watch her watch him, gauging her reaction.

"Can you forgive him?" I ask. "He wants that so badly."

"Why are you so easy on him?" she says, with no rancor, only depletion. "Why do you always give him another chance?"

"I guess I believe in second chances." I shrug.

"He's had more than that," she says succinctly.

"Can I ask you one more thing?" I'm not sure what I'm asking, even though I think I sort of know. She nods, looking sleepy. "What did you mean the other day in the kitchen—his secrets? You meant the hidden bottles, that stuff, right?"

She sighs, a long, exhausted, purging sigh.

"Tilly," she says. "I'm tired. And I love you. So let it go for now."

"I can't," I answer quietly, thinking of my father in the hallway, of his hands against the glass of Valerie's room, of some strange unspoken tie that binds him to Ashley and her mother, of Ashley's request that I understand it all too.

"It's years old," she murmurs, fading fast. "Years behind us now. Before Mom died." Her lips quiver, and she's asleep.

I look up to find my dad frozen in the doorway, his face a veil of worry, of guilt, of disquiet. I hadn't even noticed him slip closer.

He dislodges the phlegm from his throat. "What was that about?"

"You tell me," I say, then reconsider. "You know what? Don't. I don't want to hear an excuse. I want to hear what Darcy knows about before Mom died. What she knows about you and Valerie Simmons."

His mouth drops open, as does mine. I hadn't even realized I'd made a connection, but somehow, even without attempting to master the jigsaw puzzle of my life, my instinct had taken the reins.

"It's n-not what you're thinking," he stammers.

"How do you even know what I'm thinking?" I stand now, firmer on my feet, firmer with myself. *Trust me, trust yourself.* Yes, this time, now, I will.

"I just . . . I just . . ." My dad's words refuse to excuse him this time.

"When was this? How long was this for?" My unchecked rage has returned, the rage that slapped Tyler, that accused my father of failing us, that chucked that photo clear into the fireplace. Those feel like warm-up acts.

I already know when it happened, of course: it was in the sixth grade, and Ashley must have uncovered it, left me a trail of breadcrumbs to stumble upon it myself, to stand by her and share the burden of the gruesomeness of her discovery that our parents were unfaithful not just to their spouses but to their families, and instead, I kicked the breadcrumbs aside, shuffling past them in my bare feet as I ran through the grass, happy and greedy and oblivious all at once. It's no wonder she hated me. I'd hate me too.

"Not long," he offers timidly, exposing his earlier excuse, betraying his guilt. "It was a mistake." His hands are open, begging me not to judge him.

"And Darcy knew? *Darcy knew?*" I am shouting in a furious whisper, trying not to wake her but wanting wholeheartedly to throttle him, strike him down right here in the ICU.

His shoulders start to shake, then his torso, and soon, his whole body is a mess of spasmodic, wracking fits of anguished tears coursing free. I don't care. I don't give one shit. I watch him tremble, and I vow that *this is it.* I will not excuse him for another moment of my life, I will not protect him, I will not offer counsel, I will not care if he returns home tonight and swallows two gallons of vodka and chokes on his own vomit.

He tries to reply but is drowned by his guttural moans. It's just as well, because right then, right when it cannot get any worse, Ashley appears behind him, her eyes swollen and pink, and says, "She's gone."

Another daughter left to face the world alone.

twenty-seven

V aleric Simmons is buried in the same cemetery as my mother, on a quiet day in the first week of November, the sky a cast of gray steel, the air cold enough to bite. The snow still hugs the ground, squishing below us as we plod solemnly to her plot. Ashley is holding up better than I anticipated, or perhaps just better than I did when I buried my own mom, but she is stronger than I am, this I understand now, so maybe it's no surprise.

She knows that I know her secret from so many years ago; she saw this washed across my face, and of course, across my father's face, when she told us the melancholy news of her mother's passing, but we haven't spoken of it. With all that has happened, it seems almost beside the point.

Tyler and I, along with Susanna and Luanne, attend the funeral. I spot my father on the periphery of the small huddle of mourners but don't move toward him to start rebuilding our bridge. There are only so many times I can lay myself down, I tell Tyler in the SUV afterward, and he nods, his eyes on the road, and I wonder if he's agreeing with me or mentally checking sports scores.

This isn't just the day that we have all gathered to bury Ashley's mom. As if fate is mocking me with gallows humor, it's also my wedding anniversary. Tyler reminded me two days ago, pulling out an old album, laughing over our Halloween-themed rehearsal dinner. He went as Joe DiMaggio; I went as Marilyn Monroe. How odd, I thought, as we flipped through the pages, the plastic crinkling, the photos yellowed around the edges, that we already were concealing ourselves before we even married.

"We should go out to dinner," he said, though his voice turned upward and it was more of a question. "Um, to celebrate."

"Okay," I said, wiping down the kitchen counters. "Okay, yes, let's." It all felt so long ago, that rehearsal dinner, the toast my father made with nonalcoholic wine, how much I missed my mother as Luanne and Susanna pressed my dress and adorned the bun at the nape of my neck with baby rosebuds. Only that part—the pangs for my mom, I thought, squeezing out the sponge, the brown water sliding down the kitchen sink drain—didn't feel like so long ago at all.

We shower quickly after the funeral and then take our time to dress, each avoiding eyeing the other's state of half nakedness. Tyler finishes first and waits for me on the downstairs couch, reminding me of how he used to wait for me back in high school. I'd walk down the stairs, and his whole being would illuminate. Of course mine did too, though now, with everything, it's easy to forget that.

Tonight, I come down, and he rises, and I try to convince myself that it's possible to regain that glow, like turning on a flash of a camera, and *bam*, that shadow of darkness is gone.

He kisses my hand. "You look beautiful."

"Do I?" I ask, matting the wrinkles in a navy dress I haven't worn since last year's graduation ceremony. It's out of season, but I didn't have anything else clean.

We eat, as we have every anniversary for the past nine years, at Bella Donna's, CJ's father's restaurant, which is as close to Italy as I've ever been. The tablecloths are made of real silk, the music softly lilting from the stereo an opera that Darcy would likely recognize. The air swims with the scent of fresh, doughy pasta. Hank Johnson greets me warmly at the door, sliding my down coat off my shoulders, squeezing both of my cheeks with his hands.

"Thank you for doing everything that you have for her," he says.

"She did it herself." I smile. "Though you know this means she has a shot at Wesleyan."

"I know," he answers, showing us to our table, pulling out my chair. "Of course, I don't want to see her go, but I also don't want to see her not go." His shoulders rise, then fall. "Welcome to life."

"It's nice being here with you," Tyler says after Hank is gone. "I'm glad that we're doing this, glad that we're celebrating."

"Me too." I nod and scan the menu, ignoring the obvious: that I'd forgotten about our anniversary until he reminded me, and that if he hadn't, the day would have passed much like any other, except that I began it by burying an old friend's mother.

"I didn't realize how close you and Ashley had become," he says, after he orders his usual chicken cacciatore, and I, breaking from tradition, opt for the salmon.

"We used to be best friends, remember?" I say.

"Sort of," he says, his eyes squinting. "I sort of remember." He falls silent, and I do too. We've grown unaccustomed to this, the meandering small talk that adds up to something substantial in a marriage. We've forged a partnership this past week built on crisis—*How is Darcy's recovery? How is Ashley holding up?*—and now, with no red lights glaring, no alarm bells blaring, as we both shift in our seats, sipping a wine that I wouldn't have ordered for myself but Tyler went ahead and did it anyway, we're left with, well, not so much. *It doesn't feel like so much*, I think, pressing the cabernet down my throat, feeling its burn as it goes.

"How's your fish?" Tyler asks after it arrives.

"Not as good as I thought it would be," I say. "I just wanted to try something new, though. But I don't think I'd order it again."

"Well," he answers, cutting his chicken and popping it in his mouth. "You tried."

Well, I think, *I did*.

twenty-eight

The snow piles on again the next week, obese golf-ball flakes; winter is announcing its early and unrelenting arrival. Tyler is working a shift at the store, some extra holiday shopping money, and though the doors to Westlake High have been shuttered due to dodgy roads, he drops me at school on Tuesday morning. College applications are due on Friday, so I have no choice but to face the mountainous pile of paperwork on my desk. The hallways are quiet, the lights dim. I say hello to Billy, the security guard, who has heard about Darcy and asks after her. She's doing a little better, I answer, forcing a smile. This is both true and not. She has been moved into the rehab wing, and her fingers are regaining sensation, no small victory, but today, she will lose two of her toes.

"They can't be saved," the doctor told us yesterday, though they'd thought for a time last week, maybe. Dante was also in the room. He'd bought her a CD player from Walmart, so she could listen to the demo he'd been laying down of their new songs. He squeezed her shoulder and told her that ten toes were overrated, and we all grinned because what choice did we have anyway? But she will always walk with a limp, always feel self-conscious in sandals, and I will always glance down at her maimed feet and feel the flush of shame that I didn't do better by her, didn't put aside my selfishness to save her in time. I try to see it from the other side, though, too, that it's a literal walking reminder of clarity, of how muddied things once got and how far I've come to actually see more clearly.

CJ's Wesleyan application is resting on the top of my files, and I sit wearily—*How many nights has it been since I slept?* I wonder, flipping through the essays and the pages that she hopes will carry her so far from here. Now that Tyler is back in my bed, he's been keeping me awake, snoring and twitching and grinding his teeth. I never realized that maybe I'd sleep better on my own. Probably because, if I really thought about it, I'd never actually slept alone in my adult life. There was always someone snuggled next to me, as if a warm body is any reason to feel secure. That day at the school carnival, I'd smiled smugly at Ashley and stated my theory: that I had a husband and a wonderful, steady pattern and *we were trying for a baby*, so what else could I possibly need? It turns out, both everything and nothing at all.

I reread CJ's application one last time before moving on to the next one. Yes, she is ready. She will soar out of Westlake and probably never glance behind her to doubt herself. Why hadn't I ever done that? Why had I always assumed that if I played it safe, tucked my life into my palm, that I could protect us all from the destruction that could seep into the cracks, under my pores, and into my bloodstream anyway?

I lose track of time as I filter through the files, all stuffed with hopes of a better future. My neck muscles flare, begging me for a reprieve, but I want to be done with these heady declarations that there is life outside of Westlake. Not because I no longer believe it. I do now. I can see this now. But because they are also constant reminders of the road I ignored, the road I didn't think to take when I had the possibility.

A knock on the door releases me from my haze.

"I saw your light on," Eli says. He has called three times since Darcy's catastrophe, but I've been too swallowed up with everything to phone him back.

"What are you doing here?" I say, smiling widely because, both in spite of and because of everything, I am happy to see him. My neck relaxes, my shoulders spread, bursting the wads of tension that are scrunched up inside of me, and I wave him in. "Didn't you hear it's a snow day?"

"Eh, sledding's overrated," he says, waving his hand, falling on the couch. "No, actually, I just had some shots I wanted to check out. I don't have the setup at home that we have here." He pauses. "How's your sister?"

I share the details, and he tilts his head and listens, watching me intently as I speak, so I tuck my hair behind my ears, embarrassed, and look away.

"How'd everything go with your houseguest, um, who was she?" I ask, unsure why I'm asking since Tyler is back now, though completely sure why I'm asking all the same.

"You can ask, you know," he says, laughing. "Yes, she was my ex-girlfriend. I think I told you about her a while ago—*Kenya girl*—and yes, she's gone now. We just had some stuff to resolve." He bounces his head. "It's resolved."

"Okay," I say, the air hanging between us. "Hey, can I ask you something else?"

"Anything."

"Your friend, the one from the avalanche. What happened to him?"

"He didn't make it." Eli's chin drops slightly toward his chest, a subtle sign that we all carry burdens, anchors that can pull us under the depths.

"I'm sorry," I say. "Did you ever go back up? I mean, did you ever go climbing again after that?"

"I did." He leans back into the couch as if the memory is releasing him. He stares at the halogen lights on the ceiling. "I went back up once, a few months later. Only once, though, and probably never again."

"Why?" I probe, a simple question that begs a complicated answer.

"Because I didn't want the mountain to beat me," he says, not complicated at all. "I didn't want it to win. There are enough things in life where it will. But this one, I couldn't. I couldn't let it. It had already taken enough."

I push my chair back and move to him now, sinking next to him on my faded purple couch and laying my head against his chest, where I can hear his heart beat a steady beat, like a metronome on my mother's old piano. We sit there as the second hand circles the clock, in comfortable, easy silence, each of us bearing our wounds, only one of us already versed in how to sew them all the way back up.

Later, after Eli has left and after I have managed to doze on my couch, I stride out the emptied hallway of the school that I have wrapped up my identity in so completely. I peer into the music room that once provided Darcy salvation and say a hushed, fervent prayer that she will one day be strong enough to find her way back. Not to here, of course, but back to her music, her antidote. After a lifetime of wanting to pin her down, of wanting her to stay, I realize that not all of us can be rooted so easily. Nor should we be. Yes, let her find her way back, wherever that might be.

I swing into the locker room, where I peed on that stick and saw that lonely solitary line, and where I was sure that I had lost everything, every link to my husband, every hope for the future. I linger outside the art room, which is locked now, but to which I have the key. I stand outside anyway, wondering how I abandoned it all—my passion for photography, my love of a crisp, captured moment—but then I remember exactly how I abandoned it, of course: for Darcy, for my family, for my father. I lost myself for them, which we all have to do every once in a while but probably shouldn't forever.

On Friday, a small percentage, but a percentage nevertheless, of Westlake's students will press their tongues against the lips of envelopes, paste on the proper postage, and send their dreams out into the world, hoping that someone will honor them. They haven't abandoned those dreams; they haven't abandoned themselves. They all have problems, maybe not mine, but problems all the same. Maybe their parents are broke, maybe they only occasionally have hot water, maybe their fathers are trying to kick a meth habit. Maybe their grandparents are serving as surrogate parents or their jeans are worn thin from too many siblings and hand-me-downs. Or maybe their friend died up on the frozen mountain under a wall of snow. But they're still climbing back up. They aren't going to let the mountain beat them. I have. I understand this now. I have. I've spent my life ushering these braver souls out into the world while finding shelter in their shadows. This isn't a life. This is a refuge.

On my way toward the car, I stop to linger in front of the trophy case, the one with the newspaper clipping from Tyler's championship game, with the team photo—him the star shortstop—tacked up next to it. I find myself in the picture from the paper: there I am, in my cheerleader uniform, taut, beaming, so much potential yet untapped. I look at my seventeen-year-old self and wonder what I would say to her now, not just as me, but also as her guidance counselor, and as someone who has been given a little more insight into the future than she thought possible.

I would tell her, I think, standing here in the hallway, as I feel the damp spread of tears across my cheeks, that life is limitless, that fear is conquerable, that if you stay concealed in the shadows, you'll never be seen. That spending the better part of your days trying to fix people might be admirable; no, in fact, it *is* admirable, but only when you're not doing so to avoid fixing yourself. You can plug up all the holes in a boat, after all, but if you never learn how to navigate choppy waters, you still may drown. I would tell her that dreams can be small, but they are still dreams, even if it is to taste an escargot in Paris or snap a timeless image of the Eiffel Tower or run down the Champs-Elysées, gaping at the too-expensive stores, the night air on your back, the lights and the stars and the electricity palpably charging around you. Even, I realize, as I stare at Tyler's grinning adolescent face, if it is to coach a college team to victory because you'll never again feel the snap of the bat and the rush from the cheer of the crowd and the dry dirt against your cheek as you slide into home plate.

I would tell her many things, I think, before I finally steer myself away. Mostly, I'd tell her that it isn't too late. That the years are long and the road is winding and that dreams float out there to be captured, but only if you're brave enough to reach up and grasp them.

twenty-nine

Tyler is watching basketball when I unlock the front door. I can hear it in the den, and I should go to him, tell him that I am back and ask what he would like for dinner, but instead, I make my way upstairs, toward the bedroom. He has been home for only two weeks and already, I can feel us slipping back to where we used to be. Which might have been okay before. Before all of this. But now, it is not okay at all, not even a tiny sliver of okay. He's come back into our bed—this is a change—but the rest of it, it's all too familiar, all a little suffocating. The way he crowds himself into the bathroom in the morning to shave, when I had grown accustomed to steaming up the mirror alone; the way, even with all of this, that he asks me what's for dinner, as if he couldn't stop at Boston Market and take care of that one small task; the way he feverishly watches the sports channels, with Austin glued to his ear, the two of them bantering about scores and errors and *Oh man, how could he have missed that shot!* when the world outside us has just proven that none of this shit matters.

I kick off my shoes and wilt into a heap on the floor, rubbing the arches of my feet, scooting toward my bureau. I open the bottom drawer, the photographic contents of my life spilling forth, just as I did before my first flash-forward, before everything un-raveled. Before.

I weed through the mess until I find it. That perfect image of my family just before my mom got sick. Of us on our front porch, radiating happiness, radiating love, me flying back into the picture with abandon, my face askew as I throw myself toward my family before the click goes off and freeze-frames the moment. This utopic shot that I've only now learned was nothing but a mask, a façade that, had I dug any deeper, would have given way under my prodding.

Darcy confessed this to me yesterday after Dante left from his daily visit, when she finally had some strength and when we'd got-ten through our sad rash of jokes about her eight-toed life.

"I wish you wouldn't be so morbid," I said.

"It's not morbid," she laughed. "It's the opposite of morbid. I'm going to have eight toes, Tilly, and if I can't laugh about that, what the hell am I going to laugh about?"

"I suppose you're right." I smiled and then laughed a little myself. "Funny how you've suddenly become the optimist be-tween us."

"Not suddenly," she pointed out. "It's taken a while."

It turned out that her memory was just fine, unaffected by her night spent under the blanket of snow. So she told me everything: that she had caught my father and Valerie when she was eight, just before Mom's diagnosis, just as we were snapping that picture on the front porch. My mother had hurriedly dropped her off at the store because she was late for a piano lesson at a student's house, so Darcy did what she always did: headed to my dad's office for a Coke. Only she didn't find a Coke. She found, instead, my father with his hands up Valerie's blouse, pressed up against the very re-frigerator that Darcy was seeking.

"Please note that this cured me of my soda habit until college," she said dryly.

"How can you find this in any way funny?" I asked.

"Oh, Till, I don't know. I was so fucking pissed for so fucking long . . . even just a few weeks ago . . ." She trailed off. "And now I'll have eight toes . . . I got so angry that I chugged a bottle of vodka, walked through the woods, passed out, and now . . . I'll have eight toes. Forever. That can't be undone."

I nodded, because maybe I could understand how this helps her let go, and she continued.

The adults in question were understandably horrified and assured Darcy that she hadn't seen what she thought she'd seen. That there was a spider up Valerie's shirt, and she was squirming so fitfully that my dad had to help her squash it before it plunged its teeth into her skin. Darcy smiled and drank three Cokes just to shut them up, and then Valerie made a big show of buying a new VCR and left out the front door, her skirt still askew.

"Dad asked me not to tell Mom because he said it would only worry her, that the store was infested with spiders," Darcy said as a nurse came in to check her IV. "I didn't believe him, but I knew that telling Mom would destroy her anyway. I mean, I was only eight, but you still know these things." She paused, reconsidering, sucking down a sip of water from a straw on her bedside table. "I don't know. I never knew if it was the right thing or not."

While she recounted the story, I did the mental math. If Darcy had caught them when she was eight, and Ashley had somehow learned of the affair when we were twelve, this was more than a short-term fling. This was a five-year fling, minimum, because who knew if he actually ended it when his youngest daughter walked in and was forced to bear the weight of his secret, of his narcissim. My fury with my father reared itself all over again, my anger rising with the blood in the back of my neck, in the throb behind my ears.

"Why didn't you tell me?" I asked softly. "You could have at least told me."

She mulls her words.

"Mom got sick, and you had so much to deal with." She gazed at me generously, kindly, and I wondered how I'd missed it all these years. "I thought it was one small thing I could to do help, knowing that you were doing all of the rest."

I looked at her, brave and smart and protective of me, her big sister, and framed her right there in my mind. *Click.* Yes, I wanted to capture that moment indelibly.

Now, I sit on my bedroom floor, on a dreary night in November, with my husband downstairs listening to basketball, and I stare at that picture from that day on the porch, which now rings so false that it may as well be someone else's family, may as well be a Photoshopped version like the ones I see from Eli's class.

I pull the photo toward me and kiss my mother's face, because she, after so many years, did not deserve this, would not want to see us fractured every which way like this. And then I rip it, the image of our perfect quintet, calmly, concisely, into tiny, glorious pieces that dot my rug like confetti, as if I just threw myself a party. I abandon it there for now; tomorrow, maybe I will tape it together, maybe I will toss it in the outside garbage to be ushered to the dump.

And then I rise to my feet, climb into my bed, and spiral into sleep.

In the morning—*surprise!*—I find Tyler snoring on the couch. Here we are back again, stuck. I nudge him on the shoulder, but he just grunts and rolls to his other side.

Darcy is expecting me. She is being released today, and Dante and I will be the ones to wheel her home. The television is still on from the night before, muted, the scenes from yesterday's games flashing behind me, the scroll on the bottom sliding along, as if a hockey game or a basketball injury might actually be breaking news.

I watch him sleeping, just like I have so many times before. His flawless skin, his hearty, ruddy cheeks, his thick swell of espresso hair. Yes, he looks just like he did when we were seventeen. Maybe that's part of the problem now. Not that time has changed him, but that it hasn't.

I can envision his future without even having to see it. I don't need to peer into a photo, catapult myself ahead in time. There he is, in a stadium, coaching that star freshman, honing his swing, the way he taps home plate three times for good luck, the way his body uncorks like a spring. I can taste the stale smell of hot dogs from the stadium, feel the resonating rays of the sun against my cheeks. Tyler is there, discovering who he is without me, without this town, and as clear as any of my visions, I know this now. I open my eyes, staring at my husband on our couch, on *my* couch, and I know that also, this isn't a vision to flee from.

I grab for a pen and paper from the desk and start to scribble a note but rest the pen as quickly as I reached for it. No, after a decade and a half, after nearly a lifetime together, I won't do it this way, not the way that he did. Not without real words, real emotion, real understanding of the crevasse that split us in two.

"Tyler." I shake both of his shoulders. "Tyler, wake up. I need to talk to you."

"Blegh," he manages, pushing my hands away.

"No, Tyler, get up." My voice is firmer now, more sure.

"What, what, what happened, what is it? An emergency?" He jolts upright, head spinning every which way, at once completely alert and still totally cloudy, convinced that he has slept through another catastrophe.

"Nothing, it's nothing like that," I say, then reconsider and sit down on the tiny space on the edge of the couch that his legs don't swallow up. "Actually, maybe it is." I take his hand, and he wipes the gunk out of his eyes with his other. "Listen, I have to go to the hospital to bring Darcy home."

"Okay." His voice comes out croaky, like he'd rather be asleep. I'm sure that he would be. "I'll be here, no problem."

"No, that's not it." I shake my head and exhale, because this is both easier and harder than I anticipated. I wish I'd thought it through, hadn't acted quite so on impulse, if only so I could have the right words, the perfect words to honor him, to honor us, to honor myself and what I'm about to do. "When I get home . . . you don't have to be here. You can go back to Seattle. It's okay. You can leave."

"No, no, what are you talking about? Of course I'll stay."

"That's not what I'm saying," I answer. "I'm saying that maybe you should go. That I was wrong before when I accused you of not knowing what happiness was." He scrunches his face, unsure, confused, wondering if this is some sort of trap. "I think you do know what happiness is, and it's not here, not for you. And I don't think that you being here is what my happiness is either."

He nods, then shakes his head, then nods again, trying to digest this.

"But I thought that this is what you wanted. I thought that *this* would make you happy."

I shrug and offer a flimsy smile. "Turns out that maybe I didn't understand what happiness was either." In this moment, I let my smile run wider, truer, because Tyler Farmer is all I have ever known, and I have loved him so fiercely that I can't believe I'm willing to give him up. And yet, I can also believe that now, with everything, I might be brave enough to try. I run my hands over his sleepy eyes, his satin cheeks. "I have loved you since before I even knew it was possible to love someone this way, Tyler Farmer. That won't change. But let's go now, away from each other, and see what other sorts of happiness we might find on our own. Because we tried together, and it's just not here anymore."

Two slippery tears coast down his perfect face, and then, down my own. He kisses me fully, for the gift I have given him—not just him, myself too—and then I rise, let my hands ebb from his, and slide out away from the shadows.

"I don't know who I am without you." My car door slams and I race down the road toward Darcy. Maybe, actually, now I do.

thirty

Ashley and Susanna gather in my kitchen the next afternoon. Darcy is asleep in the guest room, which isn't much of a guest room anymore, more likely her permanent room, at least as permanent as she'll ever allow something to be. Tyler is gone, was gone when I got home from the hospital late last night. He left me a note saying he'd call when he reached Seattle, and he probably will, and that will be fine. But I won't hover near the phone, won't frantically check my e-mail if he doesn't. That will be fine too. There is life out there, both after and before, and it's time to embrace that.

Ashley pulls a towel over my neck and shoulders, securing it in the back, as I perch on my mother's old dining chair.

"You sure you want to do this?" Susanna asks. It's only three o'clock, but we are drinking cabernet because, though it flies in the face of logic, I feel like celebrating. Ashley gamely came when I called; she had spent the better part of the past week sifting through her mother's belongings and with the task nearly finished, she didn't know how to spend her time.

"I mean, what am I supposed to do now?" she says, scissors in one hand, wineglass in the other. "I've spent so long taking care of her that I feel like it's all I know how to do."

"You'll figure it out," I say, both because I can relate and because I know that she will. Ashley Simmons has been a lot of things, but a defeatist in the face of adversity was never one of them. This I see now; this I admire.

"I haven't done this in a while," she admits, placing the glass on the table, running her fingers through my silky yellow hair. "Are you sure?"

"I am." I nod. "I'd like to try something new, you know? Why not? It can always grow back." I think of Darcy's two toes, and how they won't, and then remember that she has already forgiven me, didn't even think that I was accountable, even though I knew that I was. But I also know I can't hold on to this for always. Because guilt, I realize, is nothing more than a prison to keep us trapped from doing what we really want. What will really bring us happiness. So I am trying to let go of that, release a few other boulders from my past.

"Okay, here we go. Don't blame me if you don't like it," Ashley says. "I got my beautician certificate, like, three years after high school." We all laugh because, *oh God*, does that feel like so long ago.

"It's something I have to do," I say, because it is something I have to do. I have realized that though I can't change the future, that doesn't mean that I can't change my circumstances to fit that future, to reach for the promise of what I'm hoping for. I sat in the bleachers and yearned to be that woman who swayed with Eli under the spinning dim lights of the prom, and by God, who's to say that it couldn't be me?

Ashley starts in the back, snipping and snipping, and layering and cutting, parsing exactly, like an artist carving a sculpture. I stare down at my kitchen floor, the strands amassing, amazed already at how much lighter I feel, how long I've been that blond cheerleader with her star shortstop husband, and how desperately I'd like to resemble something else now.

I've tasked Susanna with the Nikon—she's not a pro but is certainly capable enough of pointing and clicking—because I want this documented, down on record, captured forever, the day that I shed my skin.

When Ashley's done, I smooth my fingers over my naked neck, feeling exposed, self-conscious but excited too, exhilarated, probably how Darcy feels when she takes the stage or when someone lingers a little too long on her beauty. I feel like someone else entirely. Which, I consider, when I finally have the nerve to peek in the mirror, shifting from angle to angle, in awe of the transition that I have made, is likely the whole point.

Luanne knocks on my door later that evening, her winter coat bursting, reminding me of the Pillsbury doughboy, and gasps, a good gasp, when she sees me.

"Oh my God!" she says, filtering her fingers through my hair without asking, the familiarity that only siblings can have. "I didn't even recognize you."

I don't tell her that I'll take this as a compliment and simply usher her inside with a grin.

"Dad's in the car," she says, refusing a seat when I offer it. "He'd like to come in, explain himself. Then I'm taking him to the treatment center."

"What treatment center?"

"Darcy didn't tell you?" I shake my head *no*. "We spoke to him," Lulu says. "He came by the hospital the other day before you checked her out . . ."

"I didn't see him there," I interrupt.

"No, you wouldn't have." She purses her lips together, as resolute as I've ever seen her. "He's been coordinating it with me so you wouldn't have to see him."

I'm momentarily grateful that even though there are a million reasons to find my father despicable, he at least has the grace to let me mourn my shattered vision of our family without interference.

"So anyway," she says, jangling her keys. "Darcy and I confronted him, said we could no longer have contact if he didn't heal himself completely. Not half-assed, not on his own." Her fingers fold into a fist, swallowing up the noise. "He balked at first, but he saw how serious we were, so he agreed. He's going back."

I try to find words but have none, so I stare at the floor, then raise my eyes to my middle sister, amazed that she, the one who always coasted, and Darcy, the one who was too angry to care in the first place, have been able to do what I have never been. Force my father's hand, insist that he do right by us, climb the mountain even under threat of an avalanche.

"Thank you," I whisper finally.

"It's nothing to thank me for," she answers. "It's just what had to be done. Not for you. For Dad."

"But you did it because I couldn't. You did it so that I didn't have to."

She sighs and leans back, resting her head against the cupboard, gazing toward the ceiling fan.

"You know, Till, Darcy told me what she told you. And she told me that you thought she should have confided in you about Dad's affair so that you could have resolved it." She looks at me now, tenderly, after thirty years of sisterhood. "But you couldn't have. You really probably couldn't have. You never had to do all of this, take care of everything. She and I would have been okay shouldering some of it if you'd let us, if you'd asked."

I shrug, because I don't know that I believe her, and even if I did, there's nothing to be done about it now. That's how it was, that's how we created and structured the hierarchy of our lives— and maybe going forward, we'll all be a little wiser, a little more intuitive, a little quicker to nurse the bruises of the ones we call our family, even if sometimes they are the ones to inflict those very welts.

The car horn honks outside, and we both startle.

"Dad," Lulu states. "He's probably getting cold. I wouldn't let him leave the engine running in case he had second thoughts."

She wiggles the keys in the air and giggles, and so, so do I. I walk her to the door, and she says, "You sure? You don't want to come out and say something?"

"I'm sure," I say, because I am. Maybe sometime soon, maybe even sooner than I anticipate, but for now, I stand on the front porch and watch her go, the freezing air cutting through my pajamas, filling my lungs, invigorating the bare skin on the nape of my neck. I stay there long after their car lights have petered out down the road, and then I move to the porch swing. In all of the years that the swing has been with us, I have never once perched on it in the dead of winter. So I sit, and I admire the view, in spite of my nearly numb fingers and my cheeks aflame with cold. I rock and I rock, absorbing the still night of the only place I have ever thought to call home, reminding me that it is so sweet to be out here, sensitive, alive, peering at my old world with fresh new eyes.

thirty-one

The Arc de Triomphe is a wonder to behold. This is my first thought when I enter the gym on prom night. I have seen it before, of course, in my premonitions, which I've had no more of and according to Ashley may never have, now that I've learned to control them rather than vice versa. But in real life, the faux Arc is more regal, more gallant than I could have hoped for. The prom committee, which I've helmed in name only the past few months, has outdone themselves. Miniature Eiffel Towers swing from the ceiling; dancing, twinkling lights circle the edges of the walls. A city of lights. Right here in Westlake.

I stand outside the clanging gym doors before going in, before stepping over that threshold. This is the first prom I've ever attended alone. I considered this as I dressed this evening, pulling up my satin shoulder strap, running my fingers over my exposed collarbone, stepping back in front of the mirror that was once Tyler's too, but that I now fill for the both of us.

I ordered a new dress off the Internet. It's well out of my budget, but I don't care. It's a deep red, reminding me of the color of the fall leaves during the season that my mother died, but in a warm, comforting way, and when I surfed past it on the computer, procrastinating on my way to look for graduate programs, I knew it would be perfect. Perfect on my skinnier frame that would soon fill out thanks to a renewed appetite and beer nights with Susie and Ashley; perfect because I didn't know when I'd have the chance again to dress up with the excitement of a sixteen-year-old who was insightful enough to be grateful that she was sixteen no longer. Besides, I couldn't even think of wearing one of the other dresses stuffed upstairs in my closet, one of the ones I'd worn before. Before. Everything now was either before or after. I was choosing after. The more uncertain choice, to be sure, but also the one that wedged open a new window for possibilities.

I'd popped into the guest room before leaving to show myself off to Darcy. She was sleeping when I went to twirl in front of her, a well-earned, solid rest, so I let her be.

We'd settled into a quiet pattern together. Her hands hadn't regained full functioning yet, but they were on their way, and, in fact, so was she. The demos she and Dante had cut had nabbed the attention of a few prime producers, and though she couldn't play for them just yet, one day soon, she would. The two of them would fly out of Westlake, together, on to brighter skies and untapped dreams, refusing to cower in the face of everything, after everything. After.

"Funny, isn't it?" she said one night when we were working through her rehab exercises. "How I always thought I was a solo act, but it turns out that I was more of a duet." I laughed along with her because it was indeed funny, especially when I'd turned out to be just the opposite.

And now, the Arc de Triomphe is glorious, and after a moment of reverence, I push the doors open, and I step inside.

The gym is pulsing, throbbing with frenzied teenagers, their hormones hopping, their senses likely dulled and heightened all at once thanks to spiked punch or their flasks tucked in their inside pockets. I wave at a few, stopping to hug CJ. Johnny Hutchinson has dumped her again; I heard the whispers through the grapevine last week. So, as expected, she wallows in the corner, her breasts exploding over a bouquet of yellow flowers sewn atop her bustline. A ploy, no doubt, designed to lure Johnny Hutchinson back in, though I hope for her sake that the mission fails, because he will be one more thing that she'll wonder if she should regret leaving behind.

"You'll be fine; go have fun," I say to her after we pull back from our embrace.

"He's an asshole," she says, her bottom lip jutting out.

"Maybe." I shrug. "But you'll be fine either way. A lot of them are assholes. A lot of them aren't. It doesn't really matter. You don't define yourself by it."

I push through the din, making my way toward the DJ and the drink station when I spot Eli. Though nearly everyone else is in a rented tuxedo, he dons instead a dark navy suit, a rich lavender tie, a magnificent aberration in a flock of sheep. He smiles widely, the edges of his eyes folding like a fan, and flags me over, then whistles when I approach.

"Wow," he says. "I must insist on buying you a drink. But only if some ambiguous fruit-flavored punch will do."

"I accept," I say, laughing. "Clearly, this is your first prom, because you learn to love the stuff. I think I crave it the rest of the year. Oh, and it's free."

"Indeed it is my first, my virgin experience." He nods. "Well, first prom since I was seventeen, to be fair. I'm hoping this one turns out a little better." We weave toward the nonalcoholic bar, and I wrinkle my brow in question. "Let's just say that a few too many rum and Cokes were not my friend that night . . . nor my date's, actually. God, she was pissed at me." He shakes his head. "Man, I haven't thought about this stuff in forever."

Funny, I think, *because I used to think about it all the time.*

Before we can scoop out our punch, the DJ clicks to a new song, a slow song, one that transports me back, too far back, to *before*. Whitney Houston blares out from the speakers. *If I should stay, I will only be in your way.*

"Oh my God." Eli scoffs, rolling his eyes. "Do you remember this?"

"I do." I nod, not just because I danced to it with Tyler, but because the DJ somehow seemed to play it every year since. I'd hear it and drag Ty to the dance floor, and throw my arms over his shoulders, swaying to the rhythm, reenacting our time from when we were seventeen, from before.

"I think it's some sort of understood Prom Song." I giggle. "I actually think I used to love this song. You know, the *meaning*— '*And I will always love you*,' and all of that. Back then, it seemed pretty deep."

"Come on," he says, running his finger down my arm, twirling me before I can think otherwise, and beckoning me to the center of the room. "Let's make the most of it."

He pulls me toward him firmly, confidently, placing his hand on the small of my back like it simply fits there. I lean into his chest, and he smells like maple syrup. I rest my head against his shoulder, like I have done before, and close my eyes and inhale the sweetness. This is what I can do for now, this is what I can offer, this is my first step back up the mountain.

When the song ends, I kiss his cheek, and we walk off, fingers almost intertwined, something unspoken between us, something silent and building, which is just as we need it to be for now.

We find ourselves on the bleachers, where I wordlessly lace my hand into his, and he, in turn, doesn't flinch, doesn't pull away, though I suspect that his baser instinct might be to do so. He is a wanderer after all.

"This is probably my last prom," I say. I am swallowing it up, absorbing it, with an equal mix of sadness, euphoria, and yes, nostalgia, too. There is still space for nostalgia, even with everything that has happened. He looks toward me with surprise. "I'm applying to graduate school." I pause. "I think. For photography."

"This is a good thing for you, Tilly Farmer," he says, holding my hand steady.

"It is. Turns out that maybe I'm not the best guidance counselor. Or maybe being a guidance counselor isn't best for me," I answer, because both are true. "You probably won't be around here much longer anyway."

"Through the spring," he says, turning back to watch the beat of swaying bodies. "They offered me a full-time position, but we'll see. I haven't made up my mind."

"I can't imagine that Westlake is where you want to stay forever."

"No, probably not forever," he says, leaning into his knees, still clasping my hand. "But it's pretty alright for now."

"I bought a ticket to Paris," I say, aglow when obvious pride washes across his face. He is the first person I've told. I did it on instinct, on a whim, the same night I bought my dress. "For April, during spring break."

"You'll love it there," he says, taking his free hand, turning my face toward his but instead kissing the curve of my shoulder. "You'll take my Nikon."

"I couldn't," I protest.

"You can," he says. "Besides, that's the only way I can be sure that you'll ever come back."

We sit there until the lights stop spinning, until the throb of the bass fades into a void of disparate voices who quickly scatter off to their parents' borrowed cars, to the few splurged limousines, off into their night of well-earned celebration. Because tomorrow, they will wake up, *we* will wake up, and we will face another day, another mountain, another moment in the after. And if we are wise, which I hope that I am now, we will seize it so mightily, clench it so close, that we will never risk that it can break free, slip through our open fingers without warning.

There is the before. And then there is the after. Happiness is what you choose, what you follow, not what follows you. These are the things I have seen, these are the things I now know, these are the things I will carry with me as I go.

Acknowledgments

This book was a true labor of love, sometimes more labor than love, and I'm deeply indebted to my editor, Sarah Knight, who read my initial miserable manuscript and thoughtfully helped shape the book in ways I'd never have dreamed of on my own. Many, many thanks to everyone at Shaye Areheart Books and Crown, who have been more generous, supportive, and hardworking than I could have asked for. Shaye Areheart, Annsley Rosner, Kira Walton, Christine Kopprasch, Karin Shultz, Allison Malec, and Jay Sones.

Elisabeth Weed—you are my Jerry McGuire. Thank you, thank you.

Thanks also to Laura Dave, Jessica Jones, Annika Pergament, Sarah Self, and everyone who entertains me throughout the day on Twitter, my blog, and various other online time-wasters. It takes a village. And of course, my last and dearest public display of gratitude goes to my family—Adam, Campbell, and Amelia, without whom this whole shindig would be meaningless.